The Hero

by

PAMELA McCORD

FROM THE TINY ACORN...
GROWS THE MIGHTY OAK

www.acornpublishingllc.com
For information, address:
Acorn Publishing, LLC
3943 Irvine Blvd. Ste. 218
Irvine, CA 92602

The Hero
Copyright © 2022 Pamela McCord

Cover design by ebooklaunch.com
Interior design and formatting by Debra Cranfield Kennedy

All rights reserved. No part of this book may be used or reproduced in any manner whatsoever, including Internet usage, without written permission from the author.

Anti-Piracy Warning: The unauthorized reproduction or distribution of a copyrighted work is illegal. Criminal copyright infringement, including infringement without monetary gain, is investigated by the FBI and is punishable by up to five years in federal prison and a fine of $250,000.

Printed in the United States of America

ISBN-13: 978-1-952112-98-0 (hardcover)
ISBN-13: 978-1-952112-97-3 (paperback)

*Fate tiptoes in on silent feet.
Only much later, if at all, can someone look back
and pinpoint the exact event
that shaped the rest of a person's life.*

Chapter 1

✶ ✶ ✶

No one was on deck when London Calloway climbed aboard her boyfriend's yacht. She descended the stairs to the lower level, her deck shoes silent on the steps. "David?" she called.

She heard a startled "Oh" and turned to see a dark-haired woman awkwardly straightening her gauzy beach cover-up as she clambered off the bunk.

"What the hell is going on?"

"Uh, hi," the embarrassed young woman murmured, head down. "Excuse me." She brushed by London to take the stairs to the upper deck, leaving behind a flustered David Rankin fumbling with the buttons on his Hawaiian shirt.

London glared, the blush of rage turning her cheeks bright red as she faced him.

"London! I thought you weren't coming by," he said lamely. "Monica and I were just—"

"I can see what you were just. You sorry son of a bitch."

"It's not what it looked like. You're jumping to conclusions. I would never—"

"You would never? Really? You would never—what? Disrespect me? Violate my trust? Too late."

"Babe, look. I can explain—"

"Don't 'Babe' me!"

"I just mean you're overreacting. Nothing happened. You can't honestly think I would prefer Monica over you. Babe, you're the one I want, and—"

"Don't bother," London said, then turned and ascended the stairs. She heard his clumsy steps climbing behind her but she didn't wait. Too mad to speak, she still almost turned around to get the burning lump of hurt and anger off her chest. Instead, when she heard him calling her name, she hurried on, unable to bear the sight of him.

◦◦❥◦◦

Hot tears stung her eyes, and she swiped at them as she drove. At a stoplight, she fumbled for a tissue, tilted down the rearview mirror, and wiped at the streaks of mascara under her blurry eyes. The Bluetooth connection in her car buzzed, but she ignored it. Her grip on the steering wheel tightened as the buzzing started again, and she took a deep breath and held it, trying to steady her nerves.

She should have seen this coming. David was rich, and *of course* there were beautiful women falling all over themselves to catch his eye. It was just a matter of time before one of them would succeed. Logic told her that. But emotions? What did they tell her? It was all jumbled up together. Anger more than pain caused her tears. She felt humiliated, and she glared through the windshield as she steered her car from the Marina to her Hollywood Hills apartment. The traffic on Sunset Boulevard was backed up all the way to her turn-off. In frustration, she pounded the steering wheel. "Damn you, David."

Not that swearing helped. She wanted nothing more than to climb into bed and pull the covers over her head.

Finally leaving the congestion behind, she maneuvered into a parking space in front of her apartment building, wiped again at her eyes, and climbed out of her black BMW.

Sure, there were problems in their relationship. There were problems in every relationship. But she'd thought he respected her enough to not fool around behind her back. How naïve could she be? But, if he hadn't strayed yet, it was clear he was well on his way. How naïve had she been?

Did she even care? His straying wasn't their main problem. Once she got past the stark feelings of betrayal, what was left was an overall disappointment in him. But jealousy? She wasn't sure it really mattered in the grand scheme of things. His lack of ambition was the overriding source of her discontent. She'd overlooked her sense of wrongness in their relationship for far too long.

When the tears dried, there was no breaking heart. *Don't I care?* she wondered, juggling her keys, her mail, and the *LA Times* as she pushed open the door with her shoulder and dropped her bundle on the desk in her office.

When her iPhone rang, she debated but finally answered. She listened for several moments, then said "I'm tired, David." She glared at the cell phone in her hand. "I feel like I'm talking to a brick wall with you." She interrupted the argument he was attempting to make. "Yeah, yeah. Look, I gotta go." She ended the call and stared out the window, oblivious to the iconic Hollywood Sign visible in the hazy distance from her window. What had she been thinking, wasting years with that reprobate.

Tears welled in her eyes and she searched around unsuccessfully for a tissue. In frustration, she shoved at the papers littering the top of her desk, sending them sliding to the floor. Burying her face in her hands, she gave in to the sobs she'd been trying to suppress. After a good cry, she wiped her eyes with the bottom of her T-shirt and leaned down to pick up the mail scattered beneath the desk.

Her eyes were drawn to a picture on the front page of the newspaper lying on the floor at her feet. Entranced, she picked it up and scanned the article below the picture, about an insurgent attack on a hotel in Afghanistan.

Who was he, this soldier staring at her from the page?

She'd been fuming until she saw him, all rugged and handsome, rifle in one hand and helmet in the other. He looked strong and determined.

There was a trace of blood on his hands. More blood on the side of his face dried in a trickle that ran past his lips, down into his stubbly beard. He was wounded, but it didn't slow him down. The fierceness in his eyes made that clear.

Why did she have such a visceral reaction to this man's picture? She'd never been drawn to a picture the way she was to this one. The shot had captured in-your-face bravery, and she couldn't look away.

She put down the paper and once again stared out in the direction of the Hollywood Sign. David, with his perpetual trust fund income, didn't need to work and had no interest in a career. He just wanted to play all day, every day. And he had the funds to do just that.

The soldier, in stark contrast, looked like a man who would lay down his life to protect the frivolous choices of men like David.

Her phone vibrated. It was Nicole Lawrence, her best friend, texting to see if she wanted to go out.

"I don't feel like it tonight. Rain check?" she texted back.

The phone buzzed.

"What's going on?"

London sighed. Involuntarily, a sob escaped her.

"Spill!" Nicole demanded.

London noisily blew her nose, prompting Nicole to say, "Never mind. Don't go anywhere, I'm coming over."

Fifteen minutes later, London answered the doorbell to find her friend, armed with a bottle of wine and a pint of chocolate chip ice cream.

"You hug me," Nicole said. "My hands are full."

London giggled in spite of herself and wrapped her arms around her best friend, then followed her into the kitchen.

Efficient, take-charge Nicole set down her bundles and rummaged through London's utensil drawer for a corkscrew. "I'll pour the wine, you dish up the ice cream."

Numbly, London followed directions. Within moments, both were seated at the dining room table.

"Cheers!" Nicole said as she clinked her glass against London's.

"Just kidding," she said. "You don't have to be cheery. What did he do now? Tell me everything."

London sighed and took a gulp of the cabernet. Then another.

"That bad, huh?"

"Oh, I don't know. I mean, if you must know, I stopped by his boat in time to interrupt *something* going on with Monica. You know, Monica? I've mentioned her before."

"They were screwing?"

"Not yet. I interrupted them, but there was some quick clothing rearrangement."

"What did he say?"

"The usual. Not what it looks like, blah blah blah. I didn't give him much of a chance to explain. I stormed off the boat." She took a spoonful of the Häagen-Dazs, savoring it. "He called, but I blew him off. A temporary solution. I'm sure I'll have to talk to him eventually."

"Are you heartbroken?" Nicole's eyes were ready to shed tears if appropriate.

"Not as much as you'd think. Mostly I'm really, really mad."

"Should we kill this bottle and open another one?" Nicole asked helpfully.

London laughed. "No. Then tomorrow I'd have a broken heart *and* a headache. One bottle should do it. And a lot of ice cream."

"Really, Nic, I'm not jealous. Just pissed. I've stuck with this relationship for a long time because I'm too damn loyal. I think I'm going to break up with him. I should have right then and there, but I just wanted to get away from him."

"I'm not surprised. Every time I talk to you, you're in a mood about David."

London took another big gulp. "This is helping me put things in perspective. I should have seen it sooner. It's not about Monica. I'm not jealous of her. I'm not even jealous of him running around on me. I'm just exasperated."

"But it had to be traumatic to walk in on him like that."

"It was. I shed some tears and called him an asshole, or words to that effect, but—" she clinked her glass against Nicole's, "thanks to you, I've come to the realization that I really don't care. He's not the man I fell in love with."

"Still, are you okay?"

"As good as I can be for now. Or maybe not. I still feel on the verge of tears." She pushed her long blonde hair behind one ear. "But they're angry tears, not sad ones." London leaned back in her chair. "You know, I bet Grandma Gracie didn't mean to turn him into a playboy."

"Probably not. I remember you guys in college, always at the library, working your asses off."

"We were. His grandmother was so proud of him. She'd be so disappointed now. I hate to say it, Grandma Gracie, but I think the trust fund ruined him. He doesn't have any ambition anymore. Now he just wants to play with his toys."

"Well, he does have some nice ones."

"And the *girls*. I hate that there are always girls lounging around his yacht. Sooner or later . . . you know what I mean?"

"Do you think David and Monica—"

"I don't know. They still had their clothes on. I might have arrived just in time to ruin the moment." She sniffed at the thought.

"You're much prettier than Monica."

"Thanks. Best friends have to say that."

"Maybe, but you are. He's an idiot. Rich guys have groupies. I think they come with the lifestyle."

"Definitely with that lifestyle. I call them Money Bunnies." A rueful smile flitted across London's face. "He's feeling like a million bucks, pardon the pun."

"With his trust fund, he'll never have to work again," Nicole pointed out. "His cup runneth over."

"I know, but life isn't all fun and games, no matter how much money you have."

"Apparently for him money is the ultimate measure of his importance. I was going to say *manhood* but thought it was too tacky."

London laughed, and laughed harder when red wine came out her nose. "I love you!"

"Thank you. I love you, too." Nicole handed her a napkin.

"That's probably exactly what he thinks. Money makes him more attractive. He happens to *be* attractive, but that's beside the point. He knows I want him to do something worthwhile, like start a business or a charity or something, put that college degree of his to work. Or even philanthropy. He has more money than he can ever spend. There's so much he could do to help people in need. But given a choice between donating to a homeless shelter or buying a new Ferrari . . . well, I don't have to tell you which one he'd choose."

London scooped up one last spoonful of chocolate chip and waved it at Nicole. "Look. I know I'm not perfect, but at least I'm trying to do something meaningful with my life. I have my writing to concentrate on. He needs a career of his own. Well, he doesn't *need* one, but I'd have more respect for him if he did."

"I have to get more ice cream." She walked into the kitchen and returned with the carton. "Want some?"

Nicole shook her head. "I'm good."

"And what about kids? What kind of father would he make, assuming he even wants kids?"

"Have you talked about it?"

"No. Yes. Well, it's another one of those instances where he wants to know what the rush is. I wasn't ready before, not that I am now, so I didn't press it, but I would have been happier if he'd taken the subject a little more seriously. He likes things the way they are. And that's great for him, but it's not for me. I sound like a stick in the mud, don't I?"

"Of course not. You're not married to the guy, so maybe it's time for you to find someone who wants what you want."

"Maybe it is time." She sighed. "Thanks for coming over and bringing relief supplies. I feel a ton better than I did."

"If you think about it, he may have done you a favor," Nicole offered.

"What do you mean?"

"Now you have a legitimate reason to break up with him."

"I guess I do."

"How are you feeling this morning?"

Nicole's call got London out of bed. "I have a headache, after all. I think from crying. And I finished the bottle of wine after you left. But I'm doing okay. I'm going for a run and then I'm planning to devote the rest of the day to my novel. Talk later?"

She stared into the bathroom mirror, lamenting the frightening apparition staring back at her. She pulled her lower eyelids down to get a better look at the bloodshot whites of her red, puffy eyes, and corralled her hair into a scrunchy. Whether or not she wanted to admit it, yesterday had taken a lot out of her, and she felt beaten up.

But she had things to do, so she brushed her teeth and splashed water on her face, rubbing her scratchy eyes with a washcloth.

London changed into her running clothes and headed out the door but, after a block, realized her mistake and turned around. Her head couldn't take the pounding.

Instead, popping a couple of Tylenols, she picked up the draft of her recently completed manuscript, *The Rand Prophesy*, and settled in to attack the final changes her editor wanted.

This was London's fourth novel, and she was in the polishing phase, trying to stay on schedule so she wouldn't get yelled at. Although her prior novels had sold fairly well, none had been the huge success all authors dream of, and she hoped this could be the one.

Hours later, ready for a break, she stretched her fingers and rolled her head to counteract the kinks in her neck. She took two more Tylenols for the lingering headache, grateful that it had stayed in the background and hadn't interfered with her creative process.

She felt a little queasy and didn't want anything heavy to eat, so she settled on soup that she sipped in front of the TV.

The droning of the television had her dozing in her chair after dinner, and she was startled awake when David called.

"Hi, babe. I would have called before but I wanted to give you time to cool off."

When she didn't say anything, he said, "You're not still mad, are you?"

"Really, David? You don't think I should be mad? Actually, I'm not mad. It's not a matter of being mad. Monica was just the tipping point. One more thing that's wrong with our relationship. I'm tired of talking about this."

"Why are you always on me? Maybe next year I'll be ready to settle down. Or not. Why do I have to be the one to change?"

"You don't have to change at all. I'm glad your life is perfect, but it's not what *I* want. I think it's time we both moved on."

"You're kidding, right?"

"No, I'm not. And I'm sure Monica would be happy if we broke up."

"Monica's nothing. Are you jealous of her? Because I can assure you—"

"I'm not jealous. You're missing the point. I don't care if you did anything with her or not. Yesterday was just a straw for the overloaded camel."

"You're not being fair."

"And you were? Go have all the fun you want. With Monica or whomever. I don't care what you do."

"You need to lighten up. We're gonna be okay."

"We're not going to be okay. I've thought about this a lot, all day in fact, and I'm done. We're over. Go live your life the way you want to, but count me out."

After an icy pause, the line went dead. He hadn't taken that very well, and she felt a little guilty about not giving in.

But not enough to change her mind.

Memories from their years together swirled in her mind, and she mourned the death of a big part of her life with tears and sadness. Had she just made the biggest mistake of her life? Maybe she and David should tough it out. It had seemed so clear-cut earlier, but now doubt kept her tossing and turning. She cried herself to sleep for the second night in a row.

She could barely drag herself out of bed the next morning. Her headache from yesterday had decided to stick around. Her heart wasn't in it as she showered and threw on jeans and a Prince T-shirt, pulling her hair into a ponytail. Maybe a Starbucks would make her feel better. There was this cloud she hoped to get rid of so she could get on with her day.

She picked up her handbag and headed out to her car where she found a crude "bitch" scratched into the driver's side door of her car. *What the hell?* At first, tears had come to her eyes, but she brushed them away before they could fall. David is such a *douche*. She was certain he was responsible, and the feelings of guilt she'd experienced the night before were replaced by anger. She pulled out her cell to call him, but he didn't answer. "You sorry bastard!" she left on his voicemail, flashing her middle finger at the phone, hoping the gesture would come through in her voice.

She called the police to report the vandalism. After an hour, an officer showed up, examined the damage, running his finger over the fairly deep scratch, then knocked on a few doors. Unsuccessful at finding anyone who'd seen the incident, he said there wasn't much the police could do since he couldn't find any witnesses. He suggested she report it to her insurance company, apologized, and left.

Oh my God, she thought, throwing up her hands in frustration. *Who can I punch?* Through gritted teeth, she called her insurance rep. On hold, her tapping foot gave away the anger boiling just below the surface. Her head was pounding. She mindlessly shuffled through the papers on her desk while she listened to the inane canned music playing on the other end of the line, resisting the urge to hum along to "Raindrops Keep Falling on My Head." Her eyes landed on the *Times*, and, once again, the soldier stared back at her.

The voice of the insurance agent startled London out of her reverie. She provided the information needed for the claim and promised to forward a quote on the repair as soon as she had a chance.

Putting down her cell, she picked up the newspaper and tried to analyze what it was that captivated her about the man. He was handsome, more real-life handsome than movie-star good-looking. But it couldn't be just that. It was the strength he radiated, the power. She'd be safe with him.

I want this man, she thought as she gazed into the intense eyes of the soldier then laughed at the absurdness.

Her irritation at David faded. The picture put things into perspective. How could she complain about anything in her life after seeing the blood on the soldier's face and the determination in his eyes. Hers were frivolous problems. His were real life.

⁂

She spent the afternoon working on the rewrite. It helped to focus her mind on something besides the events of the last couple of days. Four Tylenols had made her headache finally go away. *No more tears,* she vowed.

A little makeup helped her look presentable by early evening as she had a barbeque to attend. The thought of blowing it off and staying home was tempting, but she'd wallowed enough. Besides, she didn't want to disappoint her friends, Cal and Anthony.

When London picked up Nicole for the party, she couldn't help noticing her friend's appraising glance.

"How bad do I look," she asked. "Is everyone going to be asking me what's wrong?"

"You look fine. I only know because you told me what happened. You don't have to talk about any of it unless you want to."

"Thanks. Since you're being sympathetic, come see what David's done now." Nicole got out of the car and walked around to the driver's side. London pointed to her car door.

"You've got to be kidding," Nicole said.

"I'm afraid not. And couldn't he even bother to capitalize the 'b' in bitch?"

They both laughed.

"Now I have to run around getting estimates for the repair, dealing with the insurance company, and driving a loaner car while they fix mine. Fun, huh?"

"Yeah. That sucks."

When they arrived at the party, Nicole dragged London through the front door and announced, "This one needs a drink, *stat*."

After hugs, Cal handed her a margarita and asked what was wrong. Nicole suggested they all go check out London's car.

"Are you going to sue him?" Cal asked as he surveyed the damage.

"God, no. I want nothing more to do with him. I'll let the insurance company handle it. He's a jerk, but it's not worth the effort of going after him. Too much trouble to try to prove it was him." She ran her finger over the scratch. "He really did a number on the paint job, though."

"Aren't you worried he might—"

"What? Be dangerous? No. I'm not worried about him taking it any further. He's a jerk, not an idiot. He just wanted the last word. Which happened to be on the side of my car."

Lounging around the pool, Nicole proposed a toast to the end of London's relationship with the vandal, and London clinked glasses, feeling the relief of knowing she had let go of that part of her life.

London finished her edits and emailed the final draft to her editor, calling to let her know it was on the way.

Her agent, Sara Carter, said the next step would be for London to review and sign off on the proofs when they arrived, and after that there was a cover design, an updated author bio, and the acknowledgments to deal with. Once she had signed off on those, it was pretty much a done deal.

"Are you working on anything else yet?" Sara asked. "You can't rest on your laurels. Take a breather if you need to, but we need to try for a blockbuster. A hundred-thousand-first-printing kind of blockbuster."

London laughed. "You're saying this one isn't the blockbuster?"

"We can always hope," Sara said. "But just in case it isn't, tape that word to your refrigerator to inspire you as you work on the next one."

London hadn't thought past *The Rand Prophesy*. She'd planned on resting up before jumping in again.

What the hell? Her agent knew what the market was like, and if she thought London needed to get a move on, she'd get right on it. Challenges kept life interesting.

Chapter 2

★ ★ ★

London and Nicole, both currently without boyfriends, occasionally went out on weekends to dance and meet people. Pre-David, London never had trouble attracting guys, and post-David, she found that was still the case, and she dated a few of them. Although none of the new guys made her heart skip a beat, she enjoyed herself.

She wasn't in any hurry for another relationship, but Nicole had been right. The male attention was great for her ego, and London decided to enjoy life for a while with no strings.

She focused on her writing and was content not having a steady boyfriend to distract her. Her first few books had achieved some success, but she was going to need a steady paycheck if she didn't step up her game and write the breakout novel Sara was asking for. Compared with the freedom a writing career provided her, the prospect of a nine-to-five job was daunting. Stress wasn't helpful to her creativity.

A few times, she'd tried to pound out that first paragraph that would grab her and start the creative process moving forward. It wasn't as easy this time, but, at Sara's suggestion, she decided to try her hand at Young Adult literature, currently a hot market.

Her concept was: strange goings-on in a college dorm when most of the students were gone for the holidays. Her first paragraph began:

> Kelly Brighton looked forward to the quiet after
> the noisy students celebrating the end of classes
> packed up and went home for the holidays. She
> hadn't wanted to go on a cruise with her parents,
> so she opted to stay on campus during the break.
> Another student, a nerdy kid named Hector, along
> with a house monitor, would share the old gothic
> house with her. She planned to keep to herself.
> Until tonight, Kelly had enjoyed the solitude, but
> then...

And that was as far as London got. "*But then...,*" what? What scary, horrible thing should happen to make Kelly sorry she'd stayed at school over the holidays? A ghost? A doorway to Hell opening in her closet? Something with fangs?

She waited a few days for inspiration to strike, frustrated at the lack of ideas.

"My agent is hounding me because I haven't started writing a new book yet," she told Nicole as they drank margaritas and exchanged glances with potential dates. "I've really been trying, but I'm just not inspired. Sara says that if I wait too long my loyal readers will find someone else to follow. The income from my last books won't last forever, and I'm starting to worry. Writing is my career. If I can't write, then what? Become a barista?"

"I think you're being a little dramatic. So it's been a couple of weeks—"

"Make that months. Months I'll never get back. I have a meeting coming up with Sara and she's going to be terribly disappointed in me."

"You worry too much. Do the Scarlett O'Hara thing and think about it tomorrow," Nicole said. "Right now, we should be focusing on finding a couple of Mr. Right Now's."

Two margaritas later, London announced to Nicole that this was the last time she would be overindulging. The club scene was getting boring, and she was tired of waking up with a headache.

Tipsy, she barely managed to kick off her sandals before toppling onto her bed, not bothering to pull down the covers, and she tossed and turned for a few minutes before falling into a fitful sleep.

Chapter 3

✶ ✶ ✶

"*Get down.*" He forcibly shoved her behind the wall, off the street.

"What are you doing?" The warning in his intense eyes alarmed her.

Just then, he spun around, sinking to the ground beside her, blood trickling down the side of his face, past his lips and into his stubbly beard.

"Oh my God! Are you all right?" she cried as he rolled onto his hands and knees, blood dripping onto his hand, before pushing himself to his feet.

He kept her behind him and pointed his rifle toward the street and fired a few rounds. He grabbed her arm and said "Let's get out of here."

✦

London awoke with a start, her heart racing. Stumbling to her desk, she picked up the newspaper and stared at the soldier's face. It was jarring. She could still smell the dust, the gunfire, the sweat on his skin. She felt the grip of his hand on her arm.

She sank into her chair, but her eyes stayed on his face.

And then, like a bolt of lightning, she knew. London flipped open her laptop, organizing her thoughts as she waited for it to boot up. Then she started typing:

The Hero

By London Calloway

Most people never meet a real live hero, but I was in love with one. My name is Juliana Curry. I was a journalist covering the war in Afghanistan when he saved my life.

My team and I were in Kabul, leaving the restaurant in our hotel when there was a loud boom, followed by gunfire, very close. Not sure which way to go, we turned toward the lobby. Our intention was to get out into the street, but we saw the insurgents, their bullets raking the hotel lobby.

Wordlessly, the three of us ran back toward the restaurant, hoping to escape through the delivery doors, but Charlie wasn't quite fast enough. I heard a sound and turned to see him crumple to the floor, half his head missing. "Char--" I started to yell, but my cameraman, Jonas, pushed me on toward the doors to the kitchen. I got through but, when I looked over my shoulder, no one was there. I started back to find him, but strong hands grabbed me, and a voice hissed, *"Get down."*

I struggled to get free. "Your friends are dead," the soldier said roughly. "Trust me if you don't want to end up the same way." He shoved me behind him and pointed his rifle at the door I'd just come through. In an instant, it flew open and two terrorists burst through, firing wildly. I cried out as I saw him get hit. The shot knocked him back and he stumbled to his knees, then he raised his rifle and fired, dropping both attackers in their tracks. Soldiers rushed past us from behind and took up positions around the front of the restaurant. The man wiped blood off his face with the back of his hand and then shepherded me through the kitchen and out through the delivery doors.

Once outside, he grabbed my arm and pulled me away from the siege at the hotel. We didn't stop until the sound of gunfire faded.

"I'm sorry about your friends. Are you all right?"

There was concern on his face. My eyes followed his gaze, and I saw the blood on my shirt. Unnerved, I said, "It's not my blood. It's yours."

He touched the side of his face. He looked at the blood on his fingers then wiped them on his pants leg.

"No. Wait," I implored as he backed away.

"I have to go, ma'am. I need to get back."

"You saved my life."

"Any one of us would have done the same. It's what we do."

I knew that he was going to leave. I didn't want to let him go.

"You can't go. You're hurt. Let me look at--"

"It's not necessary." As he turned to go, he stumbled as his legs gave way.

Kneeling beside him, I started to unbuckle his helmet. He put up a hand to stop me, but I brushed it away, and gently touched his hair, sticky with blood, searching for the wound. He protested, but I took a couple of tissues from my bag, which remarkably was still slung over my shoulder, and dabbed at his head, trying to stop the bleeding.

He struggled to get to his feet. I couldn't dissuade him so I helped him stand. He leaned on me for a moment, then straightened.

"Look," I said, "you're weak. If you go back there, your guys will have to take care of you. Do you want them to worry about you on top of doing their jobs?"

"That won't happen," he snapped, but his eyes lost focus and once again he slumped against me.

"We should get you someplace where you can be taken care of."

"It's not necessary." He pulled out a sat phone and called his base. "This is Captain Westfall. I need assistance."

"We'll have you out of there in a jiffy, sir," came a voice through the receiver.

I helped him slide down against the wall of the building that was sheltering us and sat beside him.

After a moment, I said, "I'm Juliana Curry. I thought you should know the name of the woman whose life you saved."

Not looking at me, he said, "I'm glad you're okay, Ms. Curry."

"I owe you so much, Captain. Can I see you again?"

He turned toward me. "Not a good idea, ma'am. You don't owe me anything."

"You can't just go. I want to thank you for real, without bullets. You saved my life. Please." My eyes pleaded, but his were determined and distant.

"No, ma'am. Really. It's not a good idea."

I returned his gaze and then saw the jeep turning onto the street. I quickly rummaged in my

```
bag and pulled out my card. As he tried to wave it
away, I tucked it in the pocket of his camouflage
jacket.
    "Please. Call me."
```

London hit "save" and stared at her words. This was good. Wasn't it? She knew it was good, and she felt an excitement she hadn't felt with any of her other books.

This would be her blockbuster. Her editor, her agent, her publisher, they'd all been pressuring her, in the gentlest way possible, to write the big one. And this was it. The idea was timely, with the unrest all over the world, terrorism targeting the most vulnerable. The world needed a hero. And she believed with all her heart that Captain Westfall was a hero. Because the soldier in her picture was a hero.

She felt a twinge of loneliness as she looked at the face in the picture. Why did he mean so much to her?

She wanted to lose herself in those eyes. Could she find him? she wondered. Surely not. He was in a war zone someplace. You don't just Google a stranger in a picture and, *voilà*, his phone number pops up. What would she say if she did find him, anyway?

The photographer's name was Simon Adjani. Him, she could Google. He had a website. Intent, London scanned the information on the page. His gallery link had a dozen or so examples of his work, but her soldier wasn't in any of them. Simon was currently in Syria. And, more importantly, there was contact information.

London printed out the page then contemplated what to do next.

She separated her emotional attachment to the soldier for now and let her business brain explore the idea that, when it was finished, having the face of the actual hero to promote her book would make excellent marketing sense.

A twinge of guilt caused her to look again at his picture. Shrugging, she packed that feeling away as well, and said to the soldier, "Sorry, but I don't know you, and it's just business."

She finally found the nerve to contact the photographer. She attached a scan of the picture to the email, and requested Simon's help in tracking down the soldier. She played the "published author" card and explained it was research for her next book. Now the ball was rolling. She traced a finger across her soldier's face and silently apologized.

An out-of-office message bounced back to her saying Simon Adjani was currently out of the country on assignment, with limited access to email. It was something of a relief, actually. She had tried, but her heart hadn't been in it. She didn't really believe that it was ethical, or fair, of her to invade the soldier's private life.

Devoting herself to her new project, words flowed quickly from her, the word count growing as she poured her heart into the novel. She could almost fall for Captain Westfall herself, picturing her soldier as she wrote about the fictional soldier.

Nervously, after two solid weeks of writing, she showed Nicole the first pages of the new book.

"I'm blown away. How did you think of it?"

"The story came to me in a dream. I couldn't get into that YA idea, and then one night I had this dream about a soldier saving my life. And I knew what to write about. Did I make him seem like a hero to you?"

"Are you kidding? What a hunky hero! I'm in *love* with this guy. Is your passport current? We should go get us some soldiers."

London laughed, pleased that she was able to put into words the magic of this man. But she didn't tell Nicole about the picture. She couldn't bring herself to share.

Chapter 4

⋆ ⋆ ⋆

Sara Carter called to say the publisher was ready to go with *The Rand Prophesy*.

It was exciting. To know that someone thought her writing was good enough to publish was heady stuff, no matter how many times she'd been published.

"So. Do you have anything else for me?" Sara's question interrupted London's reverie.

"Yes, actually, I do. I've been working on something you might like."

Sara laughed. "That's great. I can't wait to see it. What's the story about?"

"It's a love story. About a soldier. I'll email you what I've done so far." She paused. "I don't want to jinx it, but I believe it could be the blockbuster you've been asking for."

"Now, I really can't wait."

London was surprised at the sudden anxiety she felt. What if Sara didn't like *The Hero*? She'd put her heart onto the pages. She didn't want to change a thing.

Waiting the couple of days it took Sara to get back to her was excruciating.

"I'm impressed," Sara said. "There are a few things to tweak, of course, but you're on the right track. I want to see more. I'll be waiting."

London laughed. "I'll get it done as quickly as I can."

The Hero

It's been a month since the attack on the hotel. I can function during the day. But the nights are hard. That's when the nightmares come. I'm doing my job although the bureau wanted me home and put up a stink when I refused to leave. I'm okay now, but--right after--that was another story. I'll try to tell it like I felt it.

That day, adrenaline kept me going. There were so many things going through my head. I couldn't go back to my hotel where all my stuff was; the siege wasn't over yet. My escort found me another place to stay. When I was alone in my room, it all fell in on me. My whole body hurt.

When I saw myself in the mirror, I lost it. Seeing the blood, *his* blood, on me, I started sobbing. I know what it feels like to come *this close* to dying...If he hadn't been there, *I* wouldn't be here. I don't doubt that for a moment. Was he okay? Was he badly hurt? My two friends were dead. And the people at the hotel.... I started to hyperventilate but managed to get myself under control.

I picked up a notebook from the hotel's convenience shop and started writing down what I remembered. Tears smeared the ink as I wrote about losing my friends. It was cathartic to purge the devastating events from my soul. I wasn't writing a story for my bureau. I was cleansing my mind, trying to make sense of the grief that consumed me. Hours later, I put the notebook aside and climbed under the covers of my bed. Finally, my brain slowed down from the frantic pace that hadn't left me in peace.

I got a slow start in the morning, lying in bed unable to face the world and my place in it. Could I stay here? Could I go back out, seeing what I had seen? Eventually wide-ranging anger propelled me out of bed. My crumpled shirt lay on the floor where I'd tossed it the night before, and the blood staining it almost sent me back under the covers. But I took a deep breath and squared my shoulders. The only action I could take, the only thing that made any sense, was to write down what happened, and I spent the rest of the day hunched over the slowly filling notebook.

I thought a lot about Captain Westfall, wondering if he was okay. I had my bureau make inquiries. The Army wouldn't give out personnel information but said they hadn't lost any troops during the attack on the hotel.

At least he didn't die, thank God. There wasn't a day that went by when I didn't think about him. I checked all the dispatches daily in case there were reports of him. I hoped he would contact me, but I knew he wouldn't. To him, saving the famous Juliana Curry was just part of the job.

Taliban attacks were increasing. There was an upswing in US troop deaths, and I saw photos of the wounded and dead--both Americans and Afghans that my fellow journalists had taken--always afraid to look at the faces of the fallen soldiers in the pictures.

I'd submitted my story about the attack, and the bureau ran with it. I suppose my chief thought that I'd paid my dues with that one. Some journalists were imbedded with the troops, but not me. I guess they thought I needed less stress for now because they had me covering "suburban" Kabul.

Within a few days, I went back into the hotel and retrieved all my things. It felt strange being back in the place where so much horror had happened, but I dealt with it the best I could, except for when I walked through the demolished lobby and saw the pockmarked walls. Then the tears came again.

Sometimes at night, I'd nurse a bottle of beer, sitting on a low wall outside the front of the hotel, and relive it all. I was drawn there. I couldn't let go. Sadness washed over me as my eyes took in the shattered glass and broken walls. Stains from the blood of people who shouldn't have died were everywhere, a horrendous stain where Charlie had fallen. I hadn't seen Jonas fall, so I couldn't pick out the residue of his life's blood. It ate away at me that I didn't know the exact spot.

I sat on the wall, sipping my beer, lost in thought. Something made me look up, and I saw him standing in the ruined lobby. Our eyes met, and I thought I saw a flash of emotion, but it was gone so quickly I wasn't sure.

I couldn't help myself; I ran to him and threw my arms around his neck. He stiffened in surprise and started to pull back, but then, to my surprise, he allowed my awkward embrace.

"Captain Westfall, I'm sorry. It's just that

I've been so worried about you. Are you all right?"

"Yes, Ms. Curry. I'm good. I've...wondered about you, too."

"What are you doing here, just follow-up stuff?"

"No. I mean, yes. Follow-up." He seemed uncomfortable. He started to say something, then hesitated.

"What?" I prompted.

"I'm glad to see you're okay." He looked at me with those inscrutable eyes. "I'm surprised to find you here, but I, uh--" He cleared his throat. "I was hoping I might see you."

My heart jumped into my throat, and I tried to keep my voice from quivering. "You were looking for me?"

"I...no...I mean--"

Sensing his discomfort, I interrupted. "I come here sometimes. I'm not sure why. I couldn't help them. My friends, I mean. This lets me feel close to them. That sounds stupid, doesn't it? Sorry." Before he could respond, I said, "I didn't think I'd ever see you again."

I surveyed the lobby, by now in the throes of reconstruction. To me, it elicited so many emotions. I'm not sure what it was for him. Perhaps he'd seen too many of these...hotel lobbies.

He was a hero, but he wasn't suave or smooth or confident. He was a warrior, out of his element. I wasn't sure how to make him comfortable, how to make sure he wouldn't leave.

"Can we maybe go somewhere and talk?" I finally asked.

"I'd like that."

London tapped her chin thoughtfully. Captain Westfall needed a first name. A cool hero's name. She'd been flipping through the phone book to find inspiration for his last name, but actually "Westfall" had just popped into her head. She liked "Jason," but wasn't sure she wanted to give the name away. She wanted a name for *her* guy, the one in the picture. Maybe she wanted to think of *him* as Jason.

She took out the newspaper and looked at his face. No, "Jason" wouldn't be right for him. So, Captain Westfall could be "Jason," after all.

She gave a short laugh. *Did I really just think about coming up with a name for a guy in a newspaper picture? Have I lost it?*

What would Juliana and Captain Jason Westfall say to each other? Why had he looked her up?

What did London want to say to *her* guy? She wanted to pour words into a letter, words to tell him of the way she looked into his eyes every day, of wanting him to be safe. She wanted to say that she couldn't stop thinking about him or that she dreamed about him. How he was her hero.

Wow. Time to go out and play. She was way too into this guy. She needed some balance, some perspective.

She picked up her handbag and hopped down the front steps of her condo, texting Nicole that she was on her way over.

"What's up?" Nicole asked as soon as she opened the door.

"Oh, you know... I felt like spending time with my best friend. Want to go out?"

"You're not really dressed for it," Nicole said. "I mean, sweat pants and messy hair?"

London looked down at herself. "Oops. I guess the idea hit and I ran with it."

"I've got wine here. Will that do, or were you thinking about picking up guys?"

"Ha ha. Wine's fine. I've been writing all day and I needed a break. I have stuff to figure out with the story, but I'm not sure yet where I go next."

"Where do you want to go?"

"Ultimately? I want them to fall in love and end up together, of course."

"So, do you want my help?"

"No. Right now I want that glass of wine you promised."

"You're kind of stingy with your Captain Westfall, aren't you?"

"Yeah. He's mine. Back off."

"Listen, I can't help it if you made him devastatingly attractive. Even *I'm* in love with him."

Both girls laughed, but London didn't laugh quite as hard.

Chapter 5

★ ★ ★

London needed a little distance from her characters to focus on what she wanted to come of their first meeting. She took a break to let her subconscious take over the task of coming up with a plot.

When she was ready to resume, she wrote the scene several different ways, and discarded each one. She wanted J&J (her new nickname for them) to jump right into the kiss; she couldn't wait for the passion to flare between them.

But she knew it wouldn't happen that way. Juliana would know Jason was skittish and respectful, and wouldn't make a play for him outright. She'd try to get into his head, though, and eventually his heart. She wasn't a roll-in-the-hay kind of girl. She was a destination girl.

So, how best to relay that in the book?

London couldn't stand the suspense of not knowing what would happen next.

The Hero

He didn't say much after we'd been seated in the bar; he just sipped his beer or stared at the

> bottle. When he looked up, his eyes were haunted.
>   I felt pain rolling off him and fought the urge to take his hand. I didn't want to scare him off.
>   "What happened to you?" I knew it would have taken something bad for us to be here like this.
>   He didn't speak right away, but I had the feeling that when his story started to come out, he wouldn't be able to stop it.

"Tell me more about Jason," Nicole said. "I mean, what does he look like? I want *details*."

London pictured him in her mind.

"I think he's mature, maybe thirty-five to thirty-eight, or maybe he's younger, just aged beyond his years by what he's seen and done, and endured. Not a fresh-faced kid. There's experience in his eyes. Not his first tour. He's lean and tough. His hair, it's kind of straggly. Messed up from the helmet. His helmet must have helped. I mean, he had blood on his face. If he hadn't been wearing his helmet, who knows what would have happened to him."

"You make it sound so real. I can almost see this guy."

"I'm good with details."

"Sure, but there's good and then there's 'this guy is real.'"

"Don't be silly. The better I describe him, the more the reader will respond to him."

"Okay, but you didn't put it in the book. You came up with it off the top of your head, like you were looking at a picture."

"I'm good. What can I say?"

Chapter 6

⋆ ⋆ ⋆

The picture was never far away. If London got stuck, she looked at it, stared at his eyes, and the words poured onto the page.

The Hero

He stared at his beer, not saying anything.

"So, why did you hope to run into me? I can see you're not at ease, that you're not comfortable being here."

He looked up at me, apparently conflicted about something. He took a swig of his beer. "This was a mistake. I should go."

"No. Stay." I touched his hand. "Please." He seemed uncomfortable but settled back into his chair.

"Why *did* you look me up, Captain? Why did you want to see me?"

"You can...my name is Jason."

I felt grief pouring off him like beads of

sweat. "Something happened, didn't it?"
He appeared to come to a decision. His eyes cleared up and he relaxed.
"No. There's nothing. I had some time, so I wanted to see how you're doing."
"Captain, you saved my life." My voice broke. I struggled to regain control of my emotions. "How do you think I am? I lost two friends that day, and all I can think about is you. You saved my life." I realized what that must have sounded like to him.
He turned his hand over in mine and his fingers curled around my hand. In his gray eyes, so somber, I saw gratitude.
"We don't have to talk about anything, really," I said, "but, please, don't go."
He released my hand then and picked up his beer.
"And you can call me Juliana."
I don't know what I expected to happen. I had my fantasies, but the reality was so much more. He seemed to trust me. I think he found whatever he thought he needed from me. The connection between us was so strong it was almost visible. We talked for a long while. About his team, about my job, about that day. The object was to be together, and neither of us wanted to leave.
He walked me back to my hotel, and I thanked him for the drinks. Impulsively, I hugged him. I could see something visceral in his eyes as I let him go. I almost, but not quite, kissed him. I backed away instead.
"Will I see you again?"
He didn't answer. Maybe he couldn't. Wartime makes everything so intense. He squeezed my hand

> and was gone.

London felt drained. She'd wanted so much more from her Captain. But she knew the timing wasn't right.

Her relationship with David never had the intensity or urgency of Juliana and Jason's connection. London longed to feel what Juliana was feeling. She wanted a hero of her own.

Wandering into her office, she picked up the newspaper, and looked into the soldier's eyes.

"Who *are* you?" She ran her fingers lightly over the face in the picture. "At the rate I'm going, I'll be saying 'I love you' to a picture unless I get a grip."

Chapter 7

★ ★ ★

Nicole sat at London's desk making hurry-up gestures while London wrapped up a business call. London laughed and tossed a paper clip at Nicole, who made a lunge for it, toppling some of the stacks of paper on the desk.

"Sorry," she mouthed as she bent to straighten them up, not noticing the horrified look that flashed across London's face.

"I'll call you back," she quickly said and ended the call.

Before London could stop her, Nicole picked up the newspaper and spotted the picture.

"Oh, my God. This is *him*. This is Captain Westfall."

"Don't be silly. Captain Westfall isn't real."

"Yes, he is. I'd know him anywhere."

London reached for the paper, but Nicole turned her back, keeping it out of reach.

"Who is he?"

"I don't have any idea. Now give that back."

"We can find him. Look, the photographer's name is right there. If we Google the photographer, we can contact him through his website."

"No, we can't. This guy is a soldier. In the war. Do you think fame is what he wants right now?"

"Of course he does. After your book comes out, and everyone knows it's him, he'll get rich. Heck, he'd be perfect to play Captain Westfall in the movie."

"He won't want this. Look at his face. Does he look shallow and greedy to you? No. He looks like the hero he is. Now, give it back."

Reluctantly, Nicole handed the paper back to London.

"Geez. Okay, you win. But from now on I'm going to be picturing this guy when I'm reading your book."

"Let's just go," London picked up her handbag and headed toward the door. "We're going to be late for the movie."

"You have a thing for this guy, don't you?" It wasn't really a question.

"No, I don't. It's just a picture, for God's sake. You're making too much of this." London wished the movie would start but knew it wouldn't be soon enough to throw Nicole off the track she was barreling down.

"I don't think so. The way you acted when I saw that picture . . . it's almost like you were jealous."

"That's ridiculous."

"If it's so ridiculous, why aren't we kidding about this and laughing?"

London didn't respond. Nicole could see right through her.

"It's okay if you are, you know," Nicole said. "Crushes are completely normal. And that's all I'm going to say about it."

Nicole smiled gamely but not with her eyes. London knew she'd hurt her best friend. By not trusting her, by not sharing, by lying about the picture.

Thankfully, the lights dimmed as the trailers started running. London glanced at Nicole, and gently squeezed her hand. She'd make it up to her somehow.

London's Hollywood Hills apartment building had a roof deck that was usually vacant during the week, a nice place for London to take her laptop and work in the open air on nice days. Desperate to mend her relationship with Nicole, London texted her friend to come over and sun with her. The fact that Nicole quickly accepted the invitation was reassuring.

London tossed a kale salad with a lemony vinaigrette and made a pitcher of iced wine coolers, which she carried to the roof and arranged on a table under a large patio umbrella. Nicole arrived almost as soon as London was finished with the preparations.

London hugged her tightly. "I was a jerk. You were right about everything. Can you ever forgive me?"

Nicole laughed as she disentangled herself from her friend.

"I *knew* it. Now, tell me everything."

"I'm obsessed with this guy. Well, not *obsessed* obsessed, but, you know."

London sheepishly confessed that she'd contacted the photographer.

"Really? What did he tell you?"

"I haven't heard anything back from him. I got a bounce-back to my email saying he's out of the country with limited access to email."

"What did you say to him?"

"Just that I was writing a book and doing research, and that I'd appreciate it if he could give me any information on the soldier."

"I'm sure you'll hear from him. How cool would it be to actually meet your soldier? He really is a hunk."

"Not just a hunk. Can you imagine what he's seen and endured? You can tell from looking at him that he's a twenty-four karat hero."

"Aren't you going a little overboard about this guy?" Nicole asked.

"Maybe. Of course, in my mind he's all the things I've said about him. But they're all projections of what I bring to the experience of looking at his picture."

"Thank you, Professor Calloway."

"Anyway, that's why it's such a preposterous notion to look him up. Could he ever live up to what I'm imagining him to be?"

"Now, that sounds rational. I'll stop worrying about you. And, by the way, I forgive you."

Nicole poured the wine coolers and handed one to London. As they munched on the kale salads, Nicole said, "What do you think will happen when you hear from the photographer?"

"There are really only two outcomes. Either he helps me find the soldier, or he says no."

"I would think the photographer would see that you're a legitimate writer and would want to help you if he could."

"Maybe. I guess we'll see. I'm torn about what I want his response to be, though. I really have doubts about meddling in my soldier's life. He's been through so much. Maybe he'd just prefer to be left alone in his anonymity. But I'm so curious about him. And I want to know that he's okay."

"Admit it. You just want to know him."

"Yes. I just want to know him."

Chapter 8

★ ★ ★

London was anxious to get back to J&J. She hadn't quite decided what would happen next, but she knew what Juliana would be feeling. This part was easy to write.

The Hero

After he was gone, and I was in my room alone, I tried to relive every moment of the night.

I had nothing of substance. He hadn't said he'd see me again or talked about why he wanted to see me. No promises were made, no plans discussed. He was gone and wouldn't be coming back.

But I couldn't accept that, so I wouldn't believe it. Spoken or not, there was a connection between us, and I was sure he felt it too.

Still, I knew if he ever came back it wouldn't be soon. And that made me sad.

I'd thought a lot about the soldier who'd saved my life in the days after the attack. Now, I

> thought about the *man*. There was a longing in me that grew with each passing day. And all I had were my fantasies.
>
> As with all great love stories, destiny had a part to play, and I knew he was my destiny. Sometimes, destiny is a big, epic miracle, but sometimes it's as small and intimate as the meeting of one man and one woman who were meant to be together. The destiny part meant that nothing could stop it.
>
> And that's how I felt. This man needed me, and I wasn't sure whether the reason was a big purpose or a small one, personal or otherwise.
>
> "Oh, Jason," I said, hugging myself. "I need you to come back to me."
>
> As the days passed, the ache in my heart receded even if the longing didn't, and the real world reasserted itself. I had a job to do, and stories were everywhere in Afghanistan.

How to get them back together? That problem was never far from London's mind. Her book would only be three chapters long if she had him rush back and declare his love. But it was so *hard* to keep them apart.

Damn it, she thought. *Maybe I'm not cut out to be a writer. I don't have the patience for it.*

Now, that wasn't a helpful attitude. She had to keep going, word by word, paragraph by paragraph, page by page.

But nothing was coming to her. She was at an impasse in the imagination department. Pulling out the newspaper picture, she said to the soldier, "What *would* you do? I don't know if you'd come back or not."

Getting no answer, she picked up her notebook and poised her pen, hoping to generate the creative process. Other than tapping the pen on the paper a few times, she failed to accomplish a thing.

She called Nicole.

"I need a new brain. If I buy you a drink, will you help me with my story?"

Nicole laughed. "I've got wine. Come over here and it will be easier to talk."

Some minutes later, Nicole opened the door with "What part do you need help with? I'd be great with the sex scenes."

London stared at her for a moment, and burst out laughing. "That's the fun part. What makes you think I need help with that?"

"Oh, okay. Then, my job will be to get the wine."

When Nicole was settled on the sofa beside her, London said, "I haven't added much since you last saw the story except the part about Juliana sitting in her hotel room thinking about Jason. She thinks they're destined to be together but doesn't think she'll see him for a while, so she's sad. I don't know when or if he'll come back. I mean, *would* he come back?"

"He *has* to come back."

"I *know*. So, tell me how we make it happen."

"Why did he come see her in the first place? Why was grief falling off him like sweat?"

"I'm thinking he must have lost some of his men in an attack. He's very close to them, like brothers, and they've been through a lot together. Maybe it's survivor guilt. What do you think?"

"It's plausible," said Nicole. "Maybe he's in an elite squad. Then they'd be even closer. What does the Army have, Rangers?"

"That's cool. I need to Google 'Army Rangers' to see if they have captains. So, anyway, he and his men are on a dangerous assignment and they're ambushed, and Captain Westfall is the only one to get out alive."

"That would *kill* him. Are you trying to crush him?"

"No, but all the books and classes on writing say you have to heap the tragedies on the heroes. And then heap more on them."

"That's so *sad*."

"I *know*. I hate that, too, but if Captain Westfall doesn't have an emotional emergency, what does he need Juliana for?"

"Then I guess we better start torturing him."

The Hero

About a month after my evening with Jason Westfall, I was walking back to my hotel after dinner with some journalist friends. Through the grimy window of a local bar, I thought I saw him sitting alone at a table. Waving goodnight to my friends, I walked into the dusky interior of the lounge. Starting toward his table, I paused, questioning whether I'd be welcome. And just watched him. He sat unmoving, staring into his glass of beer.

He seemed lost; I don't know how else to describe it. I couldn't bring myself to intrude, so I turned back toward the entrance. He looked up then. I wasn't fast enough to escape undetected, so I smiled awkwardly and raised my hand in greeting.

He didn't smile. He just looked at me, his face hard to read. Then, reluctantly it seemed, he stood.

"Ms. Curry. Nice to see you again."

Of course, he would be unfailingly respectful. Even if I could see in his eyes that what he said wasn't true.

"Captain Westfall. I'm sorry to intrude. I saw you through the window and wanted to say 'hi.' But you don't look like you want company right now, so I won't stay."

If he'd wanted me to go, he seemed to reconsider. "I have a lot on my mind. Please, don't leave. Can I buy you a drink?"

He pulled out a chair for me. I was torn about what I should do but nodded my head in spite of my discomfort.

The conversation was stilted and awkward. We made small talk for the time it took me to finish the cocktail he'd ordered for me, then he apologized.

"I'm sorry; I'm not good company tonight. Maybe it would be better to do this another time."

"Or you could let me help," I said.

"What is it you think you could help with, Ms. Curry?"

"If I knew what was eating you alive, I'd tell you how I could help. I'm a good listener, and you look like you lost your best friend."

A curtain fell over his eyes, and I felt him pulling back.

Appalled that I'd made things worse, I said, "I'm sorry. I don't want to intrude on your...pain."

As I turned to go, his hand caught mine. There was naked pleading in his eyes.

"Don't go. I'm sorry."

I couldn't help myself. I touched his face and brushed the hair back from his forehead.

"Let's both go." He looked at me questioningly, then threw some bills on the table and followed me out the door. It was only when we got to the sidewalk that I saw what kind of shape he was in.

He must have been in that bar for quite a while.

Once again, I draped his arm over my shoulders so I could support him. He leaned on me before righting himself and managed to walk almost unassisted.

"Do you need to be somewhere?" I asked.

"No. Nowhere."

What could I do? I took him to my hotel room. I helped him sit on the side of my bed, and he slumped forward, so I untied his shoes and took them off. Turning down the bedcovers, I pulled his T-shirt off over his head.

I stood back and put my hand over my mouth, stifling a sob. There were scars and bruises and cuts on his body, some healed, some fresh. Whatever he'd been through, it broke my heart.

"Jason, get in." I guided him into the bed and pulled the covers up over him. He was out as soon as his head hit the pillow.

He groaned softly as he rolled over. I smoothed the bedcovers and tucked them around him. And then I kissed him. It was only a gentle kiss--I doubt he even felt it. I suppose it was wrong, but I did it, and I wouldn't take it back.

Now what? He was curled on his side, a lump under the covers of my bed.

I sat at the room's only table and wrote in my journal in the dim light from the lamp beside the chair. Then I read for a while, but time passed so slowly. I tried to get comfortable in the chair or resting my head in my arms on the table.

At some point after midnight, I lay myself down on the bed next to him, on top of the covers, fully dressed, and slept with my arm across his body.

I woke early to find his hand holding mine and allowed myself to stay beside him a little while longer. I had intended to get up before he could awaken, to avoid any awkwardness or embarrassment he might feel, so I pulled away from him, gathered what I needed, and headed toward the bathroom.

He was sitting on the side of the bed fully dressed when I came out, my hair still wet from the shower. He looked like he didn't know what to say.

"Did I..." he started.

"No. I assume you're wondering whether anything happened between us. It didn't."

"I'm sorry about last night. I wasn't myself."

"You have nothing to apologize for. As always, you were a perfect gentleman."

I started across the room toward the phone on the bedside table. "I'll order some breakfast to be brought up."

"No. Thank you, but I have to go." He stood and brought his hand up to his head.

"I imagine you're not feeling so great this morning. I think you tied one on last night." He didn't answer. "You need food, and I'm not going to let you leave until you've eaten something."

I stood right in front of him. "Are we clear, soldier?"

"Yes, ma'am."

I'm not sure, but I may have seen traces of a grin cross his face. "In the meantime, you can get cleaned up if you want."

Maybe it's strange that I would have all these feelings for a guy I'd only seen a few times, but he saved my life. Something happens to you when you owe your life to someone. The feelings are intense and raw. The fact that he's attractive has nothing to do with it. Well, not completely. Like the old movies used to say, when someone saves your life, you belong to them forever. That's what it feels like. Really.

Chapter 9

★ ★ ★

"Jason spent the night in Juliana's room. Aren't you proud of me?"

"So, how *was* he?" Nicole asked with a grin.

"Get your mind out of the gutter. Nothing happened. I mean, *that* didn't happen."

"Ha."

"Seriously, I *love* this book. I'm having so much fun writing it."

"Well, if they didn't do it, why did he spend the night?"

"He had too much to drink. Actually, he's still there. She ordered breakfast."

"What happens next?"

"I'll let you know after I write it."

The Hero

He was still in the shower when breakfast was delivered. I was glad because I was afraid of the awkwardness of not knowing what to talk about. At least, with food, we'd be able to ease into it. I ran downstairs and picked up a toothbrush for him while he was still in the bathroom, and left it at the door so he would find it when he came out.

I think the smell of food brought him out into the room, and he sauntered over to the table to inspect our spread. His hair was still wet, and he ran his hand through it as he sat down. I poured coffee for both of us and sat down opposite him, trying not to notice how strong and sexy he looked. He obviously had no idea the effect he had on me as he sipped his coffee. I came pretty close to letting out a moan.

We ate in silence, for what seemed like a long time, until I couldn't stand it anymore and started the small talk.

"How are you feeling this morning, Captain?"

"Could be worse. I guess I owe you for...uh--"

"Of course you don't. It was the least I could do."

Damn, this wasn't easy. He was like a code I needed to break. I was saddened to think that when breakfast was done there would be no reason for him to stay.

And so it was. After we'd eaten everything and finished the coffee, he stood, and I stood. When he didn't walk to the door, I felt a glimmer of hope. And I knew that it was going to be up to me to take this where I wanted it to go.

"Look, Jason, before you go, I'm not going to beat around the bush. Maybe for you, saving my life was in the line of duty, but, for me, it changed everything. My emotions are so close to the surface, so right there. You mean something to me. And I don't just mean gratitude. I think about you. I miss you. I don't know anything about you, and you know very little about me, but it doesn't change a thing. I want you in my life."

I waited. Maybe I'd gone too far, but I had nothing to lose at this point. I wanted him to see me. I wanted to be as important to him as he was to me.

His face reflected the confusion I was sure my little speech had caused in him. I let out a breath and turned toward the door.

But he caught my arm and pulled me into an embrace. As I tilted my face up, he kissed me, a kiss I will never get over. His lips were gentle but greedy, and I sank against him, my mind spinning webs of desire. I threw my arms around his neck, and he picked me up and carried me toward the bed.

And then set me down beside it and let me go.

"I can't do this," he said.

He turned, but I sidestepped around him. "What just happened here?"

"I'm sorry, Juliana. I can't give you what you want."

"I'm not asking you for anything."

"Yes, you are. And you know it. I have to go."

"No. Not until you tell me what's really going on here."

I could see the effort it took for him to talk. That whole fight or flight instinct was playing out on his face. I was prepared to let him go if that was what he really wanted, and I stepped aside so he could leave.

But Jason softened. He took my hands in his. "There have been women in my life. My buddies and I, we hit the bars sometimes on our nights off, and there are always women. But those...dates...are just exercise. No strings, no future. A woman like you, though. That's a whole different ballgame. I can't be in love. It's too hard, too dangerous for me."

I didn't want to hear what he was saying. It wasn't registering.

"You're a woman I *could* love. Back home, in the states, things would be different. But, here...here everything is intense. Every moment is precious because it could be your last. You feel things more deeply here. And we have this connection between us. I don't deny it."

"But I wouldn't ask anything of you. I promise."

"Ah, but you wouldn't be able to help yourself. Like now." He sighed deeply. "I'm going to go now. It's really for the best."

Seeing the look on my face, I guess he felt bad because he bent to kiss my forehead, but I stood on my tiptoes and kissed him on the mouth. Then I stepped back and said, "You're wrong. You need me as much as I need you."

London felt bad because she knew he was right. A soldier like that, he needed to concentrate on staying alive. Juliana would be a distraction that could get him killed.

But, damn it, they had to be together, and she had to figure out how to make it happen. If she tried to force the story, it wouldn't feel right, and she wanted it to be perfect. She needed inspiration, something to propel her toward where to take their relationship.

She decided she needed to research the whole Special Forces thing further. Where would Jason be, anyway? A base somewhere close to Kabul, another assignment far away, another *country*?

Or maybe she needed to focus on Juliana. What was her life there like? What was she working on?

She called Nicole.

"Once again, I've sort of painted myself into a corner and don't know how to get out. I could use some suggestions."

"I'll do what I can, but first, though, the *real* Captain Westfall, you know, in the picture—did you know that there was all this controversy over the picture?"

"What are you talking about?"

"You're not the only one who was taken by that picture. People are blogging about it. Some are saying that the faces of the soldiers should never have been shown, and that it could put them in danger. Others are saying what a cool picture it is, like a movie poster."

"I hate that. I don't want anyone else to be talking about him. What if someone else writes a book about him? Oh, my God, I'm so screwed."

"Well, not really. I find it hard to believe that there are a bunch of books being written about him at this very moment. In fact, I find it hard to believe that there's even *one* book besides yours being written. Besides, a lot of this is from right after the article came out. By now, most people have probably moved on."

"Then, why—"

"I thought you'd want to know, that's all."

"Well—"

"Really. It's okay. I just thought it was interesting. Sorry."

"I accept your apology, but only because I'm so relieved I don't have to worry about it now."

"Thank you."

"By the way, I got you a picture frame."

"A picture frame?" London asked, puzzled.

"For your soldier. Get with it, girl."

London smacked her forehead with the palm of her hand. "Duh. I can't believe you thought of this and I didn't. Thank you."

London wandered into her office and found the newspaper picture. She picked up a pair of scissors but put them down again. "Don't be mad, but I think I want to wait until the book is finished before I frame him. I don't want to jinx it or anything. Then I'll set it on my bookshelf so that I can look at him any time I want."

Nicole smiled. "No problem. I totally understand. Now, back to your problem."

"Back to my problem. Juliana and Jason had breakfast together, and when he was going to leave, Juliana gave him a speech about her emotions, and he told her he had a connection with her, and then they kissed."

"Finally."

"Kind of. Because then he told her that he couldn't let himself fall in love with her because it would be too dangerous for him."

"Huh?"

"Think about it. If he's sitting there in his foxhole, or wherever they sit, he can't have his mind wandering to Juliana. He has to pay attention. Or he could get killed."

"But other soldiers have wives and girlfriends. Why can't he?"

"I haven't quite worked that out yet, but I think it's because of the Special Forces thing. He doesn't have a whole platoon backing him up. There are only a few of them, and they have to stay alert."

"That makes sense."

"We sound like airheads, don't we?" London giggled.

"Yes. Sadly."

"I was thinking... what if he had to rescue her again. Then he wouldn't be able to deny that fate was forcing them together."

"Sounds good," Nicole said. "What would he be rescuing her from?"

"I don't know. Maybe she's kidnapped by insurgents, or her jeep breaks down miles from civilization and he finds her."

"I like either one of those. And, don't forget he still has to tell her why grief was dripping off him."

"His defenses will crumble when he's with her again, and then he'll spill his guts."

"Or, now that they've kissed and sort of declared their feelings, does he still have to have that grief thing?" Nicole asked.

"Kind of. I mean, that's why he was drinking alone in that bar. I suppose I could rewrite that part and leave it out, but I think he's got to be suffering. I'll think about it."

She wrapped up her strategy session with Nicole, promising to let her read the part about the kiss, and pulled up Google on her laptop.

"This is London."

"Hello," said an unfamiliar voice on the cell. "This is Simon Adjani."

"Simon Adjani?" It took her a moment. "Oh, the photographer. Oh my God! Thanks for getting back to me. I wasn't sure I'd hear from you." She was in the kitchen pouring a cup of coffee and pulled open a drawer searching for something to write with.

"Yes. Sorry it took awhile, but I've been on the move."

"I can imagine. You know why I contacted you. I was hoping you could help me locate the soldier in the picture I emailed you." My heart was racing. This could actually happen.

"There was a lot of interest in that photo. It caused quite a stir," he said.

"Really? Why?"

"I think maybe it touched a nerve."

London was less than pleased to hear about the others. But Simon had called her back so she still might be successful. "Anyway, I'm writing about Afghanistan and thought he might be able to provide me a good perspective for my story. Is it possible for you to help me find him?"

"Unfortunately, no."

"But—"

"I make it a practice not to out any subjects appearing in my photos."

"But, don't you get a release from them or something so you have permission to use their images?"

"When possible. In war zones, however, I protect their identities as much as possible. For their safety."

"Isn't publishing his picture on the front page of a major newspaper as dangerous as telling me his name?" London was frustrated at his responses.

Was he aware of the controversy concerning the picture, and sensitive to the suggestion that he'd made an error in judgment? She could almost feel him withdrawing through the phone, and realized she'd gone too far.

In a stilted voice, he said, "Not in my opinion. I'm sorry I can't help you." Click.

She hadn't meant to offend him. Or maybe she had. "Ah, well. It was a pipe dream anyway."

Chapter 10

★ ★ ★

The Hero

I'd been assigned a story about an Army medical team traveling to a remote village where insurgents had inflicted heavy casualties.

I'd never been on a helicopter before. Not sure how I had missed out since they were everywhere in Afghanistan.

Besides me, there were three doctors, three soldiers, and the pilot. About forty-five minutes into the flight, the sound of the rotors changed. Tensions rose in the chopper as we heard the pilot radioing our position before telling us all to brace for a hard landing. Honestly, there wasn't time to be scared, maybe because of adrenaline, maybe because of disbelief that we were in trouble.

We hit the ground roughly--I banged hard against the door, and my face bashed into the back of the seat in front of me, a blast of pain shooting through my cheek and lip--then the chopper canted to the side and tumbled. Two of the soldiers were tossed out early on, and others were ejected by the momentum of the helicopter skidding and bouncing along the ground before smashing into some boulders and breaking apart. The screeching and creaking and other noises, too numerous to describe, stopped, and we were left with an eerie silence before voices started asking if everyone was okay.

I couldn't move. I knew I was on the ground, but my legs were trapped, and the pain was excruciating.

One of the soldiers and a doctor were at my side within moments, telling me to be still. I tried to sit up, but the pain stopped me.

"We need to get you out from under there," the soldier said. "There's a piece of the tail section on your legs."

So much was going on around me. There were other injured people, and everyone was helping each other. Two of the men tried to free my legs. The pain was awful, but I bit my lip to keep from crying out. Both of them were bleeding but still helping me. I think I went in and out of consciousness because I don't remember being removed from the chopper. Once I was free, one of the doctors checked me for broken bones. He checked my eyes and examined my scalp.

"You've got a pretty good bump on your head. How do you feel?" he asked me.

My voice came out in a croak. "Not sure. I hurt." He had to lean in to hear me.

"How's...how's everyone else?" I managed to get out.

"Everyone's alive, but there are injuries. Some bad."

"We need to get to cover, Doc," a soldier said, glancing around the area. "Okay if I try to move her? We're in insurgent territory, and they'll be coming to see if they can take hostages."

He put his arm under my shoulders and lifted me to a sitting position. "Your leg is broken, maybe both of them. You won't be able to walk, so I'm going to have to pick you up. This is going to hurt."

I cried out from the pain and grabbed onto his arm. He paused briefly, and I said, "No. I can do this."

I gritted my teeth and made a heroic effort to be brave.

The men had already been forming a barrier from whatever pieces of the wreckage they could carry, and we were all corralled between the barrier and the valley wall where we had landed. There were boulders dotting the area where we'd gone down, which gave further cover.

I could hear the pilot on his radio, shouting "Mayday" over and over. The soldiers were conferring with each other and checking their weapons, pulling ammo out of the chopper body so it would be easy to access.

I kept fading in and out, and I had trouble following what was going on. But I was alert enough when I heard the first bullet ping off the helicopter wreckage, and I heard my companions yelling, "Get down! Get down."

And I was alert enough to be scared out of my mind.

Bullets were flying everywhere. Even one of the injured soldiers, his leg in a hastily applied splint and one arm immobile, was shooting with his good hand.

Someone fit a helmet to my head. It was big and fell down over my eyes, but it offered protection that I wasn't about to turn down.

I wanted to help. There were so few of us. At my pleading, one of the soldiers asked if I could shoot and handed me a sidearm. I'd done some hunting with my dad when I was young, and I probably remembered enough to be able to use the gun. No rifles were available, but considering that I was semi-incapacitated by my broken leg, the handgun was about all I could handle anyway. He made sure it was loaded and ready to fire and asked me if I was sure. Nodding, showing a bravado I didn't really feel, I lifted my head over our barricade and scanned the area. Seeing movement, I squeezed off a shot, and winced from the recoil, then manned up and aimed at anything I thought might be a target. I might not have actually hit any of them, but I thought my laying down fire could slow them up a little and help our guys.

The fire raining down on us grew more intense, and I saw one of the doctors take a bullet in the shoulder. I fired in anger at the spot where I'd seen the rifle flash. Miraculously, I nailed the bastard. The soldier kneeling next to me said "nice" and flashed a brief smile before he turned back to his position.

Some of the insurgents were maneuvering to get above us. They knew we were vulnerable as there would be nowhere for us to hide if they were behind us. We concentrated our fire, trying to pick off the ones we could see.

A mortar or something hit in front of the chopper, and the concussion sent us sprawling. I think I smacked my head. When I opened my eyes and could focus, I saw explosions kicking up dust in the hilly area where the insurgents were hiding. "What--" I started to ask but was cut off by the sound of choppers overhead. My soldiers started cheering as the heloes touched down.

Then it gets fuzzy. I think I passed out, and when I was aware of my surroundings again, I knew I was on one of the helicopters: the noise of the rotors, the vibration of the chopper. I sighed in relief and opened my eyes.

"You certainly pull out all the stops to get what you want, don't you?"

In confusion, I looked toward the voice. My vision wasn't clear, but I thought I saw Jason sitting on the floor beside where I lay.

I closed my eyes tightly and tears started to flow. I missed him so much, I couldn't stand it. I was hallucinating, and it was breaking my heart. Then I passed out.

When I woke up again, I was in a hospital room. I opened my eyes to see the doctor on his way out the door.

"Where . . ." was all I could get out, but it was loud enough that he heard me and turned around. He came back to the bed and leaned over me, the little flashlight in his hand shining in my eyes.

"Welcome back, Ms. Curry."

"Where am I?" I croaked.

"You're in the hospital in Kabul. You've been out for two days."

"What's wrong with me?" I asked.

"You have a concussion, and your right leg is broken. But you're going to be fine." He started back out of the room but paused. "Someone's been waiting to see you."

It didn't really register with me. I was so tired. I turned my head to the wall and closed my eyes.

"You're such a *girl*, Juliana," a voice said. "I tease you a little about the extremes you'll go to for a date with me, and you burst into tears."

I turned my head toward him. Jason smiled down at me.

"You *were* really there?" I asked in a broken voice, and he nodded. I was overcome with emotion and I started to cry, softly at first, and then with great, heartrending sobs.

Through my tears, I could see the alarm on his face. He didn't know what he'd done, or what he *should* do. "I'm sorry. For whatever I did. Are you okay?"

I nodded my head.

"I'd say we can't keep meeting like this, but you didn't laugh at my last joke," he said, trying again.

I couldn't focus on his words. I just wanted to look at him. I don't know what emotions were reflected on my face because I was feeling so many things, but whatever he saw he sat down on the bed and took my hand in his.

His gray eyes looked so serious and concerned. I asked him to raise my hospital bed, and when he stood up, I really saw him for the first time. He was a mess, his hair straggly and his uniform dirty and crusted with dried blood.

"You look like hell, in a heavenly kind of way," I said to him softly. "Are you hurt?"

He looked down at himself. "No. This time, it's *your* blood."

"Come closer," I croaked, my voice scratchy and raw. I took his face in my hands and kissed him.

He gently pulled me into an embrace, and we held each other for a long time until I reluctantly let him go, and he stood.

"How are the guys who were with me?" I asked.

"Everyone's alive. Some are in worse condition than others."

"Who--"

"I think the pilot got the worst of it. One of the doctors got shot. Some other injuries. I'll tell you all about it soon, but right now you need to rest. I'll come back in a bit after you've had time to get some sleep."

I tried to protest, but he kissed me again then turned and left.

A nurse came in to find me wiping my eyes.

"Ah, what's wrong, honey?"

I couldn't answer. I was so devastated that he was gone again.

"Do you want your eyes to be all red when your soldier comes back?"

"What makes you so sure he's coming back?"

"He hasn't left this hospital in two days. There's no chance he isn't coming back."

"Really?"

"Yes, really."

"I don't know why I'm so emotional."

"How could you not be after what you've been through?"

```
    Her comments made me feel much better. And she
didn't know the half of it. I had been through a
lot the last couple of months. The hotel attack,
the loss of my friends, and now the crash. And that
didn't even take into account the emotional toll
that being apart from Jason had caused me. So, she
was right. How could I not be emotional?
    Mollified, I asked for a mirror, and saw the
sympathetic look on the nurse's face.
    I felt heartsick as I saw the bandage around my
head and the bruises on my face. I almost felt
self-conscious that he had seen me like this but
knew that was insulting to Jason. He wouldn't have
cared, any more than I would if the situation were
reversed.
```

London stood up and stretched. She'd been bent over her laptop for hours, concentrating on this section of her book. It was still early, and she made a quick list of all the things she needed to accomplish. Reading over the list, she decided that right now she wanted to talk about her book, so she blew off the other tasks and called Nicole.

"Can you come over? I've made some progress on the story and want you to read it. If you want to. I'll order a pizza."

"Of course, I want to. Anything *significant* happen yet?"

"Depends on your definition of 'significant.' You can see when you get here."

Her friend arrived with a bottle of wine. They placed their pizza order then settled themselves on London's beigey sectional sofa.

"How's the real estate business?" London asked, sipping her wine.

"Pretty good, actually. We're finally starting to see inventory picking up. It was pretty lean there for a while. I'll be happily depositing a couple of commission checks before long. Maybe we should plan a vacation or something."

"I could go for that. I feel like my fingers are going to drop off. Or carpal tunnel syndrome will set in. I love my story, but writing can be exhausting sometimes."

"So can showing houses. Ah, well. These are the days of our lives." London laughed. "By the way, I heard from the photographer."

"The photographer? Oh, the *photographer*." Nicole brightened. "And?"

"And nothing. He said he wouldn't help me. I think I pissed him off when I said his picture might have put the soldier in danger. I guess he was aware of that whole internet blogging controversy. He hung up on me."

"It was a long shot. We don't need him."

"No, we don't."

London handed Nicole the pages and gave her a few minutes to read over the new section.

"Really good," Nicole said, putting it down. "So, now they can move forward with their relationship?"

"I suppose so although I think Juliana is going to be sent home to recuperate."

"But Jason can come visit."

"He's in the Army. He can't just pop over."

"Surely he could get a leave and spend it in New York with her."

"Well—"

"Here's my idea: She's upset because she's called back to America, and she won't be able to see Jason. Once she's home, he shows up on her doorstep. On leave. They spend a week together. Sex is wonderful." Nicole looked smug at her story fix.

"She has a broken leg."

"People with broken bones have sex. I'm sure there's a way."

"I don't know."

"You *want* them to be together, don't you?"

"Of course, I do. But—"

"You don't want to write the sex scenes, do you?"

London sighed deeply. "Well, my mother could read it. My friends. I don't want them to be thinking… whatever it is they would be thinking."

Nicole burst out laughing. "You are such a prude. I can't believe you just said that."

"Go ahead and laugh. I didn't say I *wouldn't* do it."

Saved by the bell. The pizza man had just arrived.

Nicole followed London into the kitchen and pulled two plates out of the cupboard. She refilled the wineglasses while London loaded two slices of pizza on each plate. They carried their dinner back to the living room, and ate in silence for a few moments.

Nicole swallowed her last bite and burrowed into the sofa cushion until she was comfortable. "So, how is he in bed?"

"Nicole!"

"Well, surely you've imagined it."

"It's a story. I haven't written it yet." She looked at her friend skeptically. "But, I'm sure he's going to be great."

Chapter 11

⭐ ⭐ ⭐

London was stuck. The direction she was thinking of taking was making her sad. She thought she should make an outline, but she'd never been good at outlines. She needed to know the ending, and she didn't have one. At least, not yet. So far, the story had come easily to her, but now she had to make it complex and rich.

How? It was complicated, spinning a yarn. Why did she even start this story when she didn't know how it would turn out? As if she had to ask. If she couldn't have her soldier, then she'd write a story she could live vicariously through.

If that's what she wanted, it should have a happy ending, right? But it didn't feel, to her, like everything would turn out okay in the end. In that event, where would that leave her outline?

```
a.  Letters declaring their feelings are sent back
    and forth between Juliana and Jason
b.  They make plans for next opportunity to be
    together
c.  Will Jason leave the Army, or is he in it for
    the duration?
d.  Juliana pines away
e.  Jason has another leave, and they meet up in
```

```
    Paris
f.  Juliana is pregnant
g.  Before she can tell Jason, he's captured by the
    Taliban
h.  OMG!!
i.  Now what?
```

Maybe that was too harsh. She didn't want him to be captured by the Taliban as it would almost guarantee a horrible end. Yeah, that can't happen.

Rolling her neck to get the kinks out, London stretched. Writing was a chore. She needed a break, so she put on her bikini and headed for the apartment pool. An hour or so of relaxation in the sun was the best medicine.

When it got to be too hot, London pulled her hair up in a ponytail and dove into the pool. A few laps and the sun would feel good again.

The Hero

Hearing someone enter my room, I turned toward the door, smiling. To see my Bureau Chief standing there.

"How are you doing?" His face was full of sympathy.

"I've been better," I croaked.

"I've got some good news for you. We're sending you home."

"What?" I couldn't believe my ears. "I can't leave here."

"Of course, you can. It's all been arranged. When they release you, which the doctor thinks will be day after tomorrow, we'll pick you up and take you back to your hotel to pack. Flight arrangements have already been made."

"But I don't want to go. I have things to do here. *Important* things."

"Now, don't argue with me. This is for the best. After you've had time to fully recuperate, we can talk about whether you should come back, but we can think about that sometime in the future."

"But--"

"I have an appointment to get to. I'll check back in with you tomorrow to see how you're doing. I know you'll be happy about this if you think about it for a while."

And he was gone. What was I going to do? I had to be here, with Jason. Especially now.

I started to cry, emotional baby that I'd become lately, but I didn't want Jason to see me this way again. He'd seen enough tears in the few times we'd been together. So, I took a deep breath to regain control and flagged down my nurse so she could get me the mirror and something to wash my face with.

No point in trying for makeup. With all the bandages and bruising, it wouldn't help anyway. Instead, I put a little Vaseline on my lips. That made me feel better.

When he arrived, I flashed my best smile (under the circumstances) and held out my hand. He saw right through my bravado, however.

"Is everything okay?" He took my hand, and bent to kiss me lightly on the mouth. I reached up and put my arms around his neck. It's so awkward trying to hug someone standing up when you're lying in a hospital bed, but he took me in his arms and didn't let go for a long moment.

When he pulled away, he searched my face. He could see that my eyes were red-rimmed, which I couldn't help, and I tried hard not to let any tears spill out.

"They're sending me home. I have to go back to America. In two days. What are we going to do?"

His eyes were somber, but he didn't speak. Instead, he sat on the bed and took my hand again.

We'd never spoken to each other, really, like this. It had been all extremes between us. The first time, when we'd met at the ruined hotel and gone for a drink, that was the only time we'd actually talked, and even then it was awkward. Well, there was also that morning, in my room, when I'd spewed out my feelings all over him. But that didn't count as the kind of conversation couples had in real life. So, what could I expect him to say when I ask him an impactful question like *what are we going to do?*

"You'll be safe there," was what he finally said. "I want you to be safe."

He wants her to be safe. Well, Juliana would not be happy with that. She wanted him to be as bummed as she was. Didn't he care that they would be apart? London could have fun with this. She'd decided to not be so glum about the future of her characters.

"I have to have a happy ending, after all," she told Nicole, who had joined her at the pool. With the weather hitting the mid-80s to 90s every day, they spent as much time sunning as possible. Not that tanning was their goal. Nothing as unhealthy as that. It was just so pleasant chatting from a prone position, glass of iced tea in hand. Nicole was able to schedule a lot of her showings and client meetings for earlier in the day, leaving her afternoons relatively free one or two days a week, and London could easily close up her laptop and take a break. "I've been reading some books on writing, and romance readers insist on a happy ending. I could buck the trend, but if no one wants to read my book, me and my sad ending would only have each other."

"Personally, I'm super happy that you changed your mind. I want Jasiana to end up together."

"Jasiana?"

"Yeah. That doesn't really work, does it?" Nicole laughed. "I guess not every twosome can have that combined-name thing going for them."

"Ha. Maybe Julion?"

"Maybe not. Where are our heroes right now?"

"They're in Juliana's hospital room. She's just been told she has to go back to America, and Jason basically patted her on the head and said she'd be safer there."

"He did *not*. I mean, he's in love, after all."

"Well, I'm sure that's the way she will see it. She probably wishes he'd break down and sob or something."

"No, no, no. There have been enough tears in the story so far to last until the end."

"I know. I have to get her to buck up. She's looking like a sniveling baby. I promise I'm going to make sure she toughens up."

Nicole raised the back of her chaise. "I have something to report."

"Tell me, tell me."

"I met someone." She smiled smugly.

"Who, where? Tell me everything."

"I was having a drink with one of my fellow agents after a brokers' open. This cute guy sat down next to me. I almost did a double-take, but I managed to stay cool. Anyway, he looked over at me and smiled, so I said hi and he said hi, and then my agent friend had to leave, so he offered to buy me a drink. Of course, I said yes. His name's Kyle Nolan and I can't wait until you meet him."

"I can't wait to meet him."

"I like him."

"I can tell. Have you seen him since that night?"

"Yes, I have. I think we're an item."

"Really? Clever of you to keep that a secret from your best friend. How long ago did this all happen?"

"Only last week. I didn't want to jinx anything. I mean, it might have turned into nothing."

"Hmm. You're an item after a week? I don't want to sound skeptical or anything."

"It's possible I might be exaggerating a tiny bit. Or maybe it's wishful thinking on my part."

"I forgive you for not telling me right away. Anyway, good for you. I suppose I won't be seeing as much of you anymore. I'll have to advertise for a new best friend."

"What?"

"Just kidding. You know you're irreplaceable."

Chapter 12

★ ★ ★

London felt jealous at being left alone while her best friend was involved with a new guy, but she didn't want to brood about it. She wasn't one to stay in a funk for long, and she was glad when the cloud of gloom floated away.

She had more uninterrupted writing time. That's how she'd look at it. She needed to ruminate on the trajectory of the story and try to figure out what she wanted to happen next.

She wanted to get to know Nicole's boyfriend, Kyle. Nicole was enthusiastic in her efforts for them to spend time together, and London had a fairly good idea of who Kyle was after meeting him.

And she didn't like him. She couldn't share this with Nicole, who was all Kyle, all the time. The problem, as London saw it, was that Kyle seemed like a player. And he had shifty eyes. She couldn't quite put her finger on what it was about him that was off-putting, but London didn't see the long-term potential of this guy, and hoped Nicole would see that he wasn't right for her. She didn't want her friend to get hurt.

Nicole had been excited to introduce her best friend to her new boyfriend, and arranged to have them both over for dinner. During the evening, Kyle hung on Nicole like a fungus. London watched Nicole chatting away not realizing her disgust. London knew it was unkind of her, but she shivered anyway at the thought. She plastered a smile on her face, turning on her charming personality.

"Kyle, Nicole's told me so much about you. You're a promoter? I'm not sure what that is."

"I make people important. I promote them."

"Interesting. How do you do that?"

"I have a Rolodex some people would kill for. And a big bank account. I get my clients out there in all the right places. You know, club openings, A-list parties, film premiers. That kind of thing. I have a talent for getting them followers on social media."

"Fascinating." London tried to muster enthusiasm, noting Nicole's approving smile.

"I could help you out."

"Me? I don't need any promoting."

"Are you sure? I mean, surely you want as much publicity as possible for your hero soldier, right?"

"Excuse me?"

"Your book. What did you think I meant?"

London flashed a stern look at Nicole. She wasn't jumping for joy that Nicole had told Kyle about *The Hero*. That she'd also told him about the picture was troubling. She didn't want a lot of people knowing there was a real man behind the fiction.

"Thanks. I appreciate your offer, but I'm good."

"I don't think you realize how much I could do for you. Introductions to important people, publicity for your book. You should reconsider."

"Thanks, but I think not. I have an agent and an editor. And a publisher. They can take care of anything I need." She turned to Nicole and asked if she needed help with dinner.

Before Nicole could answer, Kyle said. "Your loss. If you change your mind, let me know."

Kyle smirked. God. She couldn't wait to get out of there.

London smirked right back. "Thanks. I'll keep that in mind. Now, Nicole, can I help you with dinner?"

London didn't know why she was so bothered by Kyle knowing about her book. So bothered that she tossed and turned all night. In the morning, she chose a challenging route up in the hills for her run. She was troubled by Kyle knowing everything, but she was more disappointed that Nicole would share so much about her with someone Nicole had only known about a minute. She didn't want Kyle in her inner circle, and she certainly didn't want him butting into her business. After two miles she was breathing hard. She flicked the sweat off her forehead. Maybe she wasn't being fair. He hadn't done anything particularly egregious to deserve her harsh feelings. By the time she unlaced her running shoes, London had decided she would make a superhuman effort to like her best friend's boyfriend.

After her shower, she texted Nicole that they needed to talk. Nicole called immediately.

"That sounded ominous. What do we need to talk about?"

"I wish you hadn't told Kyle all about my book. I don't know him at all, and you barely know him. Didn't you think he was a little pushy?"

"No, I thought he was offering to help. I'm sorry for telling him. I probably should have asked you first, but I'm just so proud of my best friend. I couldn't help bragging about you."

Slightly mollified, London said, "It's okay, I guess. I just don't really talk about projects I'm working on until they're done. Except with you, of course. Don't worry about it. You're right. It was thoughtful of him to offer."

Maybe Nicole was right, and London had taken the conversation with Kyle the wrong way. So what if he knew. *What could happen*? She cringed.

She joined Kyle and Nicole for dinner again that week, meeting them at California Pizza Kitchen on Hollywood and Highland. Was it her imagination that Kyle looked at her funny? She tried to dismiss her concern and smiled at him. She didn't know him well enough to know if he just had Resting Bitch Face. She chuckled inwardly at the thought.

"What's so funny?" Nicole asked.

"Nothing's funny. I'm just happy for the chance to get to know Kyle better."

Nicole left for the ladies room, leaving London with Kyle.

"How's the book coming?" he asked.

"Moving right along," she responded.

"Ready to take me up on my offer yet?"

"No. Thanks, anyway." She shifted uncomfortably and wished Nicole would hurry up.

"I was talking to one of my partners about you—"

"You *what*?"

"Don't get your panties in a bunch. I just was discussing how we might be able to track down that soldier for you."

"You can't do that. It would be an awful breach of his privacy." She was horrified at the direction of the conversation. "How many times do I have to tell you I'm not interested in working with you?"

"Don't get nasty about it. They were just preliminary discussions. Geez. What's wrong with you?"

Before she could answer, Nicole rejoined them. She seemed to notice the tension at the table and said "What's up with you guys?"

"Nothing's up, babe. I was just asking London how her book was coming. She said it's moving right along. That's all." He gave London a sharp look that she took as a warning.

Nicole immediately looked nervous. "She doesn't like to talk about her work in progress," she said.

"I didn't realize that I was overstepping. I'm so sorry, London. I hope you can forgive me."

London nodded and kept her mouth shut. *If you can't say something nice . . .*

It took a superhuman effort for her to be civil to Kyle, and she was sure he knew it. His conversation the rest of the evening was innocuous and shallow.

Nicole relaxed when it didn't appear that a fight was about to ensue. London noticed with dismay that Nicole was enthralled with Kyle. The side he showed London was obviously different than what he allowed Nicole to see. And London had a pretty good idea which one was the real Kyle.

She wanted to vomit when Nicole snuggled under Kyle's arm and looked at him adoringly.

Lying by the pool the next afternoon, Nicole apologized.

"I didn't know he would bring it up again," she said.

"It's okay, I guess, but I wish he'd focus on his own life and keep his nose out of mine. He said he had somebody he works with trying to track down the soldier. *My* soldier. That's going too far, don't you think?"

"Did you tell him you didn't think he should do that?"

"Of course."

"Then he'll probably drop it. I don't think you need to worry about Kyle. He's a good guy."

"I'm sure he's just great," she responded. But London couldn't shake the feeling that Good Old Kyle's interference would come back to bite her in the butt.

Kyle was too interested in her story, but maybe she wasn't being fair. She was a published author, so maybe it was normal to be curious. That curiosity wasn't really a problem, but his unwelcome interest in the soldier was. She didn't want his privacy invaded. Which was ironic since she'd taken her own steps to track him down. She hadn't made peace with herself for that, given her belief that it could place an unwelcome burden on him if his identity were to become known.

The Hero

I'd told Jason that I was being sent back to America. He was sweet about it, but what could he really say? I wasn't expecting what he did say.

"Juliana, it's best that you go. I can't always be here to save you."

"I know that, but we could still see each other sometimes when you're around. If I go home--"

"I'm not going to be here. My team leaves for a new mission in the morning."

"Where are you going?"

"You know I can't tell you that."

"But it's dangerous, isn't it." It wasn't even a question.

"You know what I do. No point in sugarcoating it, is there?"

"How can I reach you? This can't be goodbye. It can't be."

He sighed and gazed at his feet. "Look, I'm all over. I'll give you the address where soldiers in country get mail, but that's the best I can do. I can't promise...I don't know when I can be in touch." He walked to the table holding my collection of cards and flowers and picked up an empty envelope. He wrote something and left it on the table.

"Bring me one, too," I said. When he did, I wrote down my contact information in New York. "Promise not to lose this. Please, Jason."

He nodded and slipped the paper into his pocket.

"Do you have to leave now?" I asked, afraid to look at him.

"No. Tonight, I can stay with you."

Damn this broken leg.

Chapter 13

★ ★ ★

Six months into writing *The Hero*, London was happy with the progress she'd made but needed the perfect ending. She just wasn't sure what that should be. She looked for inspiration in books and movies, anything about Afghanistan and combat. There were numerous military biographies and autobiographies by Special Forces and other enlisted men. The depth of coverage by these men and women who had lived the life and felt the need to unburden their souls deepened her understanding of what her hero must have endured. It was eye opening, the horrors they faced, their giant hearts broken by the grimness they saw, the sorrows they witnessed.

But the ending of her story eluded her. Now and then, she even asked the soldier in the picture what he thought should happen. *Still waiting for an answer.*

But often words came to her, almost without trying. Her story unfolded, and feedback she got on it kept her going. Her agent urged her to try to finish it, as she felt confident that she could find a publisher.

She still let Nicole read all the new parts after instructing her not to share with her boyfriend. And Nicole had promised. Maybe it worked because Kyle was pleasant and left the topic of her book alone.

She didn't hate spending time in his company as much, and it was a relief not having to pretend for Nicole's benefit that he was not her least favorite person.

The Hero

I'd been back in New York for a few weeks and had almost adjusted to hobbling around on crutches. Which was getting old. My family and friends were over just about every day checking on me and asking whether I needed anything. The Bureau was letting me work from home for a while longer. I guess they realized I wasn't pleased to be banned from Afghanistan. Not that they saw it that way.

I thought a lot about the last time I'd seen Jason. It was hard, not knowing when, or if, I'd see him again. He'd stayed with me my last night in the hospital until I made him leave around midnight. I wanted him to get some rest before he had to head out the next morning. Believe me, it wasn't easy to let him go.

We didn't really say anything earthshaking. It was more that we comforted each other. I learned the gentleness of him. The protectiveness. I was afraid for him, but I couldn't show it. Yes. I will be safe, but I can't know that he will be. He loved his men. He trusted them with his life, and I knew they could trust this man as well.

Looking at my face, he tried to ease my fears. To the extent he could.

"At one of the outposts, there was a kid, probably nineteen or twenty. He was always gung ho, talking about wanting to be a hero like his dad. He worshipped the old man. We kidded him about being all talk, that he hadn't been tested yet. That he had to wait in line to be a hero. That there were a lot of guys in that line ahead of him. But he took it all in stride and never let go of his dream. One hot July day, in a particularly egregious firefight, that kid actually stood up and yelled 'Geronimo' as he blasted a jihadi off a roof. We'd almost walked into an ambush. His shout alerted us in time to duck for cover and return fire. We didn't lose anyone that day. It turned out he made a pretty good hero after all."

"It's nice to know there might be someone watching your back," I said.

"There are a lot of people watching my back. We all watch out for each other. We all mean to come home in one piece."

He knew I needed reassurance, but he wouldn't lie to me. He told me that no matter what happened I'd be in his heart. I cringed inside at the "no matter what happened." Those words mean the worst is on the menu. He meant, without saying it directly, he might never come back. A hard truth I have to learn to live with.

I know he will miss me, but I didn't try to pry the "L" word out of him, or make him promise me anything. Even if I wanted to.

I made room for him, and asked him to lay down beside me. My hospital bed was awkward, my cast was awkward. Hell, *I* was awkward. And still he did his best to hold me in his arms. That was the closest we'd ever been, and I reveled in it.

"I'm going to miss you every day until I see you again," I said. I could feel myself choking up, but I didn't cry. He didn't need to go off to fight worrying about leaving me behind in a puddle of tears. He'd seen enough of them that I was afraid he would think I was emotionally unstable.

"And I'll be missing you," he said. "Every moment. I never expected to find someone like you."

I could see in his eyes that he was sincere, if I'd ever doubted it. And I could see how hard it was for him to stay stoic. And I could see that he really didn't want to leave me.

"You can't miss me every moment. Promise me. You need to focus on staying safe. You can't be distracted by thoughts of me, no matter how much I want to believe that you are thinking of me." Then I almost did cry.

"I promise. To stay safe. To come back to you."

I could finally breathe after that. I lay in his arms, trying to capture in my memory the way it felt to be held by him. I would need to remember. When I was alone again.

I tried to snuggle up to him, but my cast and the pain of moving made it difficult. Even with all of the things that weren't perfect, however, it was still the most wonderful night of my life.

So, sue me if I feel like moping around now. I don't know where he is, or how he is. Or if he's all right.

My days were spent mostly reading and writing. I keep a journal, which helps me remember dates and facts, which, in turn, helps me when I'm doing a story. I'd floated a couple of ideas to my boss for articles I thought would be interesting, and now I was working on them. It gave me something to occupy my mind.

My cast would be coming off in a few days and

not a minute too soon. I was so tired of being limited in what I could do, and using crutches was hard. Luckily, since I was working from home, I could stay off my leg most of the time and hop if I had to. Not really the best idea. There was a big red "X" on the calendar marking the day the cast was coming off.

The day before D-Day, as I liked to call it, I decided I'd print a little ode on the cast, and I spent the morning thinking about what I should write. I came up with a whole opus, but when I bent over my leg to try to actually write on the cast, I saw the problem with my big idea. One of them, anyway. It was awkward. Also, the cast had a rough surface so it didn't look great when I started to write. So, I changed the first word into a heart (sort of a crooked, messy heart) and wrote "Jason" underneath it. And smiled.

My sister Edie came by in the morning to go with me to my appointment, and then we had lunch, and a glass of wine, to celebrate my new freedom of movement. She'd only laughed a little at my feeble attempt at cast art. Of course, she knew all about Jason. I'd told her everything once I got home. She had all sorts of uplifting things to say about how we'd be together again someday. I listened with a smile on my face, not wanting to burst her bubble or mine.

By two days after the cast was off, I was getting around really well, and when the doorbell rang I didn't even have to hobble a little bit. Still feeling happy at being able to walk (almost) like a normal person, I had a big grin when I opened the door. And it froze on my face.

Because Jason was standing in my doorway, looking hopeful and sheepish. And me? I was standing in my doorway feeling ridiculously happy.

What could I do but lunge at him and throw my arms around his neck? He kissed me and then held me at arm's length for a moment, just looking at me.

"No cast, see?" I said.

In response, he stepped into the room and shut the door behind him. He set his duffle bag on the floor and took off his coat. He hesitated for just a moment, looking at me for cues, pulled me to him, and kissed me passionately, then picked me up and carried me into my bedroom.

What I said earlier, about the reality being so much more than the fantasy—let me just say that again, with emphasis. I love this man, and he proved that he loves me, too. We didn't leave my bedroom for a dozen hours. And even that wasn't enough. What happened in those twelve hours I won't share with anyone. They belong to us.

There were words we *should* say, but now wasn't the time. We'd waited so long, and been through so much, we wanted our fantasy.

In the morning, I let him sleep while I threw together the best breakfast I could imagine, and carried it in to him on a tray. He didn't make a show of saying I shouldn't have, just looked at me with grateful eyes and thanked me.

Later, showered and dressed, we took a walk in the City, the autumn air crisp, the fall colors seeming like they had been painted just for us.

"What were you like as a kid?" I asked him. "I mean, we don't know each other very well, do we? I was kind of precocious, I think. I loved books and read all the time. I was regularly at the library. And I started writing short stories, mostly about horses. I was crazy about horses."

He laughed. "I can't say I was into horses. I liked to read, too. When I got a chance. There was just me and my mom, and I helped out a lot around the house. My dad worked late, which was good."

"Why was it good?"

He looked away. "I was close with my mom, but he was more distant."

"What's your mom like?"

An odd mix of light and sadness came into his eyes. "My mom was my best friend. She loved me and protected me. I tried to take care of her, too. She was a wonderful woman."

"Where are your parents now? Are you still close?"

"My parents are gone."

"I'm sorry. What happened to them?"

"They're just gone. I don't want to get into it."

I was surprised and, I confess, a little hurt, but let it go. "Okay, then. Tell me something else."

"I guess I was a normal kid. I went to high school and then college. Then when the towers came down I chose a different path for my life."

"So you enlisted because of 9/11."

"Yes. It turned out to be a good choice for me. I finally was where I wanted to be. The military structure agreed with me, and I pushed myself to be better, always better."

"You are a hero, after all."

"I'm no hero. I'm just doing my job."

"I can think you're a hero if I want to," I said playfully.

He smiled and put his arm around me and kissed the top of my head. When he talked, he seemed so strong and sure, and I rested my head on his shoulder, content to be with him.

We strolled along hand in hand, content. At least, I was.

Until we sat on a park bench, and his smile turned somber. "I tried to stay away from you. It messes with my head to be thinking about you, but it was like I had a hole in my chest that wouldn't be filled until I saw you again." He slumped back against the bench, not wanting to look at me.

This wasn't what I was expecting. I didn't know what to say to him. Should I be happy that he couldn't fight his feelings, or should I feel sad because he thought he needed to? I stood and walked a few feet away, my back to him. When I felt him come up behind me, I said, "How am I supposed to feel, knowing you don't want this?"

He turned me around, pain in his eyes. "What am I supposed to do? When I leave here, I'm a world away from you. My life is so fraught with danger and ugliness. You know. You've seen it. That's my life."

"But you can get out."

"This is my life. I belong with my team."

"But--"

"Where do I fit in a civilized world? How do I go out to dinner, play golf, care about balance sheets or sales figures when I've blown a man apart with my rifle, when I've held a dying buddy in my arms as he drew his last breath? How do I care about anything else?"

"I can't answer that. In time, maybe you could put it behind you." I was grasping at straws, trying to find the words to convince him. "Don't you want more? A family, children, a home?"

"I don't look for the future. I live minute to minute, day to day. I have to. It keeps me alive."

"So, you're sorry you came here?" I was hurt and angry and shook off his hands. "Why *did* you come if that's the way you feel? I don't want...I don't want you to.... Damn it all."

I was losing it. I could feel myself pulling away. "I'm sorry this didn't turn out the way you wanted."

As he started to answer, I walked, then ran, from him. Coming up out of the park, I stopped dead as I realized what I'd just done. And I was appalled at my selfishness. My hero was struggling to come to terms with the way he felt, and I'd just thrown it in his face.

When the realization hit me, I turned back into the park to find him and apologize, but he was gone. I didn't know where he would go or if he would come back. I waited on the bench for an hour, but he never returned. So I went home, feeling like the jerk I was.

Walking into my room, I saw his duffle bag still sitting on the floor. He had to come back here, then, at some point. I'd have to wait.

While I waited, I thought about everything that had happened between us, about what it had taken for him to come here. And how hard it would be for him to come back after the way I'd acted.

I didn't sleep much that night, spending it on

the sofa so I could listen for him. Waking from sporadic sleep as the sun came up, I was frantic. I didn't have any way to contact him. I didn't know where he was. What if he just went back to Afghanistan?

I showered and washed my hair, tears blurring my eyes, unable to stop blubbering. I had never felt worse in my life. I called Edie, but even she couldn't make me feel better.

I couldn't focus on anything. I picked up a book, turned on the TV, put down the book, turned off the TV. Finally, I plopped on the sofa and stared at the door.

Around noon, there was a knock. I glanced at my reflection in the hallway mirror but couldn't do anything about the red puffy eyes now. When I opened the door, he took a step back.

"Look, I just came to get my stuff. I'm sorry to intrude."

"Jason." My heart was in my throat. "Oh, my God, I'm so very sorry. My behavior was inexcusable. Can you forgive me?" I reached out to him but dropped my arms, not daring to touch him until I could see that he wanted me to.

Instead, I stood aside. "Please, come in."

He walked past me, eyes cast down.

"Jason." I almost whispered it.

He stopped but didn't turn. I walked around to face him. I could see the grim set of his mouth. He was remote, guarded. Angry?

"I think we should talk. Yesterday, what I did, I...it was incredibly cruel. I knew it almost immediately, but when I went back to find you, you were gone. I thought, I hoped, you'd come back last night. I slept on the sofa waiting for you."

Well, poor me. I realized it sounded like I was making it all about me, which wasn't what I intended. I opened my mouth to explain, but he spoke first.

"It's not important now." He started around me toward my bedroom.

I put my hand on his arm to stop him. "There's nothing more important. I was wrong," I said, louder than I meant to. My voice lower, I said, "I love you. I'll never forgive myself for what I did to you. I'm not like that. I'm really not." I waited a moment, and when he didn't answer me, my heart sank. I looked in his eyes, searching for forgiveness. I was crushed by the sadness I saw. I lowered my eyes, sighed and said, "What you went through last night, I'm sure you can't wait to get away from me."

For a second, he didn't do anything. Then he took me in his arms, burying his face in my shoulder. I held him like my life depended on it. When I felt him start to pull away, I took his face in my hands and kissed him gently. He finally looked into my eyes.

"If you let me, I'd like to try to explain," I said.

He nodded but didn't speak.

"I was scared. I had this pretty picture in my head, of you and me, our idyllic future. I thought...I thought because you were here that you saw that, too. And then it all seemed to be falling apart. It was like you were being ripped from my arms. My disappointment got the best of me, I guess, and I just went off. I didn't let you say what you wanted to say. Whatever you wanted to say. I just reacted to my fear." I took his hands, my eyes pleading with him. "Please, Jason. I--"

"I'm sorry if I hurt you," he said, squeezing my hands. "I came here because I needed to. I needed you." His eyes looked so tired and defeated. I'd done that to him.

"Are we going to be okay?" I asked. "Or do you still want to get your stuff and go?" I searched his face for reassurance, or anything to make me feel like we were going to get through this.

He didn't smile, and his eyes were haunted.

"I can't tell you everything is okay. How can it be? You should be with someone who can be here for you. That can never be me." He rose from the sofa where we'd been sitting. "I should go."

I stood, too, blocking his path. "No. Just no. I'll be whatever you need me to be. If you want me to love you the rest of my life, I'm in. But, if you can't bear the strings, if you just want now, I will let you go when you need to, and we can say goodbye." I tried not to let my eyes give away how much it took for me to make that promise.

He ran his hands through his hair, clearly conflicted. He was like an unattainable goal to me. What he said about the frivolousness of life here...I couldn't deny what he said. I could understand that feeling, on a much lower level, because of my own experiences in Afghanistan. I could only, maybe couldn't even, imagine what his experiences had been.

Chapter 14

⭐ ⭐ ⭐

The bar was dim and noisy. The two men sat at a corner table, relaxing as they took in the bustle of the young upscale crowd packing the good-sized bar.

Kyle picked up his beer and took several swallows, emptying the bottle and signaling the server.

"Things are good?" the other man asked.

"Oh, yeah. Good plan, my man." He clapped David on the shoulder. "Thanks for turning me on to the chick."

"Hey, no problem. You having any issues with hanging in there?"

"I'm good. She's good, too, if you know what I mean." Kyle wiggled his eyebrows suggestively.

"Just one of the perks."

"I do like my perks," Kyle said, slumping back in his chair.

"Thanks for keeping me in the loop about my ex. I know she'll come around eventually. With you filling me in, I expect to have another chance real soon."

"Yep." Kyle reached over with his beer and clanked it against David's bottle. "I'm sure we can arrange something."

Chapter 15

Sitting around the pool, London was about to ask if Nicole wanted more tea but paused when her friend spoke.

"Kyle loves the last part, too," Nicole said as she adjusted the string tie on her red bikini. London had to squelch the uneasy feeling that came over her. Since Kyle had been in Nicole's life, London had had the opportunity to get to know him, and observe him, and she wasn't warming up to him. He hadn't done anything sketchy lately, but London was ever alert.

"He thinks there should be more battlefield action, though."

"What?" London had to tamp down the sudden surge of irritation. "It's a love story. The battle scenes are just background."

"That's what I told him. But you know how guys are."

"I'm not writing this for *guys*. It's a romance novel."

"Just passing on his thoughts. You don't mind, do you?"

Do I mind? Seriously? London stifled a deep sigh. "No. It's fine. Just so he knows it's my vision, and I don't plan to add more battles."

"Yeah. That's what I thought you'd say."

London hoped Nicole couldn't see right through her. If it had been someone else but Kyle, like Nicole, maybe she would have felt receptive to the idea, but it seemed like this guy was trying to horn in on *her* hard work. And still she couldn't put her finger on what bothered her about him.

London bit her tongue. *If you can't say something nice....* Nicole glanced at her and London nodded, tight smile in place.

"He's mentioned working on trying to contact that photographer," Nicole added helpfully.

"Son of a—Nicole, I told you the photographer won't give out information on the soldier. He thinks that's invading his privacy."

"I told Kyle that, but he says that just because you didn't have any luck, he might get somewhere with the photographer, or one of his colleagues might, and you don't own the soldier, and, if he wants to check him out, he doesn't need your permission."

"Really, Nicole?" London asked, incredulous at the words that had come out of her best friend's mouth.

"I know. I tried to talk him out of it. Really. I agree with you, but what am I supposed to do?"

"You could get rid of him."

"Would you? Get rid of your boyfriend just because I didn't like him?"

London frowned.

"What do you see in him anyway?"

"Don't you like him?"

"Oh, I'm *thrilled* to have someone who's almost a complete stranger poking around in my business. The story is mine, not Kyle's."

"You *don't* like him."

"What do you want me to say? You know I'm private about my book. And you know he keeps interfering. And you especially know I don't want him to track down the soldier. If *he* liked *me*, he'd respect my wishes on this."

"But—"

"Nicole. I'm trying. I really am. I know you care for him. For the life of me, I don't know why. He seems like the kind of guy a gypsy fortune teller would tell you to steer clear of." She sat on the edge of the pool and kicked her feet in the water. "I want you to be happy. If it's with him, then I'll deal. I mean, I'll try to be more open-minded."

"I don't want you to put yourself out."

"Look. You want me to not be mad? Maybe you shouldn't repeat what Kyle has to say about my book. I can't help what I feel. I'll get over it. Don't worry about it."

Nicole picked up her tote bag. "I have to go meet Kyle for dinner. See you later."

"Nicole—" London tried, but the speed with which Nicole left only emphasized to her that she'd hurt Nicole's feelings.

"Okay. Have fun, and I'll talk to you tomorrow," she called after her.

Alone again, London smacked her forehead with the palm of her hand. She felt guilty but wasn't sure if she wanted to fix it. She had a right to be mad at the intrusion. But Nicole was right. London did not like Kyle, and she didn't think pretending otherwise would work for very long. She couldn't help blaming her best friend, however. If Nicole hadn't been so gabby about her book, there wouldn't be a problem. Maybe she'd be able to let some of her anger go if she slept on it, but she didn't think she could forgive and forget quite so quickly. She wanted to wallow a little bit.

The early morning sun made it easier to convince herself that she should make up with Nicole. She lay in bed awhile going over their conversation. It weighed heavily on her, being on the outs with her best friend. She might not trust Kyle, but she supposed she could be civil and fake it for as long as she didn't get called out on it, so she called Nicole on her cell and apologized. And with some fast footwork convinced Nicole that London was glad for her.

Dodged another bullet, she thought, happy that Nicole didn't seem to be mad at her, but not happy about having Kyle as a permanent fixture in her friend's life.

She was angry, though, and concerned. Kyle was going too far. What if he succeeded? What if he found the soldier and disrupted his life in some way? London fumed. She'd soft-pedaled it to Nicole, but now she wondered if she'd been direct enough. What Kyle was doing was wrong, and intrusive, and potentially dangerous. And London was powerless to stop him. Something was just off about him. What was Kyle *really* after?

And what about Nicole? London's anger toward Kyle could conceivably spill over onto her best friend. It was something else she could hold Kyle responsible for.

London wandered into her office and sat down at her desk. Flipping through stacks, she pulled out the newspaper and lightly touched the face looking back at her. "I'm sorry if I got you into something you won't like. I hope he's just kidding."

There was nothing she could do at the moment about Kyle. Best to just ignore him. If he persisted in his intention to find the soldier, she couldn't stop him anyway. If it came up, she'd deal with it in whatever way seemed appropriate at the time.

Chapter 16

★ ★ ★

London was getting some pressure from her agent to get a draft of the book done. Sara thought there might be commercial potential in the story, and she'd already shopped the idea to publishers. She needed something to show them.

If London could get all the way through a first draft, her editor was on board to do a quick turnaround. All the weight was on London now, so she needed to devote some serious time to getting the book done.

The Hero

"Look," I said, "can't we just start from the beginning? Pretend I didn't blow up at you. Pretend that you can say what you wanted to say. Can't we be together for however long we have, and be happy? Tell me what you wanted to tell me when you said you fought the urge to come here."

"What's the point?"

"The point is for us to be together. You came here for a reason. I want to know what it is."

When he didn't respond, I said, "You won't say now, will you? You're using this as an excuse to backtrack. But I say we need to fight for us. Don't pull away from me. You're here because you need me, and I need you. We can fix this. I know we can."

"It's not a good idea. Coming here was a mistake. I knew it but couldn't stop myself. I didn't stop myself."

"Give me closure, then. It's too late to pretend all this didn't happen. The emotional damage is already done. When you leave, you're still going to have feelings for me. You will miss me. So, let's give each other everything we can for this moment in time, and then say goodbye."

His resistance was palpable. He didn't want to let me inside his walls. I knew the chink I'd seen yesterday was real, but now he wanted to plaster over it and go back to his regimented life. I thought about my options. I played with the idea of seducing him, but I knew as soon as I thought this that he would be offended by the blatant manipulation.

Instead, I turned my palms up and said, "I don't know what else to say. The decision is yours." I turned, meaning to get his duffle bag, but he stopped me.

"You win," he said simply.

I stopped and looked at him.

"Now what?" he said.

"Now, we figure it out, Jason." If I'd won, I didn't feel victorious. I felt beat up and bruised. What had I actually won? A few extra hours to fall more deeply in love with him only to lose everything when he left?

I started a pot of coffee. He leaned against the counter watching me work. We both needed a breather from the high anxiety of the past twenty-four hours. I made small talk while we waited for the coffee to brew.

We took our cups and sat at the kitchen table. I don't deny it was awkward at first, but when our first cups of coffee were done, and I'd refilled them, things got easier between us.

"I'm glad you came back."

"Me, too," he said under his breath.

"I make good coffee. See, you could do worse." I smiled tentatively.

When he laughed, I almost sighed in relief.

The doorbell interrupted us, and I opened it to find Edie standing in the doorway.

"I was worried about you, J. You sounded so down this morning, I thought I should check up on you."

She brushed past me and stopped dead in her tracks when she came face to face with Jason.

"Are you--" she started.

"I guess I am. You must be Edie?"

Edie turned to give me a sly smile. "Not now," I hissed.

Jason pretended he didn't see this interaction, and I stepped forward and said, "Yes. This is my sister Edie. Edie, Jason."

She extended her hand, and he took it.

"We were having coffee. Want some?" I asked.

"I can't really stay. I was running errands and just wanted to pop my head in and say hi."

"Well, you can at least stay a few minutes. I want you and Jason to get to know each other."

"How long are you in town?" she asked, and I

```
wanted to kiss her.
    "I'm going back tomorrow afternoon."
    Now, at least I knew how long I could keep him.
Not a lot of time, but I'd make the most of it.
```

Time to take a break, London decided. Her story was shaping up, but she wasn't going to lock herself in and write until her fingers fell off.

Checking her phone, she saw a text from Sara asking how it was going, and she replied that she was on top of it. After dinner, she'd try her hand at an outline that detailed how the book would end.

She was only a week away from her book tour for *The Rand Prophesy*. "Tour" actually amounted to a couple of book signings at local bookstores, but it was exciting nonetheless. She'd already found the perfect outfit for the occasion, so she was all set. Invitations had been sent out, and Sara would be there, along with other industry people.

Sara wanted her to pitch *The Hero* to publishers, so London needed to prepare a synopsis and short thumbnail. This was all getting real for her.

```
                    The Hero


    It was nice, seeing him with Edie. He was light
and respectful. Smiling. Everything between us had
been so intense. I hadn't really seen him interact
with anyone else. This was a side of him I didn't
know.
    When Edie got up to leave, she hugged Jason and
said, "You're a hero to us. You saved my sister's
```

life. Twice. As far as we're concerned, you're one of us now. For whatever it's worth, you'll always be welcome as part of our family."

He seemed taken aback as he thanked her for her kind words.

"I'll talk to you in a couple of days," she said to me, giving me a big hug. "Can't wait to hear everything."

Closing the door behind her, I said to Jason, "I didn't know she was coming over, but I'm glad you got to meet her."

"Me, too. You're a lot alike."

"I know. We used to wear each other's clothes when we were younger." I wandered down the hall to my bedroom. He followed and sat down on my bed where I joined him.

"So, tell me about your family," I said, leaning back against the headboard.

"I don't have any family," he said quickly.

"Why not?" I asked, and stopped, remembering him saying he didn't want to talk about them. "I'm sorry. I don't mean to pry. You don't have to tell me."

He glanced at me as if considering his answer.

"I don't want to talk about that."

"Is it the reason you don't want to let yourself get close to someone?"

He didn't answer me.

"I'm sorry. I'm curious about you. We're so close in some ways but like strangers in others."

"We didn't do anything the normal way."

"So, is it all going to be over between us when you leave tomorrow night?"

I could see him tense up at my question.

"It's for the best."

"You keep saying that, but soldiers get married and have families. I know it and you know it. Why do you insist on holding me at arm's length?" I was getting angry that I couldn't get through to him. "You say you don't have any family? Well, you do. You have me. You're choosing not to have any family."

"Maybe I am. Maybe it's--"

"Don't you dare say it's for the best one more time. It's not healthy to push everyone away. Why are you so insistent that this...that we...can't work out?" I wanted to scream. This wasn't getting us anywhere and I didn't want to say something I'd regret later, so, instead, I pushed up off the bed. "I'm getting a glass of wine. You want one?"

He got up, too, and followed me back to the kitchen.

"Wait." He put his hand on my arm. "I don't want to push you away. It's too hard to talk about my mother, about my life. She died, and he was gone, and I was raised by a series of foster families."

"But--"

"Let me talk. You wanted to know. I didn't fit in, with any of them. It wasn't always their fault. I was damaged and angry and closed off. But I made myself finish school. I knew I had to be able to take care of myself. I couldn't rely on anyone else. Halfway through college, I started to come out of my cave, and let people in. I met a girl, fell in love. It was good for a while. For various reasons, it didn't last. Then came 9/11, and I enlisted, and I found where I belong. That's it in a nutshell."

"Thank you," I said. "I had no idea." I could see in his eyes that he struggled with being vulnerable to me. Maybe the parts he left out would be revealed in time. I could wait.

I found an open bottle of chardonnay in the refrigerator and got glasses out of the cupboard. Before I could reach up, he took me in his arms and kissed me hard. I melted into his kiss, then felt him step back.

"I can't fight you anymore," he said.

"Shhhh," I said. I leaned against the counter and pulled him to me. "I'm not doing anything to you. I'm trying to tell you that I love you. What we could have together is amazing. I feel scared, happy, hopeful. But mostly I feel love. Come to me and stop fighting."

* * *

I watched him sleep. Finally worn down by fatigue, and maybe a little alcohol, he'd told me the rest.

"I need to know," I'd said. "Everything."

"Why would you want to let ugliness into your thoughts? The past is best left buried."

"Show me the worst. Together, maybe we can heal your soul."

"The worst." He gave a short, cold laugh. "My father was a monster. Drunk, mean. Dangerous."

"Jason--"

"Please. You wanted to hear this, so let me say it, and then it's done."

I nodded silently.

"Abusive relationships. You can't pick up a newspaper without reading about some family. A child, a wife. My father was abusive. He didn't need a reason. The sun was shining: beat the kid. He ran out of beer: beat the kid. He always said if I told anyone it would be my mother who paid the price.

"My mother. She protected me as best she could. He beat her, too, and she took the blows meant for me when she was able to. I think she wanted to leave, but he threatened her. His threats were never empty.

"She could feel when he was going to go dark. His voice would get loud. And slurred. Sometimes she hid me. And I had to listen, ashamed that I was too little to protect her.

"One day when I was ten, we heard swearing and raging coming from the family room. Mom shoved me into the linen closet, frantically arranging towels and sheets around me to make me invisible. I hid in the stifling closet, trembling as I heard his loud voice, and my mother's frightened one. And I cried as silently as I could, clutching a towel against my mouth so no one could hear me.

"Then she screamed, and I heard a shot. My foot caught in one of the sheets as I scrambled to get out of the closet, and I fell. By the time I got to my feet, I heard the door slam and the sound of tires squealing.

"I knew what a gunshot sounded like, and I knew what I would find. But I still wasn't prepared. Tears blurred my vision when I saw my mother, blood like a crown around her head. I begged her to hold on. I shook her gently, and she moaned. She was alive. I dared to hope. She called my name and gripped my arm, but whatever she wanted to tell me never passed her lips. When her hand dropped, I knew she was gone.

"The neighbors must have heard my screams because the man who lived next door and his teenage son were suddenly there. He had a baseball bat clenched in his hand. He called the police, and they took me home to stay with them until they could figure out what to do with me."

His eyes reflected the hatred he felt for the father who didn't deserve to be called by that name.

"He's serving forty years to life. I hope he dies in prison and I never see him again. I won't be at his funeral."

And he turned away from me. Maybe unburdening himself would save him in the long run. He'd told me the worst.

As I looked at him curled peacefully on his side, his breathing even and soft, I wondered at the gentleness of him. Deep in the recesses of his psyche, pushed down and sealed off, was pure horror. I wanted to fix the damage that had been done to him by a father who'd tortured and humiliated a young boy. My Jason had been beaten down and made to feel fear every day of his childhood by a sadistic man who sneered at his son's cowering and tears.

I couldn't truly comprehend what it must have been like for that little boy. My childhood had been happy and secure. My parents never once lifting a hand in anger against my sister or me.

I now knew that some of the scars I'd first seen on his body in Afghanistan had come from his father.

So few hours were left to us. Not nearly enough.

> I couldn't bear to waste any of them in sleep. I curled up next to him as close as I could get. My hand sought his, my heart happy as I felt his fingers curl around mine.
>
> I could understand, now, something about Jason. His life had been spent avoiding letting anyone in, courtesy of his father and the string of foster homes he'd been shuffled among. He couldn't give himself to me, body and soul. It just hurt too much.

Writing that part made London sad, but she knew her soldier was damaged, that love with him wouldn't be easy or certain. Still, she hoped that Juliana would be able to break through his barriers and bring him home.

It was time to make a final push and finish her story. She'd promised Sara that she'd try to get a draft to her within the month. The end was in sight. The last couple of weeks, the book had dominated her every waking moment, and she'd have to continue that regimen until it was done.

Things had cooled somewhat between Nicole and her. Apparently, Nicole hadn't been as quick to overlook her rant against Kyle as she'd thought. And London's resentment that her friend had chosen to consort with the enemy was real when she knew the enemy liked to push London's buttons. With the excuse of having to work on her book, she hadn't had to examine the friendship minutely. She could straighten everything out after her book was in the hands of her agent. She missed Nicole's unbridled exuberance as she listened to London's updates, but the book was flowing smoothly, and she didn't need her friend's help to make the story work.

Chapter 17

★ ★ ★

Saturday would be the book signing for *The Rand Prophesy*. London read over the published novel, deciding on passages she would read to the assembled multitude. Or the few people who could be coerced into attending. She was excited that her parents and one of her sisters were flying in, and Nicole would be there so she would have moral support even if no one else showed.

She liked the prologue. That was a definite. That and the first chapter were probably enough. It had been a couple of years since she had done a book signing, but Sara told her not to worry. Sara would be there, and if things started to drag, she could ask London key questions to highlight interesting parts of the book.

It was a bustling afternoon at the Barnes and Noble at Burbank Town Center. London was pleased with the turnout and got positive feedback from the attendees. Which attendees didn't include Nicole. London was frankly surprised that her best friend hadn't come to support her, and she awkwardly fielded questions from her mother about Nicole's absence. Their relationship was strained but not over. It was possible that Kyle hadn't wanted to go, but Kyle was such a promoter, she was surprised he wasn't there trying to network.

Sara requested an update on the status of *The Hero*, leaving London with the feeling that she couldn't slack off now just because *The Rand Prophesy* was out there spreading its wings.

"What's going on with my lovely ex?" David inquired, bellying up to the bar at the Chateau Marmont. "Is she seeing anyone?"

Kyle sipped his beer, resting one foot on the railing around the foot of the bar. He waved one hand dismissively. "Nothing much to report."

"Why not?"

"She and Nicole are kind of on the outs."

"That's not good. You need to fix this."

"London doesn't like me. I don't know what you want me to do."

"I want you to convince Nicole how much she misses her best friend. You could get them together. You could talk to London. See if that helps."

"I told you she doesn't like me."

"And why would that be?"

Kyle shook his head. "I don't like her either?" When he saw David's stern look, he added, "I guess it could be because I made some suggestions about the book she's working on. I told you about that one, right? The soldier one?"

"Yeah. So?"

"So you know it's based on a real guy. I might have said that I was going to track him down. Pissed London off."

"You asshole. You know why you're supposed to be doing this, right?"

Kyle shrugged.

"You better know. I want to know what's going on with London. She won't take my calls or texts. You're all I got. Now go fix it."

"Why do you care what she's doing? You're not seeing her anymore."

"Have you seen her? Tall, blonde, beautiful. Besides, it's not your business why I do anything."

"Fine. I'll suck up to her. I'll tell Nicole that I'm sorry London misunderstood my interest in her book. They'll work it out."

"Soon. It better be soon."

"Who are you, Don Corleone?"

"I'm your friend. And your client. I've paid your company enough money to get me and my friends access to A-list events. You owe me. Is that clear enough for you?"

"Anything for the client."

After the Barnes and Noble event, curled up on her sofa with a mug of coffee, London thought about what she could or should do about Nicole. For one, she could stop worrying about what Kyle might find out about the soldier. She hadn't gotten anywhere with the photographer. Why would he have any better luck? It couldn't be that easy to track down a face in a picture. The Army wouldn't be forthcoming about the identity of one of its own. Probably nothing at all would come of this whole problem, so she might as well try being nicer to Kyle.

She took a deep breath and texted "Got plans for dinner?"

After a few minutes, Nicole texted back. "No. No plans."

"Why don't you see if Kyle wants to join us?"

"Hm. Okay, I'll check with him and let you know."

When Nicole texted back they were available, London crossed her fingers that Kyle wouldn't do his best to make the evening a miserable one.

London was nervous, hoping she could be pleasant to Kyle, knowing it was important. She greeted them both at CPK with a big hug and bigger smile. When they were seated, she promptly ordered a bottle of wine. Something to take the edge off might make conversation flow more easily.

Nicole apologized for missing the book signing. She didn't meet London's eyes as she said she'd come down with a migraine at the last minute.

London waved it off, ignoring the pang of hurt squeezing her heart. "Maybe next time."

"I'll be there for sure," Nicole said, still avoiding eye contact.

Taking a silent breath, London asked Kyle how he was. He responded nonchalantly that things were great.

She was surprised when he said, "I want you to know that I'm sorry for poking my nose into your business. It won't happen again."

Nicole seemed pleased and looked to London for her reaction.

"I appreciate that, Kyle."

He's such a jerk, she thought as she smiled and nodded, *I know it's all for show.*

But Nicole, bless her heart, piped in to talk about a movie premier Kyle had taken her to, and London turned her attention away from Kyle, the snake.

This wasn't going to be easy, but if Nicole was in love with Kyle then London was going to have to make the superhuman effort to at least not hate him. That's what a friend would do.

London needed a great ending for Juliana and Jason's story. But she wasn't sure Jason could overcome the emotional burden he'd been carrying most of his life.

Child abuse, on its own, was beyond bearable. Add in the horror of his mother's murder... how does anyone get over something like that, especially a child?

The life Jason had chosen for himself was appropriate. He hadn't been able to save his mother, but now he could save others. He was strong and no longer anyone's victim. He'd made himself invincible to spit in the face of his father.

The murder must play over and over in his head, tormenting his soul. London was sure he questioned everything. The what-ifs alone... what if he hadn't been hiding in the closet? What if he were bigger, stronger? What if he hadn't made his father mad? Maybe he could have convinced his dad not to hurt her.

Could he put this all behind him? Apparently not. He'd tried to keep

Juliana at arm's length for as long as he could.

Characters in a novel are individuals, with thoughts and histories and agendas. She couldn't just make them fall in love and live happily ever after. They had to act according to their natures.

Would Jason go back to Afghanistan and realize he couldn't live without Juliana, or would he go back to Afghanistan and bury his longing for her until it no longer had the strength to torment him? London had a sinking feeling it would be the latter. Unless Juliana found a way into the depths of his psyche. She had to find a door that would let her in before he could slam it shut and lock it.

Chapter 18

★ ★ ★

The Hero

I knew he would leave soon. And I had to let him. I had poured out my soul to him, to do with what he would. If he needed to put me in a pretty little box so that he could survive, I'd promised to abide by his decision.

I didn't sleep much our last night as I lay next to him. Instead, I concentrated on the smell of him, the feel of his skin, his hand in mine. I relished every moment, knowing I would need the memories to sustain me in the lonely time ahead.

Determined to make our last day together memorable for him, too, I promised myself not to ask him for anything it would be difficult for him to give, like promises, or a future. I'd smile and let him return to the world of war and brotherhood that he needed.

That was my plan anyway. When we were up and around, however, over scrambled eggs and orange juice, he said, "I don't know how to leave you."

I paused, coffee cup halfway to my lips, and looked at him. "You leave me by planning to come back. You take me with you in your heart, and know that I'll be here loving you."

"You...you'll want a life. I can't ask you to wait for a future that's uncertain at best. You'll get lonely. I can't ask you to wait."

"I'm in love with a hero. What mere mortal man can compete with that?" I said it lightly so he'd think I was kidding, but in my heart I meant it.

He didn't laugh. He was as serious as I felt.

"Against my better judgment, I fell in love with you. There's a string connecting my heart to yours, and I'll feel the pull of you wherever I am." There was something heart-wrenching in his eyes when he finished.

"I know. I feel it, too." I was afraid to trust my ears. He was saying things I thought I'd never hear from him. He was talking about a future for us.

He pulled me close and rested his chin on the top of my head, and sighed deeply.

Safe in his arms, I said, "We can make this work. If we try. I'm willing to try."

He had opened the door and let us talk about the what-ifs. What if he came back to me? What if he tried to make a life away from his unit? What if we had a future?

Despite my hopes, I hadn't expected him to consider a life with me. He'd spent so much of his life protecting himself from emotional ties. Falling in love, I mean. He was completely devoted to his team. They couldn't hurt him like a lover could.

> When he left for the airport, we hadn't made any real plans, but he'd left the door open. He told me that he loved me, with tears in his eyes. It squeezed my heart until I didn't think I could breathe.
>
> "I'll try to keep in touch when I can," he promised, kissing me deeply before he walked through my door. I watched after him as he got in the taxi. Then he was gone.
>
> I was alone again. But I wasn't sad. At least, for now, I had the lingering glow his words had ignited in me. And he didn't tell me not to wait for him. Because he will come back.

London felt so much lighter. There was hope for a future for Juliana and Jason. She hadn't had to manipulate the story at all, it had come to her naturally, and it worked.

Her first thought was that Nicole would be happy about it. It had been awhile since she had shared every plot point with her best friend because of the friction between them over Kyle. But it was because of the Kyle issue that she felt she needed to reach out to Nicole again. Part of her patch-things-up plan.

London wanted things to get back to normal, and it would be up to her to follow through on her plan, not just make a showy stab at it. She called Nicole and asked her to come by to talk about the book.

"Can I bring Kyle?" Nicole asked.

London gritted her teeth and said, "I think we'd get more accomplished if it were just us, but it's up to you."

She couldn't believe Nicole had asked that. It was such a sore point with London, and Nicole knew that. She supposed that's why her friend had done it. She wanted to find out if London meant what she said about making up with Kyle. But London couldn't help being disappointed in her.

So, who should tag along but snake man. Nicole held his arm, and sat close to him on the sofa, and the two of them read the new pages together.

"I like the way it's going," Nicole said.

"Yeah. I can see the soldier playing Jason's part when they make the movie. If he can really act, that will just be icing on the cake," Kyle said to London, his lip curling up at the corner in a sneer camouflaged as a smile. Nicole only noticed the smile part.

"I doubt there will be a movie, and I doubt the anonymous soldier will want to be in it anyway."

Kyle flashed a cloying smile at Nicole as he responded. "You never know what can happen. Why close any doors?"

"Some doors should never be opened," London said.

Nicole was watching both of them closely. *You're watching*, London thought, *but you're not seeing*.

Kyle couldn't help himself even under Nicole's scrutiny. He said, "Let's just leave that up to me, shall we?"

I hate him. London once again had to fight with herself to keep from ordering Kyle out of her house. As it was, she had to listen to his pointed comments and see the gleam in his eye as he enjoyed pushing her buttons. Why didn't Nicole see it?

Later, she had to ask herself if her friendship with Nicole was as strong as she'd always believed it was.

Chapter 19

✯ ✯ ✯

London wasn't sure if it was the bitter taste the ordeal of being in the same room with Kyle had left behind, but she felt the need to write something dark into the story. She didn't want it to go in that direction, but the words wanted to come out, and she let them.

The Hero

I woke once again in a sterile white room, the buzz of machines filling my ears. Turning my head caused a sharp pain to shoot through it, and I let out a groan.

"J. You're awake." I heard Edie's voice through the fog in my brain and tried to focus on the face bending over me.

"What--"

"Don't talk. You need to keep still."

I squinted, my vision blurry. When I tried to talk again, my voice had trouble getting out, and my hand went to my throat.

"You're going to be okay, Juliana." Edie spoke gently.

"What happened?" I managed to croak out.

"We don't know. Someone attacked you last night."

"Attacked?"

"Yeah. Don't think about that now. When you're better, we can talk."

I tried moving my various body parts, to see what was injured. It seemed to alarm Edie to see me squirming, and she tried to get me to be still, but I wanted an inventory. Arms and legs worked. My head hurt, my neck hurt. Some of my lower region hurt, and a feeling of horror surged through me.

"Was I--" I couldn't bring myself to finish the question, but Edie knew what I was asking. I could see it in the color draining from her face and the tears that started in her eyes.

The enormity of what had happened fell on me with a weight that threatened to smother me. I turned my face away from her and shut my eyes, and tears of my own started to flow. Despite her pleading, I didn't turn back to her, and after a while she left the room, leaving me to process the overwhelming horror I felt.

I'd been so happy. My thoughts were always on Jason. He'd been gone for two and a half weeks, and I still hadn't come down from my cloud. Now, I couldn't summon those warm, happy memories. They had been supplanted by the ugliness pressing on my soul.

But that wasn't the worst of it. Weeks later, after I'd come home from the hospital, after the endless police reports, after the pain in my heart eased enough that I could breathe again, I started to notice things. My clothes didn't fit right. I was hungry all the time. Most ominously, I often felt like throwing up.

When I told Edie about my fears, she immediately grasped the significance. But what could she say? Who could know what to say to someone who had been raped and now appeared to be pregnant?

And I didn't know what to do about it. I was so resentful for what had been done to me and for its legacy.

Edie asked if I'd told Jason about what happened. I told her he couldn't know. He had enough to worry about wherever he was, just trying to stay alive. She argued that he had a right to know, but I didn't want him to worry about me. Besides, I didn't know where he was. I hadn't heard anything from him since he kissed me goodbye at my door.

I could hardly let myself think about Jason after the attack. I felt damaged, or dirty, or *something*. It was almost that I didn't want to tarnish him, like I wasn't good enough for him. Completely ridiculous things for me to be feeling. *Everyone* knows it isn't the victim's fault.

I never considered terminating the pregnancy. It wasn't the baby's fault how it came to be. I didn't know what I would feel like once it was born. Whether I'd want to keep it or not, that would remain to be seen.

It was Edie who finally asked whether Jason and I had used protection. I started to snap at her that it wasn't any of her business. Until I understood what she was asking. The attack had been so front and center, and the pregnancy had followed so closely, I had never considered that the baby might be Jason's.

"No. We didn't. Not every time. I had no idea he was going to show up, and then, well, you know. Oh, Edie. Do you think it's possible?"

"There are only a few weeks separating Jason's visit from what happened after. I think it's definitely possible."

I was afraid to hope, but suddenly the baby became important. When I saw the doctor shortly after, I asked her whether it was possible. Based on how far along the baby was, she confirmed that it could be Jason's. And the ultrasound I had weeks later showed that my baby most probably was a girl.

I felt joy for the first time in months. It was tainted joy, but at least there was a glimmer of hope, and I allowed myself to fall in love with my baby.

A cloud lifted, and I started living again.

When I was six months along, the police notified me that they had arrested the man who attacked me, and I was temporarily drawn back into the darkness of those days right after the rape. I didn't want to see the man. I didn't want to ever see him, but there was going to be a trial, and I wouldn't be able to avoid being face to face with him in a courtroom.

And, then, there was the media attention swirling around the story. My fellow journalists still in Afghanistan texted their support. The story had gone international.

At the arraignment, the judge accelerated the trial date, and it was scheduled for a month before my due date. I became obsessed with thoughts of the trial, and not in a good way. There were meetings with the DA's office, and questions from the media. I holed up in my apartment as much as I could, and leaned on Edie for emotional support.

When the trial date arrived, I was a wreck. Even though I hadn't seen my attacker, there was DNA evidence. I was warned that the DA's office would be showing pictures of me, and there would be graphic testimony from the emergency room doctors who treated me after the attack. The thought of hearing it, of other people hearing it, was horrifying to me. I sat in the row behind the prosecution's table with my head down, not wanting to look at anyone.

I felt a hand on my shoulder and glanced up into the face of the last person I expected to see. I knew everything would be all right now. Jason dropped onto the bench beside me, his eyes gentle and concerned. I let out a sob, and got awkwardly to my feet. If he was put off by my eight-months-pregnant body, he didn't show it. He put his arms around me and murmured words only I could hear. When I stopped shaking, he pulled back and looked at me, wiping away tears that had escaped and were rolling down my cheeks.

"Why didn't you tell me?" he asked. There was no accusation in his voice. I think it was regret that he hadn't been here to protect me.

"I didn't want you to worry. I was afraid something bad would happen to you if you were worried about me."

"You were never far from my mind, Juliana. I--"

Just then people started streaming into the

courtroom and I had to move to the prosecution table. I held his hand for an instant as I walked away, and softly said "Thank you."

I saw Edie enter. She gave Jason a quick hug and they sat next to each other, talking quietly.

The trial was a blur to me. I remember being on the stand and answering questions, and I remember looking at the defendant. I'd seen pictures of him after his arrest, and cringed at the thought that I'd been touched by the man in the photo, who had dirty, stringy hair, a shaggy beard and a grease-stained trench coat. For the trial, he'd been given a make-over. Clean hair, wearing an ill-fitting suit. Looking angry. I could barely bring myself to look at him.

When I was warned that the hospital's graphic testimony was imminent, I begged Jason and Edie to leave. It was embarrassing enough having a courtroom full of strangers see and hear intimate details about me. I didn't want those I loved to watch. Later I learned that Jason had slipped in to hear the testimony. He said he had to know what I'd suffered.

Somehow, I got through that day. I think it was only possible because I knew Jason was there. I wasn't alone.

Afterward, I allowed Jason and Edie to comfort me. We had a quick dinner, and then Edie left us alone.

Jason put his hand on my enormous belly. "Edie said it could be mine."

"Yes. It has to be yours. It has to be. I couldn't bear it otherwise. It's a girl."

"I hope she's mine, too, but even if not,

everything will be okay."

"How can it be?" I could feel tears welling up but steeled myself against them.

"Because, I'll be here. I'll be her father. I'll love her, just as you will, no matter what. My tour is almost up, and I don't plan to re-up. I can find something to do here. You don't have to be alone."

"How did you know?"

"Edie. My unit got a message to me in the field. When I called her, she told me what had happened to you. She told me that you needed me. I got here as quickly as I could." He dropped his head. "I'm sorry I wasn't here to protect you."

"You were busy protecting America. You're my hero. Now and forever. Don't you ever forget that."

I told him that what had happened to me was like a bad nightmare, but I was awake now. He may not have saved me this time, but how many people can say they have their own personal hero? He saved my life twice, which is two times more than anyone else ever has. And from now on, we would save each other.

Well, that tied it up in a bow, didn't it? London hadn't known that her dark turn would give her an ending for her story. Now, J&J could live happily ever after.

London was exhausted. She called Sara to say she'd finished, and then emailed the whole novel to her. She wasn't quite ready to tell Nicole yet.

Chapter 20

★ ★ ★

It was hard to wait for Sara to finish reading *The Hero*. London had to consciously keep occupied so she wasn't watching the time pass. She'd invested so much of herself in this project. Had she done it as a tribute to the soldier? London wasn't sure. She just knew she was proud of it.

The wait wasn't really that long. Sara read the book in a day. She assigned it to her best editor, with instructions to get it done fast. She took time to send a "loved it" text to London, and placed some calls to the largest fiction publishing houses. Sara had a feeling that this was going to be big.

"Clear your schedule," Sara said. "When your edits get back, I want you to jump on them. It's crunch time, baby. I'm getting great responses from publishers, and I don't want them to forget about us."

The edits arrived within days. London read them over and set them aside for a short while to let them percolate. When she finally sat down to make the changes, she was inspired. There was magic on the pages. On the final read-through, even though she'd written the story, she read it like a stranger would, enchanted and enthralled and carried along with the narrative, her heart pining away for Juliana and Jason's future together.

She got the final back to Sara, and settled in to wait for the publishing world's reaction to her love story.

London heaved a sigh of relief. It was a great feeling to have the project finished and in the hands of the people who would shepherd it onto bookstore shelves.

There was no word on her book's progress for several months. London didn't mind. She'd been down this road before and knew it was close to a year for a book to go through the process. She'd devoted so much time to finishing it that she'd neglected her life. Now, maybe she could concentrate on her life instead of Juliana's.

Reluctantly, she'd let Nicole read the final, finished product, but then she'd been delighted with her friend's glowing review. Of course, Nicole shared the book with Kyle, but so far he'd only made nice, non-snarky remarks. He didn't mention the soldier at all. He congratulated her on an interesting story and left it at that. Maybe he was really trying.

Things were almost back to the way they'd been before Nicole had crossed to the dark side. London knew she wasn't being fair. Nicole had always been a phone call away, and it was London who had pulled back from the relationship. Nicole was there for her *if* she would be nice to Nicole's boyfriend. Now that the book was in the pipeline somewhere, she wondered if she'd overreacted, been too harsh in her assessment of him.

What could he do, anyway?

Chapter 21

⋆ ⋆ ⋆

Sitting by the pool with Nicole one hot afternoon in August, applying a fresh coat of sunblock to her arms, London shared that she felt at loose ends with her book being finished. If she wanted to support herself as a writer, she needed to start the next story.

"I don't like this part, coming up with a new idea, but reading helps to inspire me. My Kindle is full. So is my coffee table. I just stack 'em up. I'll be a hundred years old before I finish all the books I've collected."

Nicole laughed. "If I think of any great ideas, I'll let you know."

"I appreciate any help I can get."

"By the way," Nicole said, "I'm showing a really gorgeous house tomorrow. It's a new listing and won't be on the market for long. You should come with me so you can see it."

"What if I like it?"

"Make me an offer," she joked.

It was a beautiful house, and its Winchester Drive address was a selling point, along with its 3,500 square feet, gated community, new construction, designer touches. Fabulous layout.

"Oh, I want it," London said. "It's just a tiny bit above my price range. And do I need 3,500 square feet?"

"I suppose not. Your apartment is really cute and comfortable. But if you should decide you're in the market to buy something, I'm your girl."

"Uh, oh," London said. "Here come the competitors for my dream house. You know I'm going to miss it."

The Slaters, an older couple, were a few minutes early but insisted on waiting outside until their son Jack showed up. It was Nicole's last appointment of the afternoon, so she wasn't in a hurry, but London wasn't so patient. When he was ten minutes late, she started looking at her watch. She could think of a million things she could be doing instead of cooling her heels waiting for someone who couldn't be bothered to be on time. It took an effort to resist the temptation to cross her arms and tap her foot in frustration. Maybe noticing her restlessness, Mrs. Slater explained that Jack was an ER doctor and had gotten tied up at the last minute but was on his way.

London was immediately contrite that she'd been so quick to judge.

She softened somewhat when a good-looking guy got out of the Range Rover that pulled into the driveway. He ran his fingers through his sandy brown hair and extended his hand, a sheepish grin on his face, apologizing for his lateness. London shared a glance with Nicole, mouthing *Wow* before smiling at the new arrival.

London smiled wickedly at her best friend, then said her goodbyes and nice-meeting-you's to the Slaters and took her leave, sparing one final glance over her shoulder at the house that got away.

Maybe someday, she mused. *Maybe someday my dream house will be mine.*

Chapter 22

★ ★ ★

London missed the daily involvement with a project she'd been passionate about. Writing *The Hero* had been her main focus for so long, she felt like she had no purpose now. She'd labored over *The Hero*, thought about, dreamed about the story more than any of her other novels. It meant everything to her. So, the question remained, what now?

Why not throw a party? She wanted to celebrate finishing her book with her friends, especially Nicole, and planned a small dinner party to thank them for their support while she worked on it. She'd have it catered so that she wouldn't have to spend all her time in the kitchen. On the guest list were Nicole and Kyle, Cal and Anthony, and her agent, Sara. She'd managed to get back on good footing with Nicole after swallowing her disappointment in her friend. Life was better without an undercurrent of anger.

The more she planned the party, the more enthralled she became with the idea of it. She had invitations printed, elegant-looking black cardstock with silver lettering. She poured over menus from restaurants she knew and restaurants she'd heard good things about. She spoke with a friend who had an extensive wine collection to find out what fabulous wines she should look for. She bought each of her guests a sterling silver keychain commemorating *The Hero* and had them professionally gift-wrapped. This little party was going to eat way into the advance she'd received for the book, but it would be worth it to be surrounded by people who had supported her.

Her guests arrived within minutes of each other. London smiled, happy to share this exciting moment in her life with the people she cared about. And the one person she gamely tried to care about.

"Your house looks great," Nicole gushed as London took her coat and handbag. "I love the way your décor matches the invitations. The black table settings and white tulips are so elegant. And I love the picture." She crossed to the easel containing the blow-up of London's book cover. "I like the silhouette of the soldier. Was it taken from the picture?"

"Kinda. I did a mock-up myself and showed it to the art person. Surprisingly, he liked it."

"Very clever. And super cool that only a tiny few of us know where the cover came from. I like being an insider."

"You will always be an insider," London said, hugging her best friend. *No matter what.*

Cal asked about the amazing smells coming from the kitchen. Even London was starting to get hungry.

"I had Cantorelli's cater for me. Doesn't it smell heavenly?"

"Cantorelli's is so fabulous. Anthony and I always go there on special occasions. It was a perfect choice for your party." He gave her a sly smile. "Can you hurry them up a little?"

She laughed. "Have another glass of wine and remember that old motto, *No Dinner is Served Before its Time.*"

"I don't think 'dinner' was the word they used in that old motto."

"Probably not, but it works, don't you think?" She squeezed his arm, and moved to greet Sara, who had just arrived.

It was Sara's first time meeting London's friends, so London made introductions and offered her a drink before dinner.

Coming back with the glass of chardonnay, London had a moment of unease as she saw Kyle speaking with Sara, and overheard him asking Sara if she knew about the inspiration for London's book.

"Of course I do. London tells me everything."

"I mean, you know it was because she was crushing on a picture in the *LA Times*, right?"

Before Sara could answer, London swept in with the glass of wine and steered Sara away from snake man.

"Sorry about that," she said under her breath. "Kyle can be obtrusive in the extreme, but Nicole loves him."

"No problem. But it seemed inappropriate the way he brought up the picture. I wonder if he's spreading that around to other people."

"I think 'Inappropriate' is Kyle's middle name. And apparently he's become my cross to bear." She shook her head. "Who knows what Kyle says and to whom? Not much I can do about it."

London announced that dinner was about to be served. Her guests filed to the table and seated themselves. As the first dish, a wonderful wilted spinach salad, came through the kitchen door, London introduced the Cantorelli's staff and promised that the remainder of the food would be wonderful as well.

She laughed at Cal as he dramatically demonstrated his love of the lemony artichoke linguini by clapping his hands to his chest and allowing his head to roll back as loud "Oh, my God's" were heard coming from Anthony.

As the last of the dessert plates were cleared from the table, with Cal exclaiming "Wait," as he swirled the last bite of flourless chocolate cake in the whipped cream before surrendering the finally empty plate, London asked everyone to stay put. From under her chair, she brought out a blue Tiffany shopping bag, and gifted each of her guests with a personally wrapped box.

"It's not much, but I wanted to express my gratitude for the love and support I've received from you all. I appreciate every bit of it. And seriously, Nicole, I could not have done it without you." She hugged Nicole, who blushed furiously.

"You don't have to thank me. It was the most fun I've had in a long time," Nicole responded.

London glanced at Kyle in time to see the slight frown on his face as he examined the memento, then dropped it back in its box and turned away from it. No *ooohs* or *aaahs* from him.

Sara noticed it, too, subtly shaking her head as she caught London's eye.

Shortly thereafter, the party broke up, with Cal and Anthony the first to leave. They hugged London and thanked her for the wonderful evening, congratulating her again on her book. With barely a nod, Kyle headed out the door behind them, followed by Nicole, who asked, "Breakfast tomorrow?" as she hugged her friend goodbye.

London nodded, thanking her for being there.

Sara stayed a little longer for one last cup of coffee before she hit the road. She smiled wryly at London, and said, "Sorry about Kyle."

"Yeah. I appreciate your sympathy." She'd have loved to dump all her resentments about Kyle on Sara but thought it would be disloyal to Nicole. Instead, she said, "He's not so bad."

"If you say so," Sara said as she waved goodbye and left.

Chapter 23

★ ★ ★

Once again, London's radar was up over Kyle. The way he'd acted at her party was troubling. She wondered if she should mention it to Nicole, who apparently hadn't noticed his questionable behavior. Dealing with the incident now seemed better than letting it fester and cloud her friendship.

Sitting in Mimi's, London sipped her coffee while she waited for Nicole, put out that she was faced again with Kyle's misbehavior.

Nicole flounced into the booth opposite London, a big smile on her face. "Last night was so much fun. Hiring Cantorelli's was brilliant. Love their food. And thank you for the keychain. From *Tiffany's*!"

"You're welcome. I should do dinner parties more often." She sipped her coffee and glanced at the menu. "I'm not sure Kyle liked the keychain. Maybe he thought it was too girly or something."

"What do you mean? He loved it. Why would you think that?"

"I don't know. He kind of made a face when he opened it."

"Well, I can tell you for sure that he liked it. He told me how nice it was."

Sure he did, London thought. *Keep the wool over your girlfriend's eyes.* "Was there something else he did?"

"Sara, my agent, said he was making a big deal about me having a crush on the soldier in the picture. I was a little embarrassed when she told me."

"I'm sure he—" Nicole stopped. "I hope you're wrong. You and he have been getting along so well. I'd be really sad if it didn't last."

"It's nothing. Kyle just has one of those personalities."

"I'm really sorry," Nicole said, lowering her eyes.

"Don't be. It wasn't a big deal." When Nicole didn't perk up, she added, "Seriously, Nicole. Everything is fine. Now, do you know what you want for breakfast?"

She felt like there was another shoe to drop with Kyle. She'd been cautiously optimistic that he wasn't as bad as she originally thought. Until now, he'd stopped trying to push her buttons. It had been months since he'd mentioned the soldier. And Nicole was happy. She liked being in a relationship, having someone of her own. She loved the glittering parties and premiers he took her to. Kyle seemed to always be there for her. London had almost forgotten what an ass he really was.

Chapter 24

★ ★ ★

Hot and sweaty from her run, London was about to head for the shower when her doorbell rang. She quickly pulled on her jeans and an oversize T-shirt. She glanced in the mirror and wrinkled her nose. *Not a pretty sight, but that's what you get when you drop by unannounced,* she thought.

She opened the door to: "What the hell do you think you're doing?"

Her mouth dropped open as she stared into the scowling face she would know anywhere.

"What—"

"Where do you get off having me tracked down and violating my privacy?"

"Wait," London managed to stammer. "I didn't track you down." She paused as she remembered her conversation with the photographer. "At least, not successfully."

She was so busy defending herself that she couldn't fully appreciate that the man who had occupied her thoughts and dreams for so long was in her doorway. Although it was hard to miss the intense eyes and broad shoulders. She opened the door farther and asked him if he wanted to come inside, but he didn't move.

"How did you even find me?" His anger didn't seem to be lessening as he narrowed his eyes.

"I didn't find you. I don't know what you're talking about."

"You had no right—"

"I'm sorry for what you think I did," London said, her own anger building. "I admit I saw your picture and was inspired to write a book because of it, but I didn't invade your privacy. I did contact the photographer, but he refused to tell me how to get in touch with you, or even your name, and I didn't try after that. I haven't done anything to you. And I don't appreciate your tone."

"Well, the guy I talked to—"

"What guy? Wait. Let me guess. His name was Kyle."

"Whatever. That guy said he looked me up on your behalf to promote your book. I have no interest in promoting your book or anything else. You know nothing about me. Let's keep it that way."

"Yes, let's," London said sharply. "Since I had no idea who you were, obviously you're not mentioned by name in my book. Your privacy, your secrets, are completely safe. Now, if you don't mind." She started to close her door.

He stopped the door with his hand. "Don't try to contact me again unless you want to hear from my lawyer."

"I wouldn't dream of it. Goodbye, whoever you are." She shut the door and stared at it, too mad to move.

"What a rude, awful man," she said to herself. "There goes one more shattered dream."

She plopped on her sofa, completely thrown off balance by what had just occurred. So many emotions swirled around her head. She was angry. He'd attacked her when she had done nothing to deserve it. His rudeness was galling. She was amazed that she'd actually seen the soldier in person. She couldn't say she met the man of her dreams because she didn't *meet* him, she was broadsided by him. She was too mad to be disappointed by how far off being face to face with him was from the way she had daydreamed it.

Her anger at Kyle and the shock of what he'd done were running neck and neck. She wanted... she *needed* to talk to Nicole, but her feelings about Kyle made that problematic. What to do?

She took a bottle of water out of her refrigerator and sat at the kitchen table while she drank it, wanting to give herself time to calm down. She buried her face in her hands as she shook her head in frustration, and stormed into her office contemplating ripping the picture of the soldier to shreds. She picked it up but stared at it instead of destroying it.

Sudden disappointment overcame her, and tears started in her eyes. "You let me down. I have no words." She dropped the newspaper, and headed for the bathroom to take the shower that had been interrupted earlier.

Running her fingers through her freshly-dried hair, she looked at herself in the mirror. *Why couldn't he have seen me when I was clean*? She narrowed her eyes. No, he didn't deserve to see her at her best.

She was at loose ends, too moody to formulate a plan for the day. Nicole chose that precise moment to call.

"Where's Kyle?" she asked through gritted teeth.

"He had some work he wanted to take care of. He said he'd be back in time for dinner. Leaving me free time for lunch. Want to go get something?"

"I don't feel like going anywhere. It hasn't been a very good day."

"Then you need company. I can cheer you up."

London couldn't muster any words right away until Nicole queried her. "London?"

"I don't want to go out. If you want to come over, I'll order pizza."

"If that's what you feel like."

"I do. We should talk. I'll call and the pizza should arrive by the time you get here."

Twenty minutes later, London answered the door and ushered her best friend in with a sweep of her arm. Nicole gave London a hug, then backed up and looked at her. "You okay?"

"I've been better. It was the morning from hell."

"So you said. Tell me everything." Nicole bounced down on the sofa.

"I had a visitor this morning. And you won't believe who."

The doorbell rang and London stood. "That will be the pizza."

Nicole joined her in the kitchen as London got out plates and napkins. "I think we need wine for this discussion," London added as she took two wine glasses down.

"It's only eleven."

London glared. "Do you want a glass or not?"

Nicole nodded and held up her hands in surrender.

"Who was it?" Nicole could barely contain her curiosity until they were seated in the kitchen with their pizza and wine.

"The soldier dropped by."

"What sol—Wait. *Your* soldier? You're kidding, right?" Nicole's big eyes reflected her amazement.

"I actually wish I were. He came to yell at me for invading his privacy."

"But you didn't—"

"No. I didn't."

When she paused, Nicole asked softly, "Was it Kyle?"

London bit her tongue, struggling against the urge to explode all over her friend. "It certainly wasn't me."

"London, I'm sorry. I thought he was all talk, and he hasn't even mentioned the soldier in a really long time." Nicole looked like she wanted to cry.

London squeezed her hand. "It's not your fault. Kyle dropped hints now and then, but I didn't believe him. I thought he was just being a jerk. It may take me awhile to want to be in the same room with him, though."

"I'm so embarrassed. Are you sure you want to even talk to me? Maybe I should leave."

London sighed. "No. Don't leave. You're my best friend. But he's not. He can't get away with what he did."

Still looking guilty, Nicole picked up a slice of pizza but put it down again. She turned to face London. "Tell me what the soldier said. What's his name?"

London took a sip from the glass in her hand, and set it down. "He didn't say. He was too busy warning me to stay out of his life or he would sue me." She shrugged. "You know, I feel the tiniest bit like a pariah. No men in my life since David. And then Mr. Hero dumps all over me." She picked up her glass again and had a couple of big gulps. "There. That's better."

"Really, London. I'm *so* sorry. Is there anything I can do?"

In her mind, London was screaming *get rid of snake man*, but instead she smiled sweetly and said, "I'm good. I'll get over it. We'll just close the book on this chapter of my life."

But, after considering it, she wasn't ready to close the chapter quite yet. She had a few choice words she wanted to share with Kyle, so she asked Nicole to give her the opportunity to speak with him in person.

"Why don't you come over for dinner tomorrow. Kyle will be there and you two can work it out. Will that work?"

"Oh, yeah. Is it okay if I bring a cast iron frying pan to smack him upside the head?"

"I fervently hope it doesn't come to that. But I'll stay out of it, and you say whatever you want."

"Do you think you could manage to excuse yourself to the market or something and give me a few minutes with him? In case you don't like what I have to say."

"So long as you promise not to kill him."

"No promises." Nicole's stricken face caused her to add, "Just kidding. I won't have any pointy objects on me."

London was sweet as pie when she arrived at Nicole's the next night. She flashed a big crocodile smile when she hugged Kyle and handed Nicole a bottle of wine she'd brought. Nicole appeared nervous, and London followed her into the kitchen, asking if she could help.

"Oh, no. Dinner's coming right along. Why don't you and Kyle just relax. I'll let you know when dinner's ready."

"If you're sure . . ."

"I am." She poured London a glass of Chardonnay, then shooed her out of the kitchen.

"Kyle, you need anything?" she called from the kitchen, and heard "no" in return.

Kyle eyed London suspiciously as she sat on the sofa as far from him as it was possible to get. She took a sip and set her glass down. "So, how have you been?"

"Fine," he responded turning away toward the television, leaning back and propping his feet on the coffee table.

Nicole popped out of the kitchen. "I forgot something. I'm going to run to the market."

"Shall I go with you?" London asked.

"No. You and Kyle just relax. I won't be long." She looked meaningfully at London.

"Okay," London replied airily.

Kyle studiously ignored her for a few minutes, feigning interest in whatever was on *Bravo* at the moment.

"So," London said leaning forward.

"So?" He looked her way.

"I know what you did, you asshole."

A wary Kyle said, "I don't know what you're talking about."

"Oh, I'm sure you do. You tracked him down. In spite of my pleas that you leave him alone, you just couldn't stay out of it."

"Big deal."

"It *is* a big deal. How'd it work out for you, huh? Was he excited to sign up for your promotional BS? Are you best of friends now?"

"He wasn't interested, for your information. So, that's that."

"Not quite. You're a sneaky, underhanded jerk. I don't know what Nicole sees in you, but since she apparently sees *something*, I'll do my best to put this behind us. But don't think for a minute that I'll forget what kind of man you are. And one of these days Nicole will see, too, and dump your ass."

"Don't count on it," he smirked. "Nice language, by the way."

"I save it for only the most deserving occasions," she responded tartly. "You qualify."

She turned to face the TV, folding her arms across her chest.

He *pffft*'d and slouched down.

At the sound of a key in the front door, London jumped up to help Nicole, taking the bag of romaine out of her hand and following her into the kitchen.

"Everything okay?" Nicole asked.

"Just peachy."

London lay in bed looking out at the gray morning. The strong breeze ruffled the leaves on the trees outside her window and caused the sheers to dance dreamily. The gloominess of the day mirrored her mood. She felt defeated. Crushed.

London hoped the wind would stay around for a little while. She wanted to run in it. She brushed her teeth and splashed water on her face. Wrapping her long hair into a knot, she wiggled into her Lycra leggings and pulled on a knit cap, then headed out the door.

The breeze on her face was exhilarating, and leaves swirled around her feet as she ran.

She had met the soldier, and it wasn't the meeting she'd imagined it would be. Her one chance, remote as it had been, to develop any kind of relationship with him was forever gone.

And it was all Kyle's fault. He couldn't leave it alone. The rage she felt caused her to lower her head and run faster until her lungs were bursting.

In her life, she'd never had such virulent feelings against anyone, and when the rain started to fall, she sank to her knees and buried her face in her hands, the sound of her sobs lost in the driving rain.

Spent, she stood and squared her shoulders. What Kyle had done was despicable, but her chances of meeting the soldier in the first place had been zero, so nothing had materially changed. She'd confronted Kyle, gotten her point across. She'd told Nicole she would put it behind her. At this point, her relationship with Nicole was the only concrete thing she could hold onto, so she made up her mind to let the incident with Kyle go. Although, if she were being honest, she would neither forgive nor forget what Kyle did.

In spite of his anger, the soldier's face was the face she'd longed to see. She played their conversation over in her head, wondering if she could have said anything to defuse the situation, but he hadn't given her the opportunity. And then she'd been too mad to fix things. Now she knew he was real and she had no idea who he was. She couldn't apologize if she'd wanted to.

"*I hate you,*" *he shouted, glaring at her tear-stained face.* Great first line for her next book.

London needed to be busy. She didn't want to dwell on the fact that she was alone. She spent more time at her computer, pecking away at the fledgling novel. She'd sketched an outline of the plot, the story of Addie Kent and Lincoln Harding, high school sweethearts who went their separate ways after college but found their way back into each other's arms, only to be torn apart by a tragic misunderstanding. She thought it had potential. More importantly, she was emotionally invested, channeling her feelings of hurt onto the pages, and the words flowed easily.

Somehow, she'd managed to avoid scratching out Kyle's eyes, feeling that her relationship with Nicole was more important to her than the satisfaction she would get from scratching out Kyle's eyes. She even braved being in the same room with snake man now and then. Because she needed her friend.

And Nicole was trying to make it right. "I had a long talk with Kyle," she said. "I made him understand that what he did was wrong. I told him how much you mean to me, and he promised to be better. He said he was a jerk because he was jealous of my relationship with you, but he knew that was immature and he promised ... *promised* ... to never do anything like that again. He actually cried about letting me down."

Sure he did, London thought before saying, "Thanks for trying to fix it. It will all be okay. I'm over it, anyway."

Kyle sat in the dark bar, looking up at the sound of someone approaching his table.

David pulled out a chair and sat down. "What's up?"

Kyle shrugged. "You're friend's not happy with me. I don't know how much help I can be keeping you in the loop on what she's up to."

"What did you do now?"

Kyle waved his hand dismissively. "I thought you might like to know that your ex is frequenting that Starbucks on the corner by her apartment. In case you could use the information."

"What, you mean every day?"

"Nah. But pretty often. Sometimes Nicole meets her there. If you just happened to stop for coffee and run into her, well, maybe it's the opportunity you've been waiting for."

"I can't drop by every day on the slight chance I'm there at the same time she is. Can't you pin it down more?"

Kyle slumped back in his chair. "I suppose I could do a little recon. I could text you if I spot her."

A week later, Kyle texted David that London had left her apartment and was walking in the direction of Starbucks. "Are you in the area?"

"I'm probably ten minutes away. Do you think that's enough time to get there before she leaves?"

"Yeah. It's a super busy place. She probably won't get out of there for at least twenty minutes."

"Thanks, man. Good job."

Standing in line at Starbucks before heading back to work on the *Addie and Lincoln* project, London felt a tap on her shoulder.

"Long time no see," David said at her look of surprise.

"Not long enough," she responded.

"Since we're both here, any chance we could talk?"

She silently glared.

"You look great," he said.

"Just the way I always look."

"Well, yeah, but . . ." He paused and looked down. "I miss you."

"You carved 'bitch' on my car."

"I know. That's—"

"I wouldn't have expected that from you."

"Look, let me order our drinks. Mocha, right? Then we can talk."

She hesitated, then said "Fine" and nodded at an empty table by the door. "I'll be over there."

Setting the cups on the table, he said, "I know I overreacted. I was pissed."

"And that makes it okay?"

"No. Of course, it doesn't. I'm trying to apologize here."

"It's a little late for that."

"You're right."

"I called the cops. You're lucky nobody saw you, or . . . . Actually, I'm sure you would have talked your way out of it somehow. Or bought your way out."

"I said I'm sorry. In fact, I want to make it up to you." He dug in the pocket of his jeans and pulled out a BMW key. "Here. Take it."

London stood up abruptly. "A *car*? You think giving me a car makes everything better? You think—"

"No. I don't think anything. I wanted to give you a peace offering. I know I screwed up bad. Not that it's an excuse, but I tied one on that night and wasn't sober when I did it. By a long shot. I can't erase it. But I promise I won't do that again."

"How did you know I was here?"

"I didn't. I got lucky. I didn't know—"

"So you carry that key around with you every day just in case?"

He sighed. "Look. I keep it in my pocket. As a reminder, or in case I run into you. One of those. I like to be prepared."

"It sounds more like you're stalking me."

"I haven't been keeping tabs. But I've thought about you. A lot. I want you to forgive me."

London thought his remorse appeared genuine, so she sat back down and picked up her mocha.

"London." He put his hand over hers, but she quickly withdrew it.

"Ouch," he said with a mock wince.

"I don't know what you want me to do. I haven't seen you in a long time. Now, you're all touchy-feely and saying you miss me, not to mention handing me a car key. What is it you're after? I'm sure it's not just my forgiveness."

"I want us to try again. I don't want anybody else. So, yeah, forgiveness isn't what I'm after, but it's the first step."

"Has anything changed? You know why I broke up with you. Have you decided to make something of your life besides being a playboy?"

"Well, I'm thinking about it."

London made a small *pfft* of disdain.

"I'll work on it. I promise. You can help me." This time, when he took her hand, she let him.

London struggled with her conflicted feelings. It would be so easy to give in. But what would it get her, in the long run?

"What happened to what's her name?"

"Who?"

"Don't play dumb. Monica. Monica in the purple bikini. I *know* you had something going with her."

David looked uncomfortable.

"Well?"

"Monica moved on. I haven't been seeing her." He shifted in his seat.

"She was never a threat to you."

"I didn't feel threatened. I felt disrespected. Among other things."

"Look, I'm sorry about that, too. But it's the past. We could start out being friends, maybe hang out sometimes, and see where it goes."

"I don't know. I don't see us getting back together. We'd be wasting our time."

"So, what else would you be doing? I'm not dating anybody right now. Are you?"

"That's not the point."

"It kinda *is* the point. Let's try again. If it doesn't work out, at least we would have tried."

"I don't know."

"Come on. Have dinner with me Saturday night. Just dinner. No pressure. Let's see how it goes."

"I know I'm probably making a mistake, but—"

"You're going to say yes, aren't you?" A big grin broke out across his face.

"Oh, what the hell. Fine. But I'm not taking the car."

***

And it wasn't so bad. She'd always had fun with David, and now she fit in somewhere again. Now, when she and Nicole got together, it was often double dating. David and Kyle seemed to like each other although London wasn't completely over her distrust of Kyle. And she hadn't forgotten or forgiven the soldier incident. She wasn't thrilled when the two guys hit it off, but she told herself she was being silly and let it go.

But she knew her relationship with David wasn't going to last. London held fast to her "just friends" pact. She was comfortable with him, but she wasn't in love with him. It was just what he'd said, it wasn't like she had anything else she'd rather be doing. But she had no illusions of anything coming of the relationship.

Of course, at first, Nicole had been aghast that London had taken him back, but even Nicole enjoyed seeing her friend with a man in her life, and had no problem with the guys becoming friends. However, it came as no surprise when London confirmed that her relationship with David wasn't romantic.

She had no interest in having a physical relationship with him, which he found hugely frustrating. As she told him, sex shouldn't be meaningless. London knew that, when the time came that David wasn't willing to settle for the platonic friendship, she would have to end it. But one thing he'd said was right. At least they would have tried.

And David always backed off when London told him to take it as it was or leave it. He probably thought he could wear her down over time. She couldn't help that. She was honest with him and planned to keep it that way.

It only took two months for London to realize that starting up with David again hadn't been a great idea.

He tried to respect her rules, but eventually he became relentless in his efforts to get her to break down and have sex with him. She got tired of it, but the reason she broke it off again was because he asked about the soldier.

She'd said no for the zillionth time to him spending the night when he said, "I know about that guy."

"What guy?"

"That soldier. I know you've got a thing for him. Kyle told me all about how he's the star of your last book."

"What!" Her eyes grew hard with anger. "That sorry bastard—"

"Why are you pining away over some guy you've never even met? You don't stand a chance with him, and I'm right here. I can't believe you want a guy in a picture more than me."

"Get out." She picked up his jacket and thrust it into his arms, pushing him toward the door. "And don't come back."

He stood in the doorway with his mouth hanging open. She shut the door in his face. She heard his fist bang the door once and, after a moment, she heard the sound of a car door slamming and the squeal of tires.

Damn it, she thought. *Damn it*. Kyle was still a snake, and she was back to square one.

In her office, she pulled out the file folder where she'd finally deposited the picture. Looking at the soldier, she started to cry. Especially since she no longer had the fantasy of one day meeting him. It was all so unfair.

The sheer futility of her attachment to this man... or, should she say, the ridiculousness of it? Was it so much to ask to find someone who could make her feel the way the man in this picture did?

"I'm sorry," she said to him. "I know you hate me. But it wasn't my fault. I'm crying because I don't have a man in my life, and you could be sleeping on the ground somewhere, your life on the line, worrying about saving lives. I'm pathetic. I pray that God keeps watch over you and keeps you safe. I know I'll never know what happens to you, but you'll be in my heart forever."

Chapter 25

* * *

Breakfast? The text from Nicole must mean she'd heard about what happened with David. She'd have to tell Nicole sooner or later, might as well get it out of the way, so she texted back to meet at Mimi's in half an hour.

Sitting at a booth, waiting for her friend to show up, London had to mentally separate Nicole from her sucky boyfriend. The only thing Nicole had done wrong was to bring Kyle into their lives in the first place. She did hold that against her. London felt like unloading on her friend but knew it wouldn't accomplish anything and could possibly cause a permanent rift between them. How many times would Nicole be willing to apologize for her boyfriend?

London stood when she saw Nicole approaching. Nicole gave her a hug and sat down, signaling the waitress to bring two cups of coffee.

"Is it true, what I heard?"

"If you mean about me dumping David, yes."

"What happened?"

London didn't answer right away, taking a moment to sip her coffee. Finally, she looked at Nicole and said, "He accused me of having feelings for the soldier."

"He what? Oh."

"Yeah. *Oh*. Apparently, Kyle told him all about the soldier in the picture. You know this is something I've been concerned about. I was uncomfortable with Kyle's interest in the soldier. With good reason. I assumed I could relax about it, but I was wrong."

"I'm sure Kyle didn't—"

London just looked at her friend.

"Are you blaming Kyle?"

"I'm not doing anything. It wasn't ever going to work out with David and now it's over."

"Yeah. Except you don't believe that and neither do I. What do you want me to say?"

"Nothing. You don't need to say anything. Look, this isn't on you. You love Kyle and you're not going to break up with him because I have a problem with him. It is what it is. I'm not sad about David. I definitely won't miss him. So, don't worry. Everything's fine." With that, she picked up her cup again and sipped, looking out the window.

Nicole was uncomfortable. London couldn't help that. She was doing the best she could to let it go. And she *really* didn't want to be mad at Nicole. She just had to do something to change the mood at the table.

But Nicole spoke first. "I don't know why he keeps doing such despicable things to you. When he's with me, he's so different. He's romantic and thoughtful. He's always treated me well, better than my last boyfriend. And I was so lonely before he came along. I keep overlooking things because I don't want to be alone again." She stared at her coffee. "Does that make me an awful friend?"

"You'll never be an awful friend. Kyle and I are never going to be close, but I'll do my best to get along with him. I don't want to be an awful friend, either."

A small, almost reluctant, smile crossed London's face. "Why don't we go shopping after this? I could use a good spree to cheer me up."

Nicole tentatively smiled back. "Sure. I got a good commission check recently so I'm ready to spend some money. It might make me feel better, too."

Chapter 26

★ ★ ★

Life must go on. One Friday night, after spending the day on a challenging chapter, she headed to the gym. Working out helped focus her thoughts, and she had no other plans.

There were quite a few people working out. Great place to pick up a date for the weekend, London thought, as she surveyed the toned, sweaty bodies lifting weights and running on the treadmills, watching their individual screens. Everyone had their earbuds in, but that didn't stop many sets of eyes from checking out the landscape. She didn't plan on trying to snag a date, but she wasn't shutting herself off from the possibility, either.

She trotted at a steady pace, quietly humming along with the music on her iPhone. Like a rogues' gallery, the faces of her men—from her seventh grade boyfriend to that guy she met at camp the summer she was fifteen, to David, and then, momentarily, to the soldier—danced in her head. Frustrated, she hit the "OFF" button on the treadmill and stepped down, wicking the sweat from her forehead with the towel slung around her neck.

"Hey, don't I know you?"

London turned toward the voice. "I'm sorry?"

"No, *I'm* sorry. You looked like someone . . . I thought you were—"

"Really? *That's* your come-on? Kind of lame, don't you think?"

"Nothing ventured . . ." said the good-looking guy in the Nike tank top. He smiled, tilting his head as he eyed her appraisingly.

She shook her head and turned away, but she heard him laugh. "What's so funny?" she said, hands on her hips as she looked up at him.

"I was laughing at myself for thinking it was going to work. I'll go think up a better line and see you later."

And, before she could respond, he was gone.

London headed to the weight machines and did an extra set on each one, exhausting her muscles to distract her thoughts. Now and then, she caught herself scanning the faces in the gym, pretending she wasn't looking for anyone in particular. When she didn't think she could do another squat or lift another barbell, she headed to the women's locker room to shower.

Fifteen minutes later, scrubbed and devoid of all makeup, hair wet and twisted into a knot on the back of her head, she stopped at the front desk to pick up the schedule of classes for the coming week. Shifting the weight of her gym bag and turning toward the door, he was suddenly standing in front of her.

"I decided not to use a line. You're too sharp for that. Instead, I'll just state my case and you can make up your mind."

"And I was looking forward to shooting you down again," London said, smiling in spite of herself.

"I *knew* that about you. You're a tough one, aren't you?"

"My friends think I'm adorable."

"I have yet to see that side of you." As she started to open her mouth, he said, "Don't say it."

"Don't say what?"

"Don't say it's because I'm not one of your friends."

"Okay. You got me."

"You see what's happening here?" he said. "We're growing a relationship."

"That's stretching it, don't you think?" She studied him. "Who are you, anyway?"

"Me? I'm the guy who's hoping you'll join him for a drink . . . or a cup of coffee. Whatever you'll say yes to."

"I doubt I'll say yes to anything right now. As you can see, I'm not at my best."

"I don't know how you could get any better," he said, his eyes crinkling into a smile.

"Finally. The line. I knew you'd get to it."

"I hadn't planned on one, but I guess that was pretty good, don't you think?"

"I have to admit, it was." She set her bag down and held out her hand. "I'm London Calloway. Coffee."

"I had to work for that one, didn't I?" He picked up her gym bag. "And I'm Alex. Alex Gilardi. Coffee it is. Want me to drive, or do you want to meet me at Starbucks?"

"I'll meet you there. In case you're a stalker." She smiled sweetly as she said it, and allowed him to carry her bag as far as her car. "The one on Baker and Cannon?"

"Sure. See you there."

"I think I'm in major like," London texted from home later. "I had coffee with a guy I met at the gym. He's *gorgeous*, and really nice."

"Who is he? Tell me everything," Nicole responded.

"Tomorrow. I'm completely wiped out. I worked my ass off at the gym. I'll tell you everything in the morning."

"Cool. See you at Ruby's at ten?"

"Okay. I have to go relive every minute of my date right now."

For the first time in months, London was happy. Alex seemed perfect for her. He was good natured and fun. They spent hours talking about everything and nothing. He was different from David, more grounded and ambitious. He was a college professor, in love with his work.

Lounging around the pool at her apartment, she let her eyes wander over him. His toned body in blue board shorts was a sight she never tired of looking at.

"I don't picture you taking any crap from your students," she said. "You're kind of impressive."

"That's me, impressive," he said, flexing his biceps in a comical gesture. "They don't want to tangle with this guy."

"I don't mind tangling with this guy," she said. "If you know what I mean."

"Oh, yeah. I know what you mean." He playfully lunged for her and she spun away with a laugh.

"Why don't we go inside?" she invited.

She loved the playful banter between them. He did seem evasive at times, but she mostly ignored it, reasoning that she didn't want to be an open book too soon in their relationship either.

London adored that he didn't appear to be taken in by Kyle. The four of them could go out together and have a great time, but Alex didn't try to bond with Nicole's boyfriend. Which was the last thing London wanted.

Nicole commented more than once that London's relationship with Alex had made her more relaxed, much less tense. She didn't have to add that she meant London was less tense when she was around Kyle. London didn't feel like she needed to be concerned anymore about what Kyle could potentially do to upset her life, other than what he'd already done. When Alex was there, Kyle was on his best behavior, his days of pushing London's buttons behind him.

When London explained to Alex about her tentative relationship with Kyle, Alex won her eternal gratitude by validating her feelings rather than trying to help her see that she was making a big deal out of nothing. She'd never before been able to get the burden of her feelings about Kyle off her chest. She'd had to keep the deepest part of her resentment of Kyle to herself. Until Alex. She didn't tell him everything, of course. Not about the soldier. Just that Kyle had gotten too intrusive into her writing, and she was concerned he had ulterior motives. And, to London's immense gratitude, Alex had her back. It was like London had won the dating Lotto.

When her doorbell rang, London called over her shoulder to Alex that she'd get it. He was hunched over his laptop at the dining room table so just mumbled an okay. As she opened the door, David pushed past her.

"Don't you think this has gone on long enough? I mean, what did I even do, anyway?" About then, he noticed Alex.

"Is there a problem?" Alex asked.

"Who's this guy?" David turned toward Alex. "This doesn't concern you."

"I think it does. I don't care who you are, if you plan on being a problem for London, then it definitely concerns me."

London stepped between the two guys. "I can take care of this." Turning to David, she said, "It's inappropriate for you to come here like this. I thought I made myself clear. It's over. Completely over."

"You haven't even told me why. What did I do?"

"It doesn't matter. It was never going to work out between us. I told you that up front, friends only. You weren't satisfied with that and I didn't want anything more. Whatever. You still should not have come here. I need you to leave."

"Why does *he* get to stay, huh? I guess he didn't mention the *soldier*?"

"Get out." She pointed at the door, and shut it firmly after he walked out.

She looked at Alex, embarrassed that he'd been witness to that ugly scene. "Alex, I'm really sorry about that. I don't know what to say."

"No problem. Do you want to talk about it?"

"Not really, but I guess I owe you an explanation." She plopped down on the sofa, and he came and sat down beside her.

"That was my ex-boyfriend, David. We broke up a year or so back but tried to go the friend route several months ago. It didn't work out."

"What was that about a soldier?"

London sighed and looked down at her hands. "It's a fictional guy in one of my novels. Remember, I told you about *The Hero*? That's the soldier. David was being ridiculous." She couldn't look Alex in the eye, and hoped he wouldn't pick up on it. She just wanted to drop the whole conversation.

He sat quietly for a moment and then said, "What do you say we go get something to eat?"

Mixed feelings of relief and guilt swirled in London's head. She knew she should feel lucky that he'd dropped the subject, but she couldn't help feeling badly that she hadn't told him the real story. All the way to the restaurant, she debated with herself whether to come clean or not. In the end, she kept her mouth shut, and Alex judiciously didn't bring up the soldier again.

She did thank him for being protective of her. "It wasn't necessary, really. David is all bluster. We broke up initially because he's a rich playboy with no ambition."

"Yeah, so far I don't see the problem. I assume there's more to the story?"

"I just lost respect for him. When he inherited all that money, he lost the ambition to do something with his life and decided to devote his life to the fun side of life. He bought every toy he could think of. He bought me stuff, too. I'm not above reproach. But, come on. At some point you need to grow up."

"But was it fair for you to try to dictate how he should live his life?"

"Of course not. But I didn't have to be part of it, and I chose not to be. I want to accomplish things in my life. I don't expect to cure cancer or anything, but I need to have something real to do. Anyway, it made sense at the time." She was getting uncomfortable with the conversation.

"So, should we order?" She picked up her menu and started perusing it.

"Yeah." He picked up his menu but put it down again. "Was that all there was to it?"

London frowned. "That's never all there is to it, is it? Something about all the girls in bikinis hanging all over his yacht. And the one that looked at me like I was the problem. Is that what you were looking for?"

"I wasn't looking for anything. Is that true?"

"Oh, yeah. It's true. I don't know for sure he was cheating on me with any of them. But, who knows? They were good for his ego." And, bingo, they'd gone where she didn't want to go.

"Do you—"

"Do I want to keep talking about this? No, I don't."

"I'm sorry. I didn't mean to pry. Subject closed."

Now she felt bad for making him feel bad. She flashed him a tight smile, took a deep breath and said, "I'm being silly. It was months ago and it's the past. We should be able to find more interesting things to talk about."

In ten minutes, the frost had melted and they were talking and laughing again.

Chapter 27

⋆ ⋆ ⋆

The Hero was finally about to be released. London had received several advance copies, and it was available for purchase in a presale on Amazon. The book would be officially launched in a couple of weeks.

She wondered if the soldier would see the book when it was out, and if he would recognize it as the contentious object of his wrath.

She couldn't worry about that. Other than a pang of *what ifs*, she was very happy to announce to her friends and family the upcoming publication and make plans for the day it would be on the shelves.

Sara arranged a couple of print and radio interviews to publicize the novel. London began formulating the talking points. She was excited at the prospect but felt a nagging concern over how to answer the question, *what was your inspiration?*

By the time it was asked, she had determined to tell the truth.

"That's an interesting question," she said to WNET radio host Scott Silver. "It came from the most ordinary place, a picture in a newspaper. I'd been searching for inspiration for another book. And I saw this picture of a soldier fresh from battle. There was something about him that got my imagination going. I tell you, Scott, when I think I might never have seen that particular picture, I get chills." She laughed. "I might be battling writer's block instead, thinking about getting a *real* job."

"Who is this mysterious soldier?" Scott asked.

"I have no idea. He was just a picture. Nothing more. And I have a feeling he wants to keep it that way."

She felt proud of *The Hero*. Seeing it in print, more than any of her other books, felt like a true accomplishment. She had a feeling that, no matter what she might write in the future, no other book would mean as much to her as this one.

Chapter 28

★ ★ ★

It was six months before London had to admit that Alex might not be as perfect as she had at first believed. The evasiveness she'd thought might be her imagination was becoming impossible to dismiss as nothing to worry about. He didn't like it if she came up behind him when he was working on his laptop, and he quickly closed the lid. He left the room when he got a call on his cell, which dinged or buzzed all the time. When she mentioned how popular he was, he frowned slightly, and laughed. It was an uncomfortable laugh, she thought.

"What don't you want me to see?" she asked him one night when his phone signaled the arrival of a text and he grabbed for it before she could react.

"What?" he asked with an innocent expression that seemed a little too staged. "It's just about work. Nothing you'd be interested in."

There was a trace of irritation in his voice that she didn't think was warranted. The little nagging concern at the back of her mind was getting bigger and harder to ignore.

Even Nicole noticed the difference. "What's going on with Alex?" she asked over the phone. "We don't see much of you guys, lately."

"He's busy with his classes. He comes home too tired to go out. He says it's just temporary and that nothing's wrong."

"You don't seem sure."

"I don't know. I think something's off, but I can't put my finger on it."

"Are you guys going to break up?"

"No. Nothing like that. At least, I don't think so. It's probably my imagination."

"What's your imagination?"

"Just . . . he seems kind of sneaky sometimes. Holding his phone so I won't accidentally see his texts or who calls him. Closing his laptop when I come into the room. Stuff like that."

"Maybe he's just a private person," Nicole offered.

"Yeah. That could be part of it." She sighed. "I'm sure we're fine."

There was nothing concrete she could point to that confirmed anything was changing in their relationship. But she couldn't be sure that he wasn't drawing away. When she asked whether everything was okay between them, he seemed surprised and was quick to reassure her that nothing was wrong.

She felt a little off-balance, however. Not quite as lighthearted as she'd been only weeks before.

It was in this out-of-kilter moment in time that fate arrived.

Chapter 29

★ ★ ★

London walked through the airport, scanning her iPhone for a text from Alex. She'd just returned from a visit with her family in Montana. Her foot caught on a duffle bag, throwing her momentarily off balance, until a hand gripped her elbow. "Oh, sorry," she said, looking up sheepishly into the face of the owner of the luggage she'd tripped over.

It was a face she'd recognize anywhere. "Oh, my God. It's you." She backed away, her eyes wide.

"Excuse me?" His obvious confusion only left her with no words until he said, "If you're all right—"

"You don't recognize me?"

"I don't know who you think I am, but—"

"I know exactly who you are. You're the soldier."

He frowned. "I'm *a* soldier. I don't know who . . . . Wait a minute. I didn't—" He tilted his head. "You look different."

"Maybe it's because you're not screaming at me. So far."

She could see that he was tensing up.

"I'm sorry," she said. "I know you thought I'd done something to ruin your life. Apparently, you saw me as the anti-Christ from the way you jumped down my throat."

Before he could run for the nearest exit, she said, "My name's London Calloway, as you know, although we weren't properly introduced. I'm a writer as you also know."

When he didn't immediately respond, she said, "We need to talk. I'd like to explain—"

"I'm sorry, Ms. Calloway, but I just got off a long flight and I'm tired."

She felt a stab of anger that he would brush her off after the way he'd attacked her. And now he wouldn't even let her give her side of it. But looking closely, she didn't see anything but exhaustion in his eyes and backed away, her anger evaporating. "Never mind. The last thing I want to do is make you uncomfortable."

When he didn't say anything, she said, "I'm sorry. Look, if you feel like it, Google me." She rummaged in her tote bag and retrieved a copy of *The Hero*, quickly jotted down her phone number and email on the fly page, and handed it to him. "Here. This is what started the whole mess. Read it if you have time, and then if you decide you want to talk to me, you have my number."

He nodded stiffly and turned away, leaving her to watch him go.

She dropped onto a bench. Her heart was racing, beating so loud she was sure anyone near enough could hear. She wanted to call Nicole but she was sure her voice would shake too much to get the words out.

London would have known him anywhere. This time, she hadn't been too pissed off to notice the determined look in his eyes, barely dimmed by fatigue. She'd also noticed that his eyes were gray. And the strong lines of his face. The way she'd imagined it so often. *Wow.*

She closed her eyes and replayed everything that had just happened. And she still didn't know his name.

She'd wanted to be mad at him, but time had taken the edge off her anger. And she admitted to herself that he might have had a reason to be hostile. And after idealizing him for so long, it was hard to give up on her fantasy. The world suddenly seemed full of possibilities. She shrugged. *Get a grip, girl. You'll never see him again.*

Chapter 30

★ ★ ★

"Lightning struck twice," London called Nicole the minute she'd put down her luggage.

"What lightning? I didn't know you got hit the first time."

"Nicole, Nicole. Metaphor."

"Oh. What happened?"

London wandered into the kitchen to pour herself a glass of chardonnay.

"London?"

"Sorry. I had to get some wine. I ran into the soldier again."

"You *did*? That's *great*. I mean, how did he act this time?"

"He didn't recognize me at first. He didn't exactly apologize, but he didn't yell at me either."

"What's his name?"

"He didn't tell me. Can you believe that I still don't know?"

"How did he look? Better yet, how did *you* look?"

"Oh, God." She headed for the bathroom mirror. "I looked like crap. Of course. My hair up in a scrunchy. No makeup because it was a travel day."

"Lucky for you, you can pull off that messy look. You're gorgeous."

"I don't know about that. But what are the chances that both times he sees me I'm looking like something the cat dragged in?"

"I don't think you've *ever* looked like something the cat dragged in."

"I could have looked better, I'll just say that."

"So, what happened? How did you leave it?"

"Basically, I asked him if we could talk and he said he was too tired. I gave him a copy of my book and told him to Google me and if he wasn't horrified by what he found out he could give me a call. Then he left."

"You'll hear from him," Nicole said. "I'm sure he'll call. It wouldn't be fair if he didn't."

"Do I even want him to? The last time I saw him he ripped me a new one. It was so unfair when I didn't do anything to deserve it."

"Yeah. I'm still sorry about that."

"You don't need to be. You didn't do anything."

"I know, but still. Have you told Alex yet?"

"No. What's there to tell, really? Since I never told him that my book was based on a real person."

"You didn't?"

"Nope."

"Are you going to?"

"I suppose if it comes up. Speaking of Alex, I gotta go get ready. We're meeting for dinner in a little while."

The letdown set in after a week. She'd been so sure the soldier would Google her and see she wasn't a psycho stalker. And call. She knew the possibility was good that he was still angry. In which case, why would he call?

She wanted the opportunity to tell her side. She deserved to clear her name.

One week, two, three. She finally stopped checking her phone every ten minutes, and shook off her disappointment. Her chance meeting at the airport had turned out to be just a footnote to *The Hero*, not a chapter.

Besides, she was in a relationship. It wasn't right for her to be daydreaming about another man. If that's what she was doing. She told herself it was just intellectual curiosity, but she caught herself gazing off into space, the face of the soldier at the forefront of her mind.

Not that she'd shared it with a lot of people other than Nicole, but one of her reasons for breaking up with David the first time was that he'd "branched out" as a perk of his newfound wealth. She hadn't liked the way she felt when she found out, and she wouldn't disrespect someone she was with by sneaking around behind his back.

London didn't hear her phone over the hairdryer muffling the sound. But she saw it vibrating on the counter, and shut off the dryer. "Hello?"

"Ms. Calloway."

Her breath caught. The voice she'd been hoping to hear.

"Yes, this is London."

"I'm Justin Beckett. You said to call."

"I did."

"I read the book." There was a long pause. London held her breath until he broke the silence. "I'm, uh . . . ." He cleared his throat. "Would you like to meet?"

When she could breathe again, she responded. "Yes, I would. Does tonight work for you?" She could have kicked herself for being so available.

"That would be fine. How about the Yard House by the airport?"

"The Yard House is good. I'll meet you in the bar?"

She barely had time to say goodbye before the call ended.

She sat on her bed clutching the phone, waiting for her stomach to stop doing flip flops. *Oh my God, oh my God.* She breathed deeply. *It was happening.* She opened her closet and put her hands to her face. *What do I wear?* She wanted to look her best so she'd have the courage to face him.

She dialed Nicole. "He called!"

"That's grea—"

"Can't talk. I have to get ready. I have to look fabulous this time."

She didn't know what she'd say to him. It was weird, however you looked at it.

She saw him first, her thoughts a jumble of excitement and trepidation. He stood when he noticed her and nodded toward the empty barstool beside him. He wasn't smiling, which made her confidence run for cover.

London didn't know what to do. Should she hug him, extend her hand? She was blushing furiously and thankful for the dimness of the bar.

He extended his hand first and introduced himself. She accepted it, grateful that he'd taken the lead. He asked if she'd like something to drink, then looked over his shoulder and signaled the bartender. She watched him as he placed their order. He looked older than she'd expected. It was hard to tell exactly, but she guessed maybe mid-thirties. She thought his eyes still looked tired, and there were fine lines on his face. His hair, straggly in the picture, was neat; he had great hair. He was a good-looking man. Her eyes strayed to his left hand, noticing the lack of a ring. Not that it meant anything. He could still be married, or some other version of "taken." He turned his head and caught her scrutiny. For an instant their eyes met and held before she looked away in embarrassment.

Once their drinks were served, they moved to a booth in a quieter area of the noisy restaurant. Sitting opposite each other, she took a sip of her wine and said, "So. Here we are."

"Yep."

"This is a lot more awkward than I imagined it would be. I mean, when I imagined it. I mean, not that I really imagined it. Oh, crap." She was babbling like a school girl.

At least he smiled. Just a small smile, but it counted.

"Mr. Beckett, I want to apologize. Not because I did anything, but by writing my book I suppose I provided the opportunity for you to be, um, inconvenienced."

She couldn't read his face. His expression gave nothing away.

"Perhaps I overreacted," he said finally. "I was surprised that someone had taken the trouble to track me down. I'm a nobody. There's no reason for anyone to be interested in me."

"It wasn't me. But I know who it was. My nemesis."

He eyed her questioningly. "You have a nemesis? That's not something you hear every day."

"Yeah. How lucky am I?" she said sarcastically.

"So, your book. Was that guy supposed to be me?"

"Yes, I guess it was. This is going to be hard to explain." She fidgeted. "I'm not used to feeling so awkward. I'm usually much more… eloquent."

He raised his eyebrows, waiting.

"Geez. I'm so embarrassed. I can't imagine what you think of me."

"So, you saw a picture of me. I don't get it. Why me?"

"I'm not even sure *I* get it. I saw that picture and I couldn't look away. In that picture, I saw what America needs. What we all need. I looked at the picture, and I had hope for the future. The fact that there are people like that, like *you*, protecting us. I guess it made me feel safe. That's the simplest explanation."

"You were asking a lot of a picture. Who could live up to that? Certainly not me."

"Please. You can't feel that way. At that one moment in time, if for no other, you did live up to it. Meeting you is a dream come true for me." She sipped her wine. "This time, I mean. Not so much the first time."

"I'm nobody's dream. I did my job. That was all. Just like a thousand other guys. I still don't see how you got an entire book from looking at a picture."

He wasn't making it easy. Maybe he was still mad. He didn't seem to be charmed by her, or pleased to be the focus of her imagination. He was distant and aloof.

"I'm a writer. I make up stories. At the time I was between books, and out of ideas. I saw the picture, and one night I had a dream about you. The dream gave me the inspiration I needed. You were so in control in the picture, so sure of what you'd just done. I saw the blood—" She peered at him sharply. "Were you badly hurt?"

"Not as badly as some. Nothing I couldn't handle." He shifted under her gaze.

"You must have seen so much. So many awful things. Are you done now? I mean, are you out?"

"Yeah. I'm out."

His words were clipped. He didn't offer more than short answers to her questions. She was frustrated by his reticence.

"Were you still active duty that first time you came to my house?"

"Yes. Your *nemesis* or whoever tracked me down, maybe he got my name from the war photographer. Bribed him or something. He asked if he could take pictures. Kind of an intrusive asshole."

"That's a good way to put it. I couldn't have said it better." She smiled, but his face remained bland. "I'm really sorry. I never meant for you to be outed like that."

He shrugged and took a sip of his beer.

"This is torture for you, isn't it? I don't think you like me much. We don't have to drag this out."

He actually grinned. "Why would you assume I don't like you? I don't know you well enough to either like or dislike you."

"You have to admit we got off to a rocky start. That first time." She frowned. "It's just . . . this is awkward enough, trying to explain myself to you. I have to say, you're not making it any easier. You're not easy to talk to."

She lifted her glass and drank the rest of the wine. "Why would you? Make it easy on me, I mean. I have no idea whether you're offended by all this, or if you think it's cool, or if you don't care one way or the other. Did you even like my book?"

"Look, why don't we start over. I'm sorry for the way I behaved. Let's put it behind us and move on. Would you like another glass of wine? If you want to stay, I'll try to be a better conversationalist."

"Do you want me to stay?" she asked.

"You're growing on me. I want you to stay."

London relaxed a little. "I was surprised you called. I kinda gave up on hearing from you. What made you decide to call?"

"I'm not really sure. I was curious. It's not every day someone writes a book about you." He looked at her. "And I wanted to apologize."

"No need. I understand your anger. Maybe I didn't at the time, but I've had a few months to calm down. We're good."

She picked up her glass but set it down again. "I don't even know where to begin. There's the book. There's my reaction to your picture. Then there's you in the flesh. My mind is racing with questions." She paused a moment. "I don't want to scare you off, so you tell me what you want to know about me." She laughed. "If anything."

"Whatever you want to tell me." He signaled for the cocktail waitress and ordered drink refills.

"I suppose the beginning is good. When I saw your picture in the newspaper, it resonated with me. Maybe it was your eyes. I don't want to sound gushy, but you looked like a hero. I don't see many of those. In fact, you're my first." She looked down, feeling awkward. "You weren't real to me. Not really. And I didn't plan to write a book based on you. I was about to break up with my boyfriend. And then I see this picture of a guy who was saving the world. The contrast with my rich, self-centered boyfriend was just too big to miss. Still, I'm not someone who gets all moony over movie stars, or guys in pictures. It was a bunch of things coming together that made me write that story. Then my nemesis tracked you down. Behind my back. I'm happy to tell you whatever you'd like to know. But it's a long story."

"Good thing I don't have anywhere to be."

She laughed. "I'm hoping to hear a little about you. This shouldn't be a one-sided conversation." She looked at him steadily. "What did you think of the book?"

"Hmm. It was interesting. It's hard to read a book about yourself without analyzing it as you go. *What was she thinking here*? Things like that. No disrespect intended, but I think it's more geared toward women."

"Yes. I admit it's a romance novel, but at least it's not a bodice-ripper. Not enough action for you?"

He shrugged.

"Say no more. I get your point."

"What do *you* want to know? I'm not that interesting." He picked up his glass, holding it in one hand, making no move to take a sip.

"Tell me why you were in the Service. Tell me what you're doing in L.A. Tell me what happens next."

"You don't ask for much, do you?" he said lightly.

He was more at ease, and London felt more comfortable, as well. Two glasses of wine definitely took some of the edge off.

"Do you mind?" She looked at him, narrowing her eyes.

"Not at all. I'm in California because it's where my family is. Pasadena. I've been catching up with everyone I left behind. I got out of the service a couple of months ago, and I don't really know what happens next for me."

"So, you were on leave when you showed up at my door?"

"Yeah. I had a couple of weeks stateside. Then your friend showed up and pissed me off. I acted rashly, and I regret it now after meeting you. You're nicer than I expected."

"Thank you. You're a ton nicer than I expected, too."

He laughed.

"Why the military?"

He looked away. "I joined because I lost my brother on 9/11."

"No! I'm so sorry."

"I needed to do something, anything, to avenge his murder. So I enlisted, trained hard and headed for Afghanistan. We took the fight to the bastards who . . . who—"

"Who tried to destroy the soul of America?"

"Yeah. You could put it that way." He took a swig of his drink. He glanced around the restaurant pensively, for a moment watching a couple of guys at the bar cheering on the Lakers.

London felt his loss. The lightness of their banter a few minutes ago was gone. "Tell me about your brother."

He looked at her questioningly. "Sorry. It's noisy in here. What did you say?"

"I asked about your brother. Tell me about him."

"His name was Stephen. He worked in the South Tower. He never had a chance." Justin gave a grim snort. "He'd have been surprised at what

I did. Within a few weeks I was in a recruiting office. I joined up when we declared war and I never looked back."

London watched him as she sipped her wine, never taking her eyes off him.

"I was over there, one place or another, for more than a dozen years. Now I'm done."

"I'm glad you're done. I'm glad you're away from that nightmare."

"Nightmare. Yeah. I lost more than just my brother. In Afghanistan, I lost men who mattered. Men I trusted with my life. Not a day goes by that I don't see every one of their faces."

"Wow. Weighty topics on the table tonight. Should we change the subject? Unless talking about it helps."

"I don't know if it helps or not. It is what it is." He glanced around the bar at multiple patrons watching multiple TVs screening multiple games. "I guess we could lighten up a little. Tell me about you."

"Well, I love to write. It's my passion. Whether I'm any good or not is up for debate. At least I've been published. It's how I support myself. Gotta keep selling those books. I've been fairly successful so far." She grinned. "Maybe *your* book will make me millions. Besides that, I have a brother and two sisters. I'm the only one in California, though."

"What about the boyfriend?"

"My boyfriend? Oh, you mean David. That's over. I broke up with him the day I found your picture."

"Uh oh. Should I feel guilty?"

"No, you shouldn't feel guilty." She laughed. "We got back together for a little while but broke up again because—" London stopped short.

"Don't stop now. Whatever you were going to say must have been good."

She blushed. "I was going to say we broke up again over you. But that topic will take some real explaining."

He raised both hands and leaned back in his chair. "Are you going to turn out to be a psycho or something?"

She laughed again. "No. Oh, the intricacies of that story. See, there was this guy. My best friend Nicole's boyfriend. He's my nemesis, by the way. When I was writing my book, he decided to try to find you. Apparently, he did. He mentioned a couple of times that he had some guys at work looking into it, but I didn't think he was serious. Although he's a promoter, so I suppose he and his associates are probably great at Googling and pulling strings. I think he thought if the book was a big success he could promote you as the hero behind *The Hero*, and in the process promote himself. I tried to protect you from him. I told him not to track you down. I was sure you weren't looking for fame and I didn't want to exploit your military service. Look at me. I knew you so well from a picture. Woo hoo." She took a sip of her wine and then said, "I'm really sorry. All this must sound so strange to you. It made perfect sense at the time, but you weren't ever supposed to know any of this. You weren't real to me."

"I'm real now, though, huh?"

"Yeah. You are really real." She shifted in her seat. "Tell me about your family."

"There's me," he laughed. "Justin Ryan. Junior. My sister's name is Lindsay."

"I like Justin. I'm glad you don't go by Junior. My mom had a city thing. London, Savannah, Dallas and my brother got a normal name. William."

"I like your name."

She was just tipsy enough to say, "You haven't said it yet."

"I like your name, London."

"I like the sound of your voice saying my name." She suddenly blushed. "*That* was a little forward, wasn't it?"

"No. Okay, maybe a little." Leaning forward, he rested his elbows on the table. "I'm sure I'd like to hear you say my name, too."

Now she was flustered. "I—"

"Just kidding."

London laughed and reached for her bag. "It's getting late. Maybe we should call it a night."

"So long as we agree to pick up where we left off. If you'd like."

"Yes. I would like." She turned to go. "I should tell you, though. I have a boyfriend."

"And?"

"And, I won't cheat on him. So if you still want to meet up again, we can, but I'll tell Alex first so he won't be worried."

"No problem." He walked her to her car, and then he walked away.

Chapter 31

* * *

London liked being with Justin a little too much. She tried to stop the memories of her evening from flooding her mind, and picked up her phone to text Alex that she was thinking about him. After several minutes, he responded that he was thinking of her, too. She texted a mushy goodnight message, but then rather than putting on her pajamas and getting ready for bed, she picked up her handbag and headed for her car. It was only nine-thirty, not really late. She wanted to be with Alex tonight. If she told him about seeing Justin, maybe she could stop feeling guilty.

He wasn't expecting her, but she was sure he'd be happy when she turned up at his door. By the time she parked in front of his condo, her focus was completely on Alex and the anticipation of seeing him.

She raised her hand to push the buzzer, but heard laughter through the door. Female laughter. She told herself it was probably the television and knocked loudly.

"Who is it?" she heard Alex call out.

London hesitated a moment, then said, "It's me."

"Uh, just a minute." She heard a few muffled noises, and waited, looking curiously at the door that hadn't opened right away.

He looked flushed when he cracked open the door. His shirt was untucked and only partly buttoned. "It's not a good time, London," he said. "What do you need?"

"I just... I was thinking about you and wanted to be with you tonight. Is that a problem?" She was still standing on the porch, and alarm bells were clanging in her head.

"I, uh, have a lot to get done for work. How about I call you tomorrow?"

She heard a thud from inside and a female voice said "Oops." She looked up into Alex's eyes. He knew the jig was up. She stepped around him into the living room, spotting an embarrassed woman in the kitchen, wine bottle in her hand.

"Oh, none for me thanks," London said. "I won't be staying."

Alex didn't even try to stop her. He knew it would be a cold day in hell before she wanted to see him again. She confirmed it with a frozen "Goodbye, Alex."

He sent one or two half-hearted texts apologizing and saying it wasn't what it looked like. But of course it was and he knew she knew that. And London didn't bother answering.

Bitter and angry, she'd come home from Alex's and plopped onto the sofa. In the dark. Her phone buzzed on the table, but she didn't reach for it, not even tempted. Tomorrow would be better, she promised herself. She just had to get through tonight.

Too tense and jittery to sleep, she trudged into the kitchen and pulled a half-empty bottle of wine out of the refrigerator then resumed her position on the sofa.

It was the situation that threw her, not so much the fact that it was Alex who'd let her down. Although she hadn't seen it coming this time, like she had with David. Alex wasn't the love of her life, but she still had an attachment to him even if her heart wasn't a hundred percent into him. She should have taken her uneasy feelings about him more seriously. Then she wouldn't have been broadsided this way.

London awoke to the anticipation of possibilities. And then remembered the breakup. She was crestfallen until Justin's face floated into her mind. Then the tiniest of anticipation showed up again. She couldn't wait to see him again, especially now. She didn't even try to kid herself that she wasn't using Justin as a way to avoid being devastated by Alex. Alex may not have been *the one*, but being betrayed was a blow to her ego. She didn't feel quite as perky as she pretended she did.

But the weird timing of it happening the night she'd met Justin for drinks. It was uncanny. Almost too perfect. Almost like fate was clearing the way for her.

What if she hadn't met her soldier? There would have been nothing in her life to blunt the pain of Alex's cheating. She'd be wallowing in it. It seemed like God had opened a door for her at just the right moment.

The knock at her door snapped her out of her reverie. She padded to the door and opened it to see Alex. She stood silently looking at him.

He shuffled his feet. "We need to talk."

"You may, but I don't." She started to close the door, but he put a hand out to stop it.

"Let me explain, London. Please."

"Why? It doesn't matter why or what or when. Or who. You cheated."

He rubbed a hand over his face in exasperation. "Look. I made a mistake. We don't have to be done over this. I won't see her again."

"See whomever you want. I don't care." Chin up, she crossed her arms over her chest.

"I made a mistake. She was an ex-girlfriend I happened to run into, we started reminiscing and things just happened."

"I don't think so. Nothing just 'happens.' You make a choice. And, as long as you're confessing, why don't you at least be honest. You didn't just run into her. You've been in touch with her all along, haven't you? The mysterious calls you left the room for, the way you freaked when I happened to glance at your phone. Don't forget the nervous way you would close your laptop whenever I got near enough to see what you were doing. Just be honest."

"I didn't want you to get upset. I was handling it. She kept contacting me. She was feeling hurt after we broke up and I tried to help her through it. She said talking made her feel better. But it doesn't mean anything. I don't have feelings for her anymore. It's you I want."

"She doesn't happen to work with you, does she?"

Alex didn't meet her eyes. "Not directly, no. She's a school counselor."

"So you see her around campus, right?"

"Sometimes. It's not like we meet for lunch every day or anything."

"Doesn't sound like a very good bet that she's going to butt out of your life, does it?"

"I can promise not to see her again."

"No. See her. Date her. Rekindle your romance. Because *our* romance is over. I've been through this before. Not something I plan to repeat. So, don't be holding your breath that I'll change my mind. It's over between us." This time she shut the door.

She changed into her running clothes. Thoughts crowded her head. She needed to run to sort things out. Before she could walk out the door, Nicole called.

"You didn't call me after you met up with the soldier. How did it go?"

"It was an interesting evening. Let's get breakfast and I'll tell you everything."

"Sounds good. I can't wait to hear."

"I'll meet you after my run.

An hour later, she was seated opposite her best friend, explaining why she had red, puffy eyes. Nicole did her part to support London and to dismantle Alex brick by brick.

After one final sniff, London told Nicole all about her *date* with the soldier.

Chapter 32

★ ★ ★

It was all she could do to restrain herself. Justin had kidded about her being a psycho, and she didn't want to give him any more ammunition. Waiting was so hard, though. She was glad she worked from home so that no one else could see the moony look on her face. Was he thinking of her, too? Once her mind was cleansed of Alex, she didn't look back. She was relieved, actually, and surprised she didn't miss him.

She'd felt a strong attraction to Justin but hadn't allowed herself to examine it. She liked him. A lot. So strange since she'd known him for such a short time. She didn't count the ton of time she'd spent enthralled with his picture.

She'd told him she had a boyfriend. Maybe he wouldn't call after all. She was crestfallen at the thought that she'd tanked her potential relationship with Justin.

But, of course, he called.

"I wondered if you'd like to get together," he said. "If Alex doesn't mind. You can invite him if you need to."

"Oddly enough, Alex and I are over. What I said I wouldn't do to him it turned out he was doing to me. If you know what I mean. I just found out."

"I'm really sorry to hear that. I know it couldn't have been easy to learn of his infidelity."

"I won't lie. It hurt."

"Are you up to a rebound date?" he asked with a small laugh.

"I want to see you. And it won't be a rebound date. If you want, it will be a real one."

"We picked a great day to come down here. It's glorious." London stood at the edge of a crowd watching the oiled bodies of weightlifters pumping iron at legendary Muscle Beach Venice. It was a comfortable eighty degrees, and a soft breeze carried odors of fried foods, sweaty bodies, and marijuana. In spite of the grittiness, there was so much to experience in this cosmos.

They meandered along the Venice boardwalk, weaving in and out of the hordes of people enjoying the beautiful afternoon. Walking side by side, sometimes their hands would brush against each other. London wondered if he felt the same electricity she did at the touch. She wanted to take his hand but, not knowing if the gesture would be welcome, she didn't. She wanted him to be the one to take that step.

It was fascinating to observe the colorful slices of humanity found in the vibrant beach city. Music from street performers added to the charm, or maybe the oddness, of the boardwalk. A young Michael Jackson impersonator danced and twirled and moon-walked on the sidewalk, and Justin dropped a five in his tip jar. "You picked a great place to spend our day together," Justin said.

"I love this place. It's so quirky and alive. And that heady scent of sunblock. It's intoxicating," she said with a laugh.

As she picked through the selection of beaded earrings on a cloth-covered card table, she felt his eyes on her and looked at him questioningly. "What happened?" he asked. "With Alex. Do you feel like talking about it, or am I out of line?"

"No. It's okay. I dropped in on him unexpectedly and he wasn't alone. He's my boyfriend, so I assumed he'd be glad to see me. And there was this woman there. Both of them were obviously embarrassed. Then I left. He showed up on my doorstep the next morning with a lame apology and a lamer excuse. It was too late, of course. I'm done." She stopped to examine a colorful beach cover-up at one of the kiosks.

"That's tough."

She spoke over her shoulder. "It was. But *c'est la vie*. I'm over it."

As they walked on, he said, "It's only been a couple of days. Maybe you should give yourself more time."

"To do what? I'm not going to change my mind. Onward and upward, I always say."

"You do?"

"No. I don't think I've ever said that before." She laughed. "What about you? Did you see that picture over there in Afghanistan?"

He hesitated. "I did. My fiancée sent me a copy."

A soft "oh" escaped her lips. "Your fiancée?"

"Yes. Gina."

"You're getting married?" She tried not to sound as deflated as she felt. "Sorry. You don't have to answer that."

"Actually, she's my ex-fiancée. She called it off last year. Can't blame her. I didn't give her much to hold on to."

"Still, it's too bad."

"Not really. I pushed her away."

"Why would you do that?" Before he could answer, she said, "I'm sorry if I'm being intrusive. Again. I don't mean to be. I should keep my mouth shut."

He shrugged. "It's okay. It was too hard having someone waiting for me. That was no life for her. And I wasn't in any hurry to come back. What I did over there was important. My unit was my family. And I wasn't done. I wasn't done settling the score on Steve's life."

"But you are back. Why?"

"It wasn't by choice." He was pensive as he gazed at the ocean. "Feel like a taco?" He turned toward a street vendor, one of many to choose from on the boardwalk.

"Sure."

They ordered a couple of fish tacos and bottles of water, and wandered to a patch of grass under the palm trees. Sitting in the minimal shade the palms provided, they scarfed their lunch and relaxed looking at the stretch of beach. London kicked off her flip flops and wiggled her toes in the grass.

"So. You were about to tell me why you came back, I believe."

She thought he wouldn't answer, and was surprised when he said, "I was wounded. Not the time in the picture. Back then, we'd just ended the siege on a hotel, clearing the floors one by one to rescue any remaining victims. There was a suicide bomber in one of the rooms who detonated himself when he thought we were close. None of us were killed, but I got hit with some of the debris from the blast. That time, I was lucky. A few months ago, not so much. I got shot."

"You did? But you look fine now. Aren't you?" He didn't answer right away. "I mean, wouldn't they want you back after you're completely well?"

"The bullet hit a rib and shattered. They couldn't get all the pieces out. There's shrapnel close to my heart. According to the docs, that's not a good thing. So, they cut me loose." He looked up at her then. She could almost feel his bitterness.

"Cut you loose." She sighed. "But you're safe now. Isn't that a good thing?"

"Nobody's safe. Ever. Didn't 9/11 teach us that?" He spoke with visible emotion. "I didn't want to leave my men. We were a team. Two of them were killed in the ambush that got me. I didn't want to leave. If I could, I'd go back in a heartbeat."

"I'm glad you're here. I'm glad you made it home. I said a prayer for you every night. I didn't know you, but I cared about you. I thought often about where you might be, what you might be going through. I wanted you to be safe. And now you are. So, I'm not sorry they cut you loose."

She was surprised at the vehemence with which she spoke. Now that he was sitting beside her, she knew how true it was. She did care about him. She squared her shoulders. "Okay?"

"I had no idea I had such a fan."

"Yeah, well, you do."

His eyes met hers and held.

London felt her cheeks grow hot. "You want to walk some more?"

He helped her to her feet. She put a hand on his arm to steady herself as she slipped her flip flops back on, then brushed the grass off the back of her legs. "I think we've had enough seriousness for one day. Let's go have fun."

London wondered if she'd been too pushy, too open with her feelings. But she didn't really believe that. He would call. This time she was peaceful and threw herself into the growing word count of her new novel. After her history with men letting her down, she should put a lid on her growing infatuation. Take it slow and easy and if anything came of it, fine, but she had her book to work on. Addie and Lincoln had broken up and Addie was crushed, sure she couldn't go on without her high school sweetheart. London was milking the emotions. She felt a rapport with her protagonists. And it kept her mind off the fact that she couldn't wait to see Justin again.

When he invited her to dinner, she said yes. Even though they knew each other so little, she felt connected to him and had a suspicion that he felt the same way.

It was so much easier to talk to him now than it had been at the beginning, back when he was furious with her. Now, there was a lightness to their conversation.

She smiled as she said, "What have you been up to?"

"I've been busy. I finally got a job and moved out of my parents' house. They were nice enough to let me crash there while I figured things out. I found a furnished apartment in Burbank. I haven't had time to accumulate a bunch of stuff, being out of the country for so long. Having done it both ways, it's a heck of a lot easier to move when you don't have anything to move except your clothes."

She laughed. "I could have helped if you wanted me to. I can carry clothes."

"Thanks. I didn't want to subject you to manual labor after only one date."

"Now we're on our second date, so you can ask me things."

"Duly noted."

"Where are you working?"

"A friend of mine has a construction business and he offered me a job. He and I used to bang nails during the summers when we were in school. I enjoy manual labor, by the way. It feels real to me."

"Well, you've got the muscles for it." She blushed. "Not that I've noticed, of course."

"Of course."

"Isn't it dangerous? I mean, with the shrapnel? Couldn't heavy lifting cause—"

"It is what it is. I can't sit on my butt all day every day, waiting to drop dead."

"But—"

"No buts. I'm not worried about it. Okay?"

"Okay. I'm sorry. I was out of line. Of course you should do what you think is best."

"I appreciate that."

London sipped her wine, not sure what to say, then changed the subject. "What does your apartment look like?"

"I don't know. Nothing special. One bedroom, one bath. A kitchen. The usual."

"What are you doing to make it yours?"

"I paid first and last month's rent. That officially makes it mine."

She laughed. "You're such a guy."

"And I'm okay with that." He picked up his menu. "What have you been up to?"

"Mostly working on my new novel."

"What's this one about? It'll be hard to follow up a book about me."

She punched his arm gently. "How quickly we become a celebrity."

"What can I say? You turned me into one."

"Good thing you're embracing it. That said, you hit the nail on the head. There's only one you."

"Now that we agree on that," he said with a smile, "what *is* your new book about?"

"It's a romance about Addie and Lincoln, two high school sweethearts torn apart by circumstances. Actually, you're to blame for this one."

"How's that?"

"After our first *meeting*—you remember the one—I pictured you saying 'I hate you' to me, then thought *what a great first line*."

"I was really a jerk, wasn't I?"

"You certainly took me by surprise. But it will all work out for the best if my new novel turns out to be a bestseller. It's not that easy to come up with story ideas, and you dropped one in my lap."

"So, you forgive me."

"I totally forgive you."

Her eyes skimmed over his profile as he ordered for them. She longed to touch him, to snuggle up under his arm and kiss him. *Back up, girl. We don't want to scare him off.*

She marveled at how light he seemed tonight. Bantering playfully. Neither brought up the serious issues they'd discussed last time. Neither wanted to spoil the mood of the night.

After her second glass of wine, he caught her holding his glance a little too long, and she blushed. She fumbled for her bag and excused herself. She walked as steadily as she could to the ladies room. Once there, she locked the door and leaned against it. *What am I doing?* Her head spun. She'd had just enough to drink to know she was definitely capable of doing something she shouldn't. *God help me, I want him.* He was handsome, of course, but there was more. Her connection with him was undeniable. She felt it pulling her toward him now. London had to decide what to do next, what she *should* do, or what she *wanted* to do. Which were *not* the same. She sighed, determined not to do anything she'd regret later.

She swung open the door and stepped into the hall. Justin was waiting for her.

"I wanted to make sure you were all right," he said.

"About that. I probably should have stopped drinking after one glass." She took an unsteady step and put her hand on his arm to catch her balance.

Being so near him, she was surprised at her self-control. She gave a small shake of her head to banish her impure thoughts.

The Santa Monica restaurant sat across the street from the beach. After dinner, they decided to walk along the shore. It was a pleasant night, both because of the company and the weather. She kicked off her sandals to feel the sand on her feet.

Glancing up at him, she asked, "Did we have our first fight earlier?"

He looked at her quizzically.

"You know, when I asked if your job was dangerous?"

"I wouldn't call it a fight."

"You were a little prickly. I was just trying to get to know you better."

"Sorry. Your question caught me off guard. I'm not counting that as a fight."

She laughed. "Neither am I." She hooked her arm in his as they walked back toward the restaurant. *Innocent, but not as good as holding hands would be*, she thought.

As she started across the sand toward the street, he pulled her back.

"Oh" involuntarily escaped her lips as desire overtook her. Without thinking, she took his face in her hands and kissed him.

He returned her kiss with a passion that matched her own. Pulling her close, he lifted her off the sand for a moment.

London suddenly wiggled to get down. "It's the alcohol. I don't know what else it could be. I'm sorry." She broke free from his arms and turned away, but he stopped her.

"Don't apologize. You did nothing wrong."

"I think I should go."

"Okay, if you want. I'll take you home."

London's thoughts were scattered. The beach at night was romantic, like a fantasy. She wanted him, but she'd been too impulsive. Now she wanted to go home and figure it all out.

She sat on Nicole's sofa, her chin resting on her pulled-up knees. It was a safe zone since Kyle was at work. She was all talked out after dissecting last night with her best friend. Nicole was in the kitchen refilling their coffee.

"What are you going to do if he calls?" Nicole asked, handing London her mug.

"After last night, I don't know if I'll hear from him."

"You kissed him. And he kissed you back. What about that scenario leads you to think he won't call?"

"I threw myself at him."

"Doesn't sound like he resisted. I know, I know. You drank too much and made a fool of yourself. Well, he drank as much as you did. Maybe *he's* embarrassed. You have to talk to him."

London took a sip of her coffee.

"So, tell me," Nicole said. "Do you think there's any potential with this guy?"

"I just met him. I don't know. What are the odds that I meet the object of my obsession and that we actually fall in love and end up together? That's crazy."

"What were the odds that you'd meet him in the first place? Stranger things have happened."

"Still."

"This blows my mind. He's the *hero*. And you met him. And you spent hours with him and then you kissed him. How romantic is that?"

"Thanks for trying to make me feel better. I'm sure everything will be okay. If he calls, I'll figure out what to do then. For right now, it's silly to worry about it."

But of course she worried about it. She almost jumped every time the phone dinged. When she did hear from him, it was a text asking if she'd like to go for a hike. Her fingers shook as she responded that she'd be there. Then she sat down to wait for her heart to stop racing.

Chapter 33

⭐ ⭐ ⭐

Justin was already at the north end of the parking lot at the Eaton Canyon trailhead when London arrived. She forced herself to look him in the eyes as she greeted him, but it was hard not to focus on his toned, muscular body, broad shoulders... the whole picture. She also noticed the dog tags around his neck that swung free as he bent to tie his shoes.

"So, you ready?" he asked, setting off down the trail. "I used to hike here with my dad and Steve when we were kids. It was close to our house in Pasadena."

"It's beautiful."

"Yeah. It was my favorite place to hike back then. It's been a long time since I was here."

He slowed his pace. "I don't know how far you want to go. It's around four miles roundtrip, but there's a cool waterfall if you think you can make it that far."

"I'm a runner. I have great stamina."

"It shows," he said with a smile, his eyes traveling to her bare legs. "But it gets pretty rugged in places."

"I never turn down a chance to see a waterfall," she said.

London fell into step beside him. Small talk and awkward laughter passed between them as they hiked.

Cresting a small hill, they sat on a rock and pulled out their water bottles. It was warm and, even though they were both in shorts and tanks,

London swiped at the sweat on her forehead. She bent to tighten the laces on her hiking boots, and straightened. Looking at him thoughtfully, she said, "Justin, I want to apologize for my . . . behavior. I had too much to drink."

"Why are you apologizing? You pretty much behaved yourself. Except for that one thing," he said with a grin.

"Because I don't want you to think I'm a . . . a . . . ho. I'm really not like that. I was nervous being with you and had too many drinks to help me relax."

"Did you just say 'ho'?" He laughed out loud. "You are the furthest thing from a 'ho' I can think of."

"Are you mocking me?"

"No. I'm sorry. But I don't think you did anything you should apologize for."

"It's just . . . I didn't want to make a bad impression. It's not the way I want you to see me."

"How do you want me to see you?" His steady gaze caused her to lower her eyes.

London could feel her face coloring. "Can you even imagine what a strange situation I find myself in? It's so weird. Newspaper, book, tripping over your bag at the airport, date . . . kiss. I won't mention you showing up on my doorstep. I don't like that part. And now, here we are. See? Weird."

"It's not something I was expecting either," he said. "London, listen. I couldn't get you out of my head last night. You're a beautiful woman. Even if you hadn't . . . if *we* hadn't kissed, I already was drawn to you." He stretched one arm at a time across his chest and rolled his head to loosen up. "Maybe the kiss never would have happened if alcohol wasn't involved. But don't be sorry for it. I'm not."

London smiled at him. She couldn't believe she'd found her soldier. She couldn't believe she was having this conversation with her soldier. In all the time she'd looked at his picture, she'd never allowed herself to tip over the edge into full-on hero worship. But now, sitting beside him, it wasn't a stretch for her to let herself fall.

All the things she saw in him drew her in. And, despite his protestations, he seemed every inch the hero she believed him to be.

He wasn't frivolous by any measure. He was solemn and deep. And she wanted to look at him. She wanted to touch his face, to run her fingers through his hair. She wanted to take him in her arms and make him glad he'd come home. But she demurred. This one, she didn't want to ruin. It wouldn't be all about sex with Justin Ryan Beckett.

―――

They were careful at first, opening up slowly and exposing bits of vulnerability, not putting a label on what was between them, searching for that moment when it felt right to give in to what they each wanted. But the time came when London couldn't wait any longer. Over dinner at Sabatino's, she asked what she wanted to know. "So. What now?"

He looked at her curiously before saying, "What do you mean?"

She felt awkward and embarrassed. She knew how hard it would be, but she also knew that if neither of them took the first crucial step, they wouldn't go any further. She owed it to herself to go for broke.

"I like you," she said. "I'd like to keep seeing you. You know where I stand, so it's up to you where we take this." She sat back and picked up her glass.

"I don't want to stop seeing you, but I'm not sure what I can promise you. I do like you. If you're good with taking a chance, I am, too."

She felt a pang of concern. "What do you mean what you can promise me? Are you saying you see this as a lark?"

He stared at his drink, rolling the glass back and forth between his hands. Looking up at her solemnly he said, "No. I don't see this, us, as a lark. I just don't know what the future holds for me."

It hit her between the eyes. The shattered bullet was real, and it weighed heavily on his mind. For her part, she'd managed to stuff thoughts of his health crisis into a drawer in her mind and turn the key.

She took a shaky breath and lifted her drink. "Here's to chances."

After the toast, she looked at him. *So, what now?*

Somehow, the mood had changed. She smiled to cover the ache she felt. Conversation during the rest of dinner was perfunctory.

Justin was quiet as he drained his glass, and said, "Shall we?"

Walking to the parking lot, he said, "That turned more serious than I intended it to. I'm not fatalistic about my future, and I'm sorry I brought you down."

She nodded, not looking at him, but felt the tiniest bit relieved. He put an arm around her shoulders and gave a quick squeeze. "Cheer up," he said. "We're good."

Then she smiled at him. "I agree. We are."

He walked her to the car and watched as she opened her door.

"London, wait."

She turned. He took her in his arms and kissed her. She curled her fingers in his hair, to capture the kiss and make it last. It took her breath away. Finally, she pulled back and gazed into his eyes, trying to read what they were saying.

"I suppose you think *I'm* a ho now," he said, smiling.

She gave a short laugh. "Get in," she said. "This can't end here."

They drove in silence to her apartment. Once inside, she dropped her things, then took his hand and led him into her bedroom.

"I don't know why I'm doing this." She put her arms around his neck. "But I can't get you out of my mind."

He kissed her deeply but resisted when she tried to pull him down onto her bed.

"What's wrong?" she asked. When he didn't say anything right away her heart sank. "*Is* something wrong?"

He didn't meet her eyes. He took both of her hands in his and sighed.

"Justin, you're scaring me."

"I don't mean to. It's just that . . . I don't think we should do this, after all," he said.

"But, you—"

""I know. I said we could try, and I meant it, but, now . . . I don't think it's a good idea."

"I give up," London said, tears starting in her eyes. She let go of his hand and walked out of the bedroom. When he followed her into the living room, she could see he was struggling with his emotions, but she was emotional, too.

"You need to make up your mind," she said. "I know this is all happening too fast. If you need time to acclimate—"

"I do, but that's not it."

She looked at him expectantly.

"You're a wonderful woman. I had no idea I'd meet someone like you and feel so drawn to you. But my life is very unsettled right now, and I don't want to hurt you."

"Then don't."

"I think in time it would be inevitable." He turned away from her.

"Why?"

He didn't answer immediately. Without facing her, he said, "I have a lot to work out. There are dark places in my soul, London. Things I did over there, things I've seen . . . I don't know if I'm capable of leading an ordinary life. My family thinks I should put it all behind me, but it's not that easy. I'm not the same man who went away all those years ago. And then there's Gina. Maybe I owe her something . . . an explanation, an apology." He turned to look at her. "It wouldn't work between us."

Now it was her turn to be silent. She studied his face. "Now tell me the real reason."

He looked at her questioningly.

"It's been my experience that when someone throws up multiple excuses, it's because there's something else they don't want to say." She gazed at him levelly as if daring him to evade her.

He shrugged. "All right. You already know the truth. I have a bullet in my chest. A bullet that could move. It might be because I bend over to pick something up. It might be because I sneeze. Hell, it might happen when I'm sitting on the sofa watching TV. I got sent home because of that bullet."

She turned her head away, unable to look at the pain she saw in his face.

He saw her brush at the tears that appeared at the corners of her eyes.

"I don't know how long I have. It wouldn't be fair."

"But we—"

"What if you were to love me? What if we fell head over heels for each other and then, poof, I was gone? Isn't it better not to let yourself get involved and take the risk of having your heart broken? I'm not a good bet."

"What if it didn't happen? Who's to say you can't live a long, long time? It's possible, right? I know this is crazy. We've only known each other for a minute, but in that minute, I lost my heart to you. What if you walk away and then live a whole lifetime? Wouldn't you regret what we could have had? Nobody knows what tomorrow will bring. I don't have a bullet in my heart, but I could step off a curb next week into the path of a bus. There are no guarantees, Justin. There are no guarantees. What if I fell head over heels for you? I already did."

She sighed and walked to her door, not waiting for an answer. "Just think about it," she said as she opened the door. "I can't force you to be with me, so go do what you need to do."

He took a hesitant step toward her, his expression unreadable, then said, "I'm sorry," and walked through the door.

"Me, too," she said softly as she shut the door.

Chapter 34

★ ★ ★

London gave Nicole an abridged version of what happened with Justin. "We were having such a great night, then everything changed. I think he's afraid to trust in us. We talked about wanting to see where our relationship could go, but when we got to my house, he got cold feet. It wasn't fair."

"What do you mean he got cold feet?"

"He thinks he's not a good bet for a long-term future. He got shot, and that's why he was sent back home. But he'd really like to be back there in the middle of the war."

"I know it doesn't jibe with the rosy future together you were hoping for, but should you take him at his word? I give him props for at least thinking about you."

"I know you're right. Just like I know he's right. But, damn it, I don't want to give up if there's any possibility we could make it work. God. Why can't he give us a chance?"

"He told you why. And maybe he'll change his mind. And, London, I don't want to minimize what you're feeling, but you haven't even known him a month."

"And yet I feel like I've known him since the first time I looked at his picture. It's weird to say I'm in love with him, but I think I *am* in love with him. You haven't met him. I hope you get the chance someday."

"I hope so, too. I've had my fingers crossed for you both. Just be patient and see what happens. You never know."

"Yeah, I suppose. But I'm not going to sit around and wait. Maybe this was a fantasy that I was lucky enough to have. Maybe it wasn't ever meant to be anything more. So, I'm moving on."

"Wow. I know you're an adult, but how very adult of you."

"I know. Don't I sound like I've got it all together?" She giggled. "Think of all the free time I'll have now to go shopping with you."

And in that moment, she really meant it.

"I'm glad you got to meet your soldier," Kyle said. London sat in Nicole's living room watching a movie with Nicole and her boyfriend.

"Thanks, Kyle." She bit her tongue and didn't bring up the fact that he'd damn near destroyed any chance she might have had with Justin by butting in.

"Yeah. Sorry it didn't work out for you."

London's guard went up. She'd enjoyed an uneasy truce with Kyle since the David incident, mainly by determining to have a good relationship with Nicole's boyfriend. She just wasn't sure whether this was a sympathetic statement or a veiled dig. She mentally shrugged her shoulders and thanked him, saying everything was fine.

Nicole had been intently watching the interplay but seemed to relax.

"He must have thought he had a psycho on his hands," Kyle added, for once not bothering to hide his snide disdain for London.

London's face turned bright red. "*Excuse* me?"

"What? I mean, you had an unhealthy interest in the guy. What was he supposed to think?" Kyle's crappy grin was too much for her to bear.

"*Kyle.*" Nicole looked horrified.

London stood, and Nicole jumped up but didn't even try to talk her into staying, instead giving London a quick hug. "I'll walk you out."

"You guys are too sensitive. I was just kidding," Kyle said.

Nicole shot him a dirty look.

One of these days, Nicole's gonna know what kind of man she's involved with. London was too dejected to give in to the fury Kyle's comments deserved. She forced herself not to dwell on what had just happened and concentrated on her driving. She wanted nothing so much as to be home curled up on her sofa, snuggled in the comfort of soft cushions and the soft throw she kept folded on the ottoman. She parked at the curb, and walked up the sidewalk toward her apartment.

Chapter 35

★ ★ ★

London stopped in her tracks as Justin pushed up from the hood of the car where he'd been lounging. "Can we talk?"

It took a moment for her to respond, then she nodded and fumbled for her keys, acutely aware of him. Once inside, after tossing her handbag onto the coffee table, she faced him. "So, what do you want to talk about?" Her arms were crossed protectively in front of her and she tried to keep her gaze steady. Not easy when her stomach was doing flip flops.

"I want to talk about us."

"I thought there *was* no us. You said you couldn't do it."

"Yeah. I said that. But I find that I can't let go. I don't want to let go . . . of you. Is there any way we could—"

"What, talk it to death? You want to rehash our conversation and then decide you were right the first time?" She turned away and headed to the kitchen. She pulled two bottles of water out of the refrigerator and handed one to Justin, then walked around him to the living room. He followed and sat next to her on the sofa. London thought briefly of wrapping herself in the throw and pulling it over her head. Instead, she stared at him. "You were saying?"

There was grave sadness in Justin's eyes, and London suddenly felt guilty for not welcoming him more graciously. She reached out and took his hand. "What do you want from me?"

"You can forgive me."

London's eyes brimmed. "There's nothing to forgive. You were honest about your feelings, your fears. You said what you needed to say." She wiped at her eyes. "What are you saying now?"

"I know I should leave you alone. I'm being selfish. My feelings for you hit me like a ton of bricks and—" He sighed deeply and cleared his throat. "I've been alone for a while now. I know it was by choice, but I don't want to be alone anymore. If I hadn't met you, maybe I'd still have my equilibrium, but you've thrown me off balance."

"I could say the same thing," London said softly. "I was doing fine, and then there you were. Maybe I already belonged to you, from the first time I saw your face in that picture. I didn't know it at the time, but how else can I explain why I fell so fast and so hard for you? Maybe my life was on hold until you came into it."

"I guess one of us should say it, then. I'll do it. I want to be with you."

"I want to be with you, too. I've been miserable since you walked away. I'm a big girl, and I'll go into this with my eyes open. If we only have moments, I'll treasure them. If we have a whole lifetime, I'll consider myself the luckiest girl in the world."

He stood and pulled her to her feet. "Thank you." He tilted her face up and kissed her, then held her in his arms.

She pulled away, eyes shining, but her heart dropped when she saw his face. "Why don't you look happy?" His demeanor triggered her concern. "What's wrong?"

"You said what I wanted to hear you say, but I can't help feeling that I'm cheating you."

"You said what *I* wanted to hear, too. And I'm super, super happy that you did. I told you, I'm in. All the way in. And I couldn't be happier about it. And, you know what? I have a really good feeling about this. I think you're going to be around a long time."

He gave a half-hearted laugh. He smiled but not with his eyes. To London, it felt like an ice pick to her heart. Her arms went around his neck, and she kissed his lips, and then held him.

When she let him go, she said, "If we're going to do this, then we have to do it with hope, and faith. And *joy*. If you can't let go of your guilt and be happy for what we can have together, maybe we shouldn't even try. It's up to you. I want to go for it. Can you?"

He sighed. "Yes."

London was relieved as she saw the darkness leave his face. He smiled tentatively as he wrapped her in a bear hug.

"Let's go get something to eat and talk about our future," she said, happier than she'd been in a long time.

"If you're sure you want to go somewhere."

"I know. I can't believe I said that. But I need to wrap my head around the fact that you really came back. I want to make sure I'm not imagining this. If we stay here, well.... I want a minute to process this before we end up down the hall."

"So let's go get something to eat and talk about our future," he said. "The room down the hall can wait a little longer."

London started glowing halfway through dinner. Now that they were *officially* together, there were more important things they could be doing, things they couldn't do in a restaurant. When they were presented with the dessert menu, Justin asked her if she wanted anything.

"Nothing on the menu," she said, looking up at him through her eyelashes.

"I know it's a cliché, but check, please." he said with a smile, signaling their server.

It was not meant to be that night. Waiting at London's front door was a tearful Nicole. She looked embarrassed when she saw that London wasn't alone and tried to go, saying they could talk later, but London stopped her.

"What's wrong?"

"I broke up with Kyle."

London almost gave a fist pump but restrained herself. Nicole was hurting. "I wish I could say I'm sorry. I mean, I *am* sorry for you being hurt; but Kyle, I never trusted him. I tried to keep my feelings about him to myself, but tonight he went too far."

"I know. I thought things were so much better. You seemed to be getting along lately. Apparently, I was wrong. I've been wrong the whole time, haven't I?" Nicole looked at Justin. "I'm so sorry about this. My timing sucks, doesn't it? You must be Justin."

"And you must be Nicole." He took her extended hand.

"That would be me. Look, you guys, I can talk to London tomorrow. I don't want to ruin your evening."

"What kind of friend would I be if I tossed you out in your hour of need?"

"She's right," Justin said. "Why don't I leave you two alone. I can see you tomorrow, London. If that's okay with you."

"Yes. We can see each other tomorrow. For sure, though, right?"

"For sure." He gave her a light kiss, said goodnight to Nicole, and was gone.

London tried to keep the disappointment she felt from showing on her face. It was like tearing her heart out to see him go.

"So. Coffee?"

Not that she needed any more coffee. But Nicole might need to talk for hours, so she settled her friend on the sofa and headed to the kitchen.

"Was it what happened tonight?" London called from the kitchen.

"Yeah. Straw, camel. It was too blatant to ignore. When I jumped on him for being an asshole, he said that he was tired of me anyway."

"Consider the source. He's the biggest jerk I've ever met. It's *his* loss, not yours." She settled on the sofa next to her friend.

"I know. Not much comfort, though."

"Well, you know he couldn't walk meekly out of your house. He had to get the last word in." London took a sip. "I wonder what his deal was with the soldier, though."

"I don't know. He's a promoter of new talent and the young and the wealthy. Maybe he foresaw your book being a big success. Which would make the soldier a big success. And then he could step in and take credit for discovering him."

"Pretty flimsy. You'd think if he wanted to ride on my coattails he would have been nicer to me."

"I could call and ask him," Nicole said innocently.

"Oh, God, no! My fervent wish is that you never speak to him again."

"Your wish is granted."

London laughed. "Let me know when you're okay so we can celebrate." She punched Nicole gently on the arm. "Just kidding."

Nicole made a face. "I don't think it will take that long. It's been coming for a while now. I should have listened to you in the first place." She sipped her coffee. "It's just, I was with him for a long time, and now I won't know what to do with myself."

"I know. It's hard. It's that missing them that gets to you. I'm really sorry. I would have tried to like him again for you." She gave her friend a hug.

Nicole pulled back suddenly, "Oh my God, London. Justin came back. And he's so *hot*. I would have recognized him anywhere from that picture although he cleans up really well. I'm sorry I interrupted you."

"You interrupted our first sexual encounter, but don't worry about it," London said with a laugh. When she saw the horrified look on Nicole's face, she added, "Don't worry. Anticipation makes it better. Tomorrow night will be amazing."

"He probably hates me now."

"I'm sure he doesn't. He wouldn't dare hate my best friend."

"So, tell me what happened. What did he say?"

"He was waiting for me when I got home from your house. Basically, he said he can't live without me."

"I'm so happy for you. It's all so weird, the way it worked out. Do you suppose you'll still have time to fit me in now and then?"

"Of *course* I'll still fit you in. You and me, BFFs!"

London picked up the cups. "You don't want any more, do you? Do you want to stay here tonight?"

"No and no. I'm feeling better now. I have to go through feeling sad and crappy, and I might as well face it. Want to have breakfast in the morning?"

"Or, you could go running with me. I think it would make you feel *much* better."

"But breakfast is so much easier."

"Easier isn't what you need right now. Trust me. I know all about it."

By morning, Nicole was in better spirits although she was slightly grumpy about skipping breakfast to do something healthy.

"Shouldn't I be pampering myself to get better?" she pouted.

"This *is* pampering yourself. You're going to feel great when we're done, and we can go to Starbucks afterward."

Between breaths, Nicole told London she didn't think she and Kyle would ever get back together. There had been an undercurrent because of the friction between Kyle and London.

London apologized for not warming up to Kyle, but Nicole waved her off. It would take her awhile to get her spirits up again, but she was resolved that she'd made the right decision to dump him.

Finally relaxing at Starbucks, London picked up her mocha, and looked at Nicole over the top. "You know how you interrupted us last night?"

"I'm so, so sorry. I knew I was in the way."

"No. That's not what I'm getting at. You weren't in the way. Don't even think that. What I was going to say was that maybe it was a good thing. Justin and I have only known each other for a really short time. We shouldn't be having sex so soon, should we?"

"That's a complicated question. Depends on so many things."

"I know. I think I jumped into bed with Alex too soon, and look how that turned out. Justin's special. I believe I could already be in love with him. I don't want to screw it up."

"Anticipation can be a turn on. If you want to slow it down, it gives you something to look forward to. If he's not okay with waiting, maybe he's not on the same page as you."

"It's just that I really want to—"

"Rip his clothes off?"

London laughed. "*Exactly*. Do you think you can fall in love with a guy from the way he kisses? I think that's all it took for me."

"Yes. I do think you can. I've had one or two of those epic kisses before. I completely agree that a kiss can melt your heart."

"I hope he isn't going to be disappointed in me if I make him wait."

"He'll be fine with it. I saw the way he looked at you. I think your kiss might have had the same effect on him."

By the time they left Starbucks, London was feeling relieved that Nicole wasn't a puddle of emotion.

Chapter 36

★ ★ ★

"You look beautiful," he said. He held a bouquet of pale peach tulips.

London smiled widely, blushing at the unexpectedly thoughtful gift. She led the way to the kitchen, filling a crystal vase with water. She set the vase in the center of the dining room table, and smiled up at Justin. The longing in his eyes matched her own. They moved into each other's arms, feeding the hunger that consumed them both.

"You know," London whispered in his ear, "I really want to see you naked right now."

"All you have to do is ask," he said with a laugh.

For a moment, she almost gave in to her desires. "I *would*, but . . . I can't believe I'm saying this, but do you think we're making a mistake by jumping into bed too soon?"

"I—"

"I want this to last. I'm kind of afraid that if we rush into the sex part it could make it too easy for things not to work out. How often have we seen each other? We could count the times on one hand."

He sighed. "I'm a guy. You can never jump into bed too soon."

"I'd think you were joking except for the look on your face."

"I'm kind of joking, but I'm not all the way there yet." He stepped around her and headed to the kitchen. "I think I need a beer if we're going to do the *just friends* thing."

"Yeah. Bring me one, too."

As they settled next to each other on the sofa, London felt guilty for putting on the brakes. But this wasn't a fling, and she wanted to give it the best possible shot at a lasting future.

"Are you—"

"Am I okay with it? Yeah. I want you too much to jeopardize our relationship. We have plenty of time. For all of it."

London saw the cloud pass over his face as if he thought he was jinxing it, but she didn't say anything. She kept the pang in her heart to herself.

He slipped down to the floor, resting back against the sofa between her knees. "There's a football game on. Okay if we watch some of it? Since . . . you know."

"I know. And that's fine. I'll just sit here on the sofa by myself and watch you watching the game."

When she saw his concerned look, she doubled over in laughter. "Just *kidding.*"

She sighed, content to have him here, happy that he was close enough to touch. She bent and kissed the top of his head.

Chapter 37

★ ★ ★

Justin had been a real trooper. He'd never questioned her desire to wait. Everything he did underlined the fact that he cared deeply for her.

London sat at one end of the sofa, watching him, and knew it was time. "I love you, Justin."

He smiled. "I—"

She didn't let him get the words out. She pulled his face down to hers and kissed him, really kissed him.

He wrapped his fingers in her hair and lost himself in the kiss. He pushed her down onto the sofa and lay on top of her, his hands sliding up under her sweater. She pulled him closer and moaned.

And then he stood up. She looked at him in surprise. "Justin—"

"I'm sorry. I shouldn't have let that happen."

She stood and took his hand. "It's time. We've waited long enough."

This night, they spent together.

And the next, and the next.

Chapter 38

★ ★ ★

The two men sat in a booth in the Chateau Marmont bar. Several empty beer glasses sat on the table between them, and their voices were tense, angry.

"What did you do?" the angrier of the two asked.

"Chill, dude. I got tired of playing nice for that ex of yours and maybe I wasn't as diplomatic as I could have been."

"Now that you and Nicole broke up, I don't have any more plays."

"There might be something," Kyle said. "If you're interested. I don't think it will get you any brownie points with her. It would just be a revenge thing."

"I'm listening," David said.

"Cool. I was tired of those bitches anyway, so this will be fun."

Chapter 39

★ ★ ★

London did a double take at the blurb on the cover of the tabloid. She stopped unloading her groceries and stared. The woman behind her in line told her to buy the damn magazine and stop holding up the other shoppers. In a daze, London barely heard her until the woman cleared her throat dramatically and waved her hand. London apologized and tossed the tabloid on top of her other items, and rushed to her car as soon as she'd paid for everything.

Sitting in the front seat, she pulled the magazine out and looked at the picture of Justin, with a caption that said "The REAL Soldier behind the Book." It was a grainy picture of Justin, showing him casually drinking a beer. That son of a bitch Kyle. There was no question he was behind this. The story was provocative, revealing what scant details of her relationship with Justin that Kyle might be aware of. And making up details when the truth wasn't titillating enough. It made her seem like a cheesy opportunist. And Justin, like a clueless sap. The main point of the story was that London was an obsessed fan who stalked a soldier whose picture she spotted in a newspaper. And that she'd tracked him down and scammed him into a sex-fueled relationship. Inside was another picture of Justin and her, his arm around her. She recognized the setting. They'd been waiting for the valet to bring their car around after dinner by the beach. Under the picture was a caption that read, "Poor guy. Does he know what he's gotten himself into?"

Chapter 40

⭐ ⭐ ⭐

How could she tell Justin about the tabloid? She felt guilty that he would have to deal with people recognizing him and bothering him, not to mention the negative online chatter she was sure would follow. The timing was so awful, given how new their relationship was.

In tears, she called Nicole. A text wouldn't do.

"Do you know what he did?"

"Who?" Nicole asked.

"Kyle. He got one of the tabloids to run a story about Justin. It's an awful story."

"I'm going to go pick one up, and then I'll be over. Don't panic."

How do you not panic when your new boyfriend finds his face plastered all over a magazine cover?

Too agitated to sit, London paced as she waited for Nicole.

Nicole made record time. She breathlessly rushed through the door when London opened it and plopped on the sofa, patting the cushion beside her for London to join her. Together, they read the story through. Twice.

"God, London, I'm so sorry."

"It's not your fault. This is all on Kyle."

"But why would he—"

"You know he didn't like me. Ever. He wasn't even good at faking it."

"Maybe so, but—"

"Maybe he was pissed that you broke up with him," London said.

"That would mean he actually cared about me."

"Not necessarily. His ego might have been hurt. That could have set him off."

Nicole's nose was buried in the story again.

"I don't know how to tell Justin about this," London said. We only just really got together. He's going to think I'm bad for him."

"Are you kidding? He can't blame this on you. You're both victims."

"But maybe I'm not worth the trouble I'm causing him."

"If he thinks that, he doesn't deserve you."

London stood and resumed pacing.

"Call and invite him over. The sooner you get this over with, the sooner you'll know what happens next."

Justin arrived with a bottle of wine and a smile. When he pulled her into his arms, he could feel her tense. He took a step back and looked at her curiously. "Is everything okay?"

"Come on in," she said.

"What's wrong?"

She shifted uncomfortably. "I have to tell you something. I feel really awful about it."

His worried look made her feel worse than she already did. "Why don't we sit down," she said quietly.

He joined her on the sofa and took her hand. "Tell me."

Her eyes were downcast. She couldn't look him in the eye. "I'm so embarrassed," she said after a moment. Then picked up the tabloid from the coffee table and handed it to him.

He glanced at the magazine, and did a double-take. "What is this?"

She could see his anger grow as he flipped through the pages.

"Did you—"

"No. It wasn't me. I didn't know. When I saw this . . . ." She didn't continue.

"Then how did it happen?"

"It was Kyle. Nicole's ex. It had to be."

Her phone picked that moment to ping. Glancing at it, she saw a leering emoji. From David. She stood, flustered.

"What is it," Justin asked.

"I don't understand," she said. "David? It was David?"

"Did you do it?" she texted back.

In a moment her phone pinged again. "With a little help from my friend. Ha ha."

"Apparently, David *and* Kyle. I guess I have two nemeses."

Justin watched her. "Well. I wasn't expecting to ever be on the cover of a magazine."

"I know, and I'm sorry. I don't know what to do."

"Forget about it. Those rags come out every few days. By next week, I'll be a has been."

"That's not funny, Justin."

"What do you want me to do? Would you rather I stomped out the door and tracked them down?"

"Maybe," she said glumly.

He pulled her into a hug. "Look. It happened, and there's nothing we can do about it now. Neither of us has anything to be embarrassed about. Just forget about it."

"What will your family think? What about my family?"

"I don't think my parents ever read tabloids."

"But their friends could tell them—"

"And if they did? Seriously, don't worry about it. Call your family and tell them about it if you think you need to. I know I haven't met them, but I'd be surprised if they weren't on your side."

She heaved a sigh of relief. "I feel so much better. Thanks for talking me off the ledge."

"That's what I'm here for."

"That's not the only thing you're here for," she said with a flirty smile. I'll open the wine."

Chapter 41

★ ★ ★

Weeks later, London sat in Justin's car outside a neat English Revival house on a shady street in Pasadena. Today, she was meeting his family.

She loved that Justin had such a close-knit family. Even though she didn't see her own family often, she called or texted with her sisters regularly. They knew about Justin—not all the details but that he might one day be someone special to the Calloways. With luck, they'd meet him soon.

Another look at the house, which was on a slight rise, and she grabbed the car door handle. Justin got out and hurried around to get the door for her, then held her hand as they walked up the pathway to the front door.

The door opened before they could knock. London was immediately drawn to the small woman with sparkling eyes who was smiling warmly at them.

"You must be London. How wonderful to meet you. I'm Kathy. My son talks about you often. I'm very happy you're here."

"I'm pleased to meet you, too, Kathy. I've heard so much about you all." She smiled up at Justin. "He babbles about you all the time."

"I don't babble," he said gruffly.

"Well, maybe I'm exaggerating a little." She laughed, and then noticed a handsome bear of a man had come up behind Kathy.

"Senior, look. It's London."

Justin Senior dipped his head to her, smiling as he clapped Justin on the shoulder. He reached out a hand. "So happy to meet you."

"Thank you, Mr. Beckett. I'm very happy to meet you, too," she responded, clasping his hand.

She liked him immediately. The resemblance to Justin was evident in the bone structure of his face and in the great hair, which was only slightly gray. They were both tall, but Justin had him by at least an inch.

As they moved into the living room, Kathy said, "Lindsay will be here in a little while. She has an art class on Saturday mornings. But she can't wait to meet you."

"I hope she likes me," London said before she could stop herself.

"As if you have anything to worry about," Kathy said with a laugh. "You seem like a lovely young woman."

London smiled. Looking around the room, she noticed more than one framed photo of two similar looking boys at various ages. The bond between them was obvious. She stared at one photo showing two handsome young men, arms draped over each other's shoulders, skyscrapers in the background.

"Those are my boys," Kathy said wistfully. "Those were happy days. I should have held on tighter."

"They look so much alike."

"They were very much alike. And not just in the way they looked. They were best friends." She pointed to the figure on the right. "That's Steve."

"I thought it might be, but they're so similar."

London squeezed Kathy's hand. Kathy looked at her gratefully.

"When Steve died—" Kathy stopped as her voice broke. After a sigh, she resumed. "When Steve died, a part of Justin died with him. He was lost without his brother. Then Justin enlisted and it was almost like we lost him, too."

"I can imagine it must have felt like that to you, having both of them gone."

"I know why Justin joined up. I can't blame him. But . . . it was hard." Kathy traced a finger over Justin's picture. "After that, when we saw him, all the light was gone from his eyes." She turned back to London. "Until now. You've brought Justin back to us."

"I—" London felt herself redden. She hadn't expected this. "I don't know what to say."

"Don't say anything, dear. Just . . . thank you."

At that moment, Justin and his father returned from the kitchen, beers in hand.

"Have you two bonded yet?" he teased.

"We're best of friends now," Kathy said. "You picked a great girl, son."

"I know." He patted the sofa for London to join him. Senior put an affectionate hand on Kathy's shoulder, perhaps noticing her sentimental mood.

London looked up at Justin, remembering his mother's words. She got misty as she savored the memory, turning away before he could see her eyes.

By the time coffee and small sandwiches had been served, Lindsay arrived.

She breezed into the living room and bent to hug her parents a quick hello. Justin stood and Lindsay hugged him, turning as London rose from her seat.

The young women smiled at each other, Lindsay's smile a touch more appraising than London's had been. She was aware of Lindsay's scrutiny and was momentarily unnerved until Lindsay turned to Justin and said, "You did good, big brother."

London glanced at the portfolio Lindsay had dropped at the end of the sofa. "What have you got there? It looks so professional. Anything you can show us?"

Lindsay smiled. "It's for my art class. I've been taking drawing and painting classes for, like, ever."

She picked up the portfolio and unzipped the top. "Now, keep in mind I'm just an amateur," she said as she pulled out a sketch book. She flipped through the pages until she found what she was looking for, then, embarrassed, hugged it to her chest for a moment. "Okay, here goes."

It was a charcoal drawing of a young man. A familiar young man. London looked up at Lindsay.

Lindsay said, "I know, it's weird. I only want to draw my brother. My brothers," she added absently.

"There are two of them," she continued, flipping a page back over. "You probably recognized Justin. Here's the one of Steve." She handed the large pad to London.

Lindsay had a good eye for capturing something lifelike and real in her portraits. London flipped back and forth between the two drawings. "I *love* them. Really. You're so good."

She handed the sketch pad to Justin. He looked at the pictures for a long moment before handing them back to Lindsay. "I had no idea, Lin. This blows me away. Wow."

Lindsay bent over and kissed him on the cheek. "I hope you like them."

"More than I can say," he murmured.

Chapter 42

✦ ✦ ✦

London and Justin had been together for months, so taking him home to meet her family at Christmas was important to her. They'd Skyped with her parents a few times, but it wasn't the same as meeting in person.

"I talked to my mom this morning," London said. "They invited us for the holidays. Any chance you'd want to come to Bozeman with me?"

"Montana?"

"Yes. They're mountain people," she said with a wink.

"Well, I—"

"And my siblings will be there. I want you to meet everyone."

"How could I refuse an offer like that?"

"I was hoping you wouldn't be able to. And with any luck we'll have a white Christmas. None of those eighty-two-degree days that so often mark Christmases in Southern California."

He laughed. "My Christmases in the Army weren't white, either. I guess this Christmas will be special in many ways."

London loved him so much. This man was the light of her life, and she could barely wait to introduce him to her family.

"Remind me again who everyone is," Justin said as they waited at baggage claim. "Jessica and Harry are your parents, right?"

"Right. My sister Savannah Callen is married to Andy. They have the twin three-year-olds, Katie and Kevin. Dallas is married to Don Hooper; and my brother, Bill, and his wife, Tara, are parents of four-year-old Cole."

At Christmastime, there were a lot of people in the house. Justin was initially overwhelmed by the crowd, but only initially. He was welcomed with open arms and hearts, and after the first couple of hours felt like he was one of them.

After Christmas Eve dinner, London and the girls congregated in the kitchen, clearing and washing dishes while the guys retired to the den to smoke the cigars her father liked to bring out for holidays and special occasions.

With five of them sharing kitchen duties, everything that needed to be done was finished in twenty minutes and the ladies sat around the kitchen table with cups of coffee.

Savannah looked from face to face, then turned to London. "Okay, tell us everything. We're dying for details."

London laughed. "It's a pretty unbelievable story actually." She hadn't told her family about the picture. They knew about the book, of course, but she hadn't told them in depth the story of how she met Justin. She suddenly was very excited to share, and covered her face with her hands. "I'm so embarrassed. I'll tell you, but you have to keep it to yourselves. And especially don't be teasing Justin about it."

"About what?" Dallas asked. "Why are you embarrassed?"

London took her coffee cup to the kitchen sink and dumped it out, then took a wine glass down and poured herself a glass of chardonnay. She sat back down and raised her glass. "I need this."

"Well, now we're intrigued," her mother said.

"Hurry up," Tara said. "We're all waiting."

"So, you know my latest book?" London asked.

"*The Hero*? Of course. I loved it," Savannah said.

"Me, too," Dallas added. "And?"

"And, the reason I ask is because Justin was the inspiration for it."

"What?"

"Yeah, *what*?" Savannah added. "I didn't know you'd known him that long."

"I didn't. Not really. Hang on a minute." She pulled her iPhone out of her back pocket, and thumbed through the photos until she found the one she wanted.

"There was this picture in the paper. It started the whole thing." She passed around the phone and everyone crowded over the screen to see the picture.

Tara expanded the photo and exclaimed, "Is that Justin?"

"Yes. That was the first time I saw him. And that picture inspired my novel."

"How did you find him? Did you track him down?"

"No. In a million years I never expected to meet him. Then he turned up on my doorstep to yell at me for invading his privacy."

"What—"

"That's a whole other story, for another time. And then months later I literally tripped over his luggage at the airport when I was coming home after my last trip out here for Mom's 65th. I recognized him immediately. He probably thought I was a psycho stalker at first, but I told him to read my book and then call me, and he did. And that's how it all began." She sipped her wine as she looked at her incredulous audience.

"That's the most romantic story I've ever heard," Dallas said. "Wow."

"I know, what are the chances of something like that happening in the real world?" Savannah asked.

"Probably zillions to one," London said. "But, really, don't let on you know about it because it might embarrass him. If you want to tell the guys after we're gone you can, but I want him to be completely comfortable with all of you." She sighed. "He doesn't think he's a hero, but he really is."

It turned out London didn't need to worry about embarrassing Justin. Her brother took care of that.

"So, how did you meet my sister?" Bill asked.

"We met at LAX. We just bumped into each other."

"You picked her up in an airport?"

"More like she picked me up."

"That doesn't sound like my sister. I didn't know she was so aggressive."

"She wasn't. She was . . . she just . . . Hell. I don't know."

"You're looking a little embarrassed there, bro. You don't know how you ended up together?"

"I, uh, maybe you should ask her."

"That's kind of a weenie answer, dude," Bill said. "Is it a secret or something?"

Justin shook his head. "It's not a secret. She wrote a book about me."

"The scary one?" Andy Callen asked with a smirk.

"Not that one."

"That only leaves one," London's dad said. "I thought it was fiction."

"It was. She just saw a picture of me and got inspired."

"Hang on a sec," Bill said. He stood and went to the doorway. "London. Can you come in here a minute?" He turned back to the guys and smiled.

She appeared a few seconds later. "What do you need, Bill?"

"What's this about you writing a book about your boyfriend?"

She blushed furiously, then mouthed *I'm sorry* to Justin.

He shrugged.

"Well?" Bill pressed.

She waved at the air to scatter the heavy layer of cigar smoke hanging in the room. "I just finished having the same conversation in the kitchen. If you must know, Justin was the inspiration for *The Hero*." She still held her iPhone and scrolled back to the photo, thrusting her phone at her brother. "Here. I saw this and the story just came to me."

Bill looked at the picture and then handed the phone around. It ended up with Justin. It had been a long time since he'd seen the picture so he stared at it for a moment, then handed it back to London.

"I told the girls not to repeat the story because I didn't want to embarrass you, Justin."

"It's okay." He picked up his beer and took a drink. "I don't care if you don't."

"I don't care. Dallas said it was the most romantic thing she's ever heard. And I agree with her."

The men all laughed, and Bill clapped Justin on the back. "Don't know how you're going to live this one down, Junior. We can be brutal with the jokes."

"Bring it on," Justin said, grinning broadly.

Harry stood. "Can I get the hero another beer?"

"Dad!" London said. "I expect that of Bill. I'm seeing a whole different side of you."

He winked. "Aren't the ladies missing you? You should run on back."

She laughed, then leaned down and kissed Justin gently before heading back to the kitchen.

Early Christmas morning, the gaily wrapped packages were soon the gaily unwrapped packages, and three tiny tots played under the festive tree in the family room while indulgent adults watched, mugs of coffee in hand.

Outside, the ground was covered in a blanket of snow, and the adults all went out to help the little ones build snowmen. The blue Montana sky was breathtaking, with big fluffy clouds and white mounds of snow that made the blue more vibrant. A crisp wind rustled leaves and caused hair to bristle with static electricity.

After a playful afternoon snowball fight, men against women, everyone was ready to relax around the big fireplace for the last time before it was time to pack for home. Jessica and Savannah brought out mugs of hot cider. Harry made a little impromptu speech about how good it was to be surrounded by family. He added "and future family" to a chorus of laughter. He got serious for a moment to tell Justin how pleased they all were to meet him and that he was welcome back any time.

London was sad to be leaving her family. She didn't know when she would be able to visit again. It made her happy, however, to watch Justin interact with them. They'd made him welcome, and she knew she needn't worry about whether he would fit in.

Chapter 43

★ ★ ★

On New Year's Eve, Justin asked if she wouldn't mind if they skipped Cal and Anthony's annual party. He said he wanted to be alone with her.

Which was thrilling. It was so romantic, it gave her chills. After spending the Christmas holiday surrounded by family, she didn't mind spending her first New Year's Eve alone with the most important person in her life. And her friends would understand.

The thought of sharing a kiss at midnight, toasting each other with champagne . . . she couldn't imagine a better way to spend New Year's Eve.

But there *was* a better way. He'd wanted to surprise her, so didn't tell her their destination as he drove north along the coast toward Pismo Beach until they turned into the Cliffs Resort. Perched on a bluff, with the ocean spread out below, the view from the resort was breathtaking. After dinner, they stood side by side at the railing looking out at the sea. The air was crisp and the sea breeze was biting, but Justin's arm around her shoulders protected her from the cold. London couldn't believe how happy she felt. She was giddy and her eyes sparkled as the waiter filled their glasses in preparation for the stroke of midnight. In spite of the other couples on the terrace, they felt like they were in their own separate world.

All London could see was Justin. As the magic moment arrived, he swept her up into his arms and kissed her deeply, holding tight to her until their kiss ended. As he let her go, he got down on one knee.

London's heart caught in her throat as he took her hand and looked into her eyes.

"I never knew I could be this happy. I want to spend my life with you, to wake up to your beautiful face every morning," he said, his voice husky. "London Calloway, will you marry me?"

Overwhelmed by emotion, for a moment she said nothing. When she said yes, it was a whisper. And then he was holding something sparkly and bright and slipping it on her finger. Her legs grew weak as she looked at her hand in his, her thoughts a jumble of excitement and awe. She'd had no idea. And yet it felt so right.

"I need to sit down," she said, never taking her eyes off the emerald-cut diamond ring.

"Of course." He led her to a bench. "I didn't mean to scare you."

"I'm not scared. Surprised for sure. And happy, very happy. And scared." She smiled sheepishly. "I mean, I'm not scared to spend my life with you. Just scared because this is so big."

"For me, too."

"I guess this means things are working out for us, right?"

"Ha ha. They worked out for us from the moment we met."

"Well, maybe not the *moment* we met. You thought I was a stalker at first, remember?"

"Yeah, well, now you will officially be *my* stalker." He laughed and pulled her into a bear hug.

London held her left hand up and admired the engagement ring over Justin's shoulder. "It's so beautiful."

"Compared to you, it's just a dusty rock. I love you, my beautiful future wife."

"I can't wait to show off my dusty rock to all my friends."

Chapter 44

★ ★ ★

Morning light nudged them awake. London buried her head in Justin's neck, curling into him. He yawned and turned toward her to engulf her in his arms. She pulled her hand out from under the covers and admired the way the diamond sparkled in the sunlight coming through the window.

"Did we really just get engaged?" she asked as she turned her hand this way and that. "I mean, I didn't dream it, did I?"

"If so, then I had the same dream."

"My parents are going to be so surprised!"

"Considering I asked your father for your hand, maybe not so much."

"You did?" A big smile spread across her face. "I had no idea!"

"I wanted to do everything right with you. This is going to last forever."

London didn't say anything, but a cold dread clutched her heart as the word "jinx" flashed through her mind.

Nicole pooh-poohed London's superstition. She refused to let her friend allow a cloud to hover over the great news she'd just shared. "Say it with me now," she said. "My future is *not* jinxed."

London was grateful that Nicole seemed so sure, and allowed herself to breathe a sigh of relief. "Thanks, Nikki. I'm so relieved."

"You're welcome. Now show me that rock again."

London lifted her hand so both of them could admire the dazzling ring.

"I'm so jealous!" Nicole said with a grin. "Not only are you engaged, you're engaged to your hero. In a fairy tale love story. Who gets that?"

"Me!" London rummaged in her handbag and put on her sunglasses, then flashed a wide smile. "My future's so bright, I have to wear shades."

Nicole laughed. "I want to wear shades, too."

Chapter 45

★ ★ ★

Cal and Anthony wanted to throw a party for the newly-engaged pair. The invitation from London's long-time friends would be hard to turn down. Cal was tall and slim, with distinguished-looking salt and pepper hair and a flamboyant manner. He owned an in-demand event planning company in Los Angeles. London had no doubt that any party he planned would be fabulous. And Anthony, Cal's handsome Italian husband, was a gifted chef. Although, she expected that Cal would insist on having the party catered so that he and Anthony could enjoy themselves with their guests.

London was thrilled at the offer, but Justin wasn't quite as enthusiastic.

"I'm out of practice," he said when they discussed it. "I haven't done a lot of partying in a long time. I guess it seems sort of frivolous."

"Frivolous is okay for a special occasion. And this is the most special occasion I can think of. It will be fun." She knew his heart carried weighty matters. It would take a lot longer before he could let himself feel free of the darkness he'd endured. Little by little, she was sure she could make him able to trust life again.

"You're right. It's nice of your friends to do this for us."

"I hope that someday you'll think of them as your friends, too. But, until then, I was wondering...." A thought had come to her. "I don't suppose you'd like to invite any of your friends?"

"I could invite Dave. Not that we hang out much, other than having a beer after work now and then. I did tell him I'm engaged, and he'd probably like to be there."

"What about guys from your unit? You've talked about getting together. Would you want to invite any of them?"

"A couple of guys are in Manhattan Beach. I can get in touch and see what they say."

"That would be great." London's eyes shone. She was curious about his Army friends. If they had dark clouds of their own. She was also curious about why he hadn't seen any of them. When she tried to pin him down, he hadn't seemed in a hurry to rekindle their bond.

Justin and Dave talked about a new construction project, and London chatted politely with Dave's wife, Cindy. Nicole was in the kitchen helping Anthony. London gazed at her iPhone. "What time will the rest of your friends get here?" she asked. "I can't wait to meet them."

"They'll be here before Cal uncorks the champagne. I talked to Billy this morning. They're curious about you, too."

"What have you told them about me?"

"Just the basics. But don't worry. I expect they're going to like you just fine."

"I wasn't worried. How could they not like me?" She smiled flirtatiously and squeezed his arm.

London was anxious about meeting Justin's friends. They knew a side of him that she never would.

She had another reason for anticipating their arrival although she didn't mention it to Justin.

"Are they bringing dates?" she asked, her eyes straying to the door. "Are they married or anything?"

"Neither one is married. I think Rick has been dating someone, but Billy's single."

"Will I like them? I mean, are they like you? Kind of serious?"

Just then the doorbell rang and London watched Anthony open the door and greet the visitors.

Justin said, "They're here."

Making a beeline for Justin but leveling a curious eye on London, one of them said "You must be the bride to be. I'm Billy." His big smile endeared him to her immediately.

"I'm the future Mrs. Beckett. Call me London. So happy to meet you." Billy was dark haired and handsome. Rick was shorter and darker, but no less handsome.

"Check out the rock on her finger," Rick said with a grin.

London held her hand up and showed off her ring.

Billy took a closer look. "Way to go, man," he said to Justin.

Justin beamed. "Yeah. I'm a lucky man."

"Where'd you two meet?" Billy asked.

London and Justin exchanged a glance. "I'll let you handle that one," she said with a smile.

"It's a long story. I'll tell you guys some other time."

"I think you should make him tell you now," London said. "It's such a *good* story."

"I don't want to embarrass you. You being a stalker and all."

She laughed. "Let me get you guys something to drink." She headed to the kitchen and motioned Nicole over as she poured the wine.

"What's up?" Nicole looked at London quizzically.

"Don't say I never did anything for you" She handed Nicole one of the glasses and said, "Follow me."

"Why, what's going on?" Nicole asked.

"You'll see."

"I couldn't carry all the glasses, so I asked Nicole to help me," London said innocently as she handed Justin and Rick a drink. "Nicole, can you give that one to Billy?"

She watched as Nicole and Billy gave each other appraising glances. It was obvious that no further assistance from London would be needed.

Chapter 46

★ ★ ★

After dinner, Cal made a congratulatory toast.

"Tony and I are so happy for London and Justin. Everyone, drink to the happy couple." After sipping his champagne, Cal continued. "London, you amazed us all. Who would've thought you'd meet your Prince Charming. Make that your *Hero*. Tony and I couldn't love him more."

More toasts followed. Nicole said, "Nothing is going to rain on your parade. You're my best friend, and I'll make sure of it."

London laughed and raised her glass, grateful for Nicole's reassurance.

London basked in the glow of all the warm wishes. Justin smiled, a little embarrassed by the attention. When all the toasts had been made, and people started to move away from the table, Rick and Billy caught up with Justin. Soon, they were deep in conversation. London watched from the kitchen doorway, glad they were reconnecting.

Rick Morgan and Billy Burns were as reticent as Justin. All of them were more serious and private than they'd been before their time in Afghanistan. But getting together was cathartic and a renewal of their deep bond.

London didn't want to horn in on their guy time, so she rounded up Nicole and headed into the kitchen to see if they could help with the cleanup. Anthony refilled their glasses and waved them away, so they took their drinks out to the patio. Even in January, the weather was mild and comfortable.

"So, what did you think?" London asked her best friend.

"I think you found me a hero of my own. I really like him." She sipped her wine. "I think he likes me, too. We have a date Saturday."

"Really? That's exciting. I wish I'd gotten to know him better before I decided he might be the one for you, but sometimes you just have to wing it."

"I'm good with that. Besides, you might not have had another chance to fix us up. This was perfect."

"I might like him better than Kyle."

"You'd probably like Attila the Hun better than Kyle," she said drily.

London smiled. "I'm really happy Justin called his friends. It's been sort of hard for him to be social. I think he's uncomfortable around people who don't see anything past their own noses. Can you imagine what it must be like? They were literally facing death every day over there, and then they come here and listen to people complain about what probably sound like really insipid things. A rude sales person, too much traffic, how the movie wasn't as good as they thought it would be. I don't know. He doesn't complain, but I watch his face sometimes, watch him watching other people. And I wonder what he's thinking. So maybe he needs this. I mean, to be around people who understand what he went through."

"You understand him."

"I do, but I just wrote about war from the comfort of my apartment. I didn't experience it for real. And I'm sure he has some fears about—" She stopped talking.

"Not about you guys. You look so happy together."

"I don't doubt he loves me, but I think he worries a lot about leaving me behind. If, you know, something should happen."

"Like what?"

"Not that he likes to talk about it, but I told you the reason he left the Army was because he got shot."

"He looks like he recovered just fine. Didn't he?"

She shrugged. "The doctor didn't get all the bullet fragments out of his chest, and left Justin with the impression that it could be a problem in the future."

"How big of a problem?"

"Big enough that he couldn't stay in the Army. If those fragments move around, they could—" She stopped talking. "I'm sorry. It just wouldn't be good, that's all."

"You can't think about that."

"I try not to, but it makes me sad. And it weighs heavily on Justin. He's more fatalistic than I am."

"Is this why you thought being happy might jinx everything?"

"Yes. I don't want to take anything for granted." She sighed. "We almost didn't happen because he didn't want to put me in a position to be left alone if . . . you know."

Nicole hugged her. "That's only *one* possible outcome."

"That's what I told him, but I don't think he believes he'll get to open door number two. Sometimes, when he doesn't know I'm watching, he gets this melancholy, faraway look on his face. And it breaks my heart."

Nicole squeezed London's hand. "If you live your life thinking everything might end, you'll miss all the great stuff along the way. You have to march ahead with your head held high. And believe. Believe until you can't believe anymore."

"I know. And I don't have a choice. I have to show him how good our life together can be." She stood. "We should get back to the party. I promise to keep the glass half full."

Chapter 47

★ ★ ★

Within weeks, Nicole was in love. She and London talked daily, and they were happy talks. Not angry, stilted ones, like during the Kyle period. London was relieved that Billy seemed to be thoughtful and attentive with Nicole.

Nicole told her that Billy had a bit of darkness in him as a result of his tours of duty. He had his own nightmares. As he grew to trust Nicole, he let her comfort him, let her tease the bad stories out of him. His reluctant sharing grew into real intimacy, drawing Nicole to him, touching her deep in her soul.

"I never knew it could be like this," Nicole said. "I've never known anyone who's been through so much. My other boyfriends seem so frivolous in comparison."

"I know exactly what you mean. It's the same for me and Justin. Justin and Billy, they're real men, not superficial boys playing with their toys. And I wouldn't trade Justin for anything."

"I really didn't see this coming. I can't believe how great things are."

"I'm so happy for you, Nicole."

"Do you realize if you'd never seen that picture, you'd never have met Justin, and I'd never have met Billy? I think it was all meant to be."

"I believe it was destiny. For us both. How many newspapers have I thrown out without even bothering to look at them? But that day, that picture? It gives me chills to think how a simple twist of fate caused all of this. So, I think it's fate that we double date this weekend. You know, to celebrate destiny?"

Nicole laughed. "I do believe that's a great idea."

Walking hand in hand along the Third Street Promenade after stuffing themselves with Mexican food at Loteria, London teased Justin that it was almost like a coming out party for them. Their first double date since they'd been together. "It was hard to share you," she said.

He grinned. "True. But it was fun. Besides, you don't have to share me tonight."

"And I plan to take full advantage of that." She pulled him into a deep kiss. "Don't listen, you guys," she called over her shoulder to Nicole and Billy.

"I'm not sharing Billy, either," Nicole replied, linking her arm through his and smiling up at her date.

"Good. We're on the same page. But first we need to walk off that huge dinner." She took Justin's hand. "Come on. We're going to walk all the way to the end of the Santa Monica Pier and back again. *Then*, we're going home."

Chapter 48

★ ★ ★

"Life is good," London said.

They sat side by side in lounge chairs on the rooftop deck of London's apartment building on a lazy Sunday morning. Spread around the chairs were sections of the *LA Times* they'd already finished with. It was pleasant to soak in the early morning sun as they sipped coffee and absorbed the rays that wouldn't become too hot to bear for at least another hour.

"Should we think about setting a date to make things legal?" She trailed a finger up his arm.

"It can't be quick enough for me," he responded. "What do you have in mind?"

"I've been thinking about it, and I know what I want to do. If it's all right with you."

"Sure. Why wouldn't it be?"

"Christmas Eve is on a Saturday this year. And there's nothing more I'd want for Christmas than you."

"You want to get married on Christmas Eve?"

"I do. My parents got married on Christmas Eve, and I always thought it was very romantic."

"If you want a Christmas Eve wedding, that's what we'll do."

"I want it to be small and intimate. Only family and close friends. Does that sound okay to you?"

"I want you to have the kind of wedding you want. Small is great, and probably a ton less stressful. We could elope tonight if you want."

"As tempted as I am by that offer, we have to share our special day with our loved ones. Both our parents would be sad if we left them out."

"I was kidding. You're going to be a beautiful bride, and I want to see you walk down the aisle. I want to say all those magic words to you and hear you say them to me." His voice grew hoarse and he looked down, his eyes red-rimmed when he looked up at her again.

Her heart melted at the emotion on his face. "No detail of the wedding matters except you and me being together. It's the beginning of everything for us. I don't care about any of the trappings of the ceremony." She suddenly smiled widely. "Except for my dress, of course. I'm going to have the best dress *ever*."

He laughed. "It will be the best dress ever just because you're wearing it."

"Way to go, future husband. Your mom taught you well."

"I try."

Chapter 49

★ ★ ★

"God, it's so hot," London said, wiping the sweat off her face.

"We should have started our hike earlier," Justin responded. "But you wanted to sleep in."

"That's right. Blame it on me." They sat on a boulder halfway through their Eaton Canyon hike. "It's Saturday. I didn't want to get up at the crack of dawn."

"If we're being honest, neither did I," he said with a laugh. "It's glorious out here. A little heat won't kill us."

"Thankfully, I have a closetful of tank tops and shorts. I'm always prepared."

"You rock those cutoffs, by the way," he said with a wink.

"Nice of you to notice."

"I always notice." He took off his baseball cap and dumped water over his head. Shaking the drops out of his hair, he leaned his head back and sighed contentedly.

"I love the smell of the eucalyptus. And pine needles. I love the smell of the mountains in general. We're so lucky." London took a long sip from her water bottle, and leaned over to kiss him. "I can't believe how great things are. I love you so much, we're getting married in a few months, and our best friends are dating. How could we be any happier?" London's words reflected more than her current state of happiness. They were an attempt to push away the fear that things might be too good to last.

"Yeah, babe. We're as happy as two clams."

The small cloud that seemed to pass behind Justin's eyes caused a chill to her heart. He appeared to be sharing in her euphoria, but London feared his was as false as was her own.

"It feels good to have everything going right for a change, don't you think?"

"I suppose."

London couldn't stop herself from pushing, the need for reassurance an unexpected emotion. "You don't sound sure."

"I'm sure about you, L. I think . . . maybe it's bad luck to revel in our happiness. You know, tempting fate or something."

"I should know better. I hope I haven't already jinxed us."

"I don't really believe we can be jinxed like that. It's just, the last time I felt on top of the world was right before 9/11 changed everything. Maybe I'm scared."

"Now I'm scared. We need to erase this whole conversation."

"No. We can't live that way. I *am* happy, London. You make me happy. I never expected to find love like this. We're strong together. We don't need to be afraid."

"I'll never be afraid as long as I have you. Not ever."

But there was that little tickle in her brain that wouldn't go away, and she vowed to herself to keep her exuberance in check. *Please, God. I'll always have him, won't I?*

Chapter 50

★ ★ ★

Justin was unusually quiet as they walked along the Venice Boardwalk on an early June morning. He held her hand and answered her questions, but in between he was lost in his own thoughts. London stole furtive glances at him and chewed her bottom lip.

"What's going on?" she asked, sipping her latte. "You're not saying much. Are you okay?"

"Yeah, I'm good. Just thinking about... It's nothing." He flashed a half-hearted smile and tossed his empty Starbucks cup in a trash receptacle.

"Thinking about what?"

She stopped. "Let's sit for a minute." She stepped over a low concrete wall bordering the boardwalk and sat facing the ocean. "Come on."

Justin joined her with a sigh. "Really. Nothing's wrong. It's just..." he blew air out through his lips. "Today's the anniversary of the ambush. The day my guys were killed by the Taliban."

"I'm sorry. I didn't realize." She rubbed his back and leaned her head on his shoulder for a moment. "I'm so glad you're here now."

"I should be there," he said simply.

"*No*. Why would you want to be back there?"

"Because I'm needed there. I could be doing some good if I was still with my team. If it wasn't for that bullet... I'd be there in a heartbeat. It's where I belong."

"You belong here with me." She looked away from him, barely containing her anger. She couldn't believe what she was hearing.

Justin didn't answer right away. He shuffled his feet in the sand and looked out at the ocean. "I'm not going back in the Army, so there's no point thinking about it."

"You think that makes it all right? Just because there's a medical reason you can't jump on a plane, you think my knowing you want to be anywhere but here with me is *nothing*?" Tears sprang to her eyes and she dashed them away with the back of her hand.

"London, that's not what I meant. I love you. I want to marry you. But I'm not going to lie. I'd be there if I could be."

"How is that supposed to make me feel?"

"I owe today to my men." He looked at her apologetically. "I can't really explain it. You . . . you weren't there."

She stood, hands clenched at her side, trying hard to keep a lid on her emotions. "So you're saying I'm incapable of understanding."

"That's not what I'm saying. Well, not exactly. But it's hard for people who haven't been through it to know what it's like."

"I can't help it if I weren't there. But to say I can't understand—"

He looked at her. "I'm sorry if I offended you, but I don't want to do this today. Today isn't about you." His eyes were getting hard. "Look. If you want to be mad at me, fine. Why don't we head back."

He stood and stepped back over the concrete wall. "You comin'?"

"Fine," she said through gritted teeth.

They walked in silence, the tension palpable.

London tried to calm herself down. She wasn't afraid he was going to leave her, but it hadn't occurred to her that he might have a secret desire to go back to fighting a war clear across the world. She couldn't wrap her mind around it. And she didn't know what to do.

Silent, she stared out the car window on the drive back to her apartment. He didn't try to talk to her.

When he pulled up to the curb, she turned and looked at him. He stared at his hands gripping the steering wheel, his mouth set in a grim line.

"Justin—"

"I think I should go. I don't want to say something we'll both regret."

She opened the car door. She hoped he'd somehow make this all right, but he said nothing.

"I'll see you later, whenever. You can call me." She shoved the door shut and watched him drive away.

Her world was imploding. This was a side of him she hadn't seen before. Pulling out her cell, she punched in a number. "I need to talk. Can I come over?"

Of course, Nicole said yes.

London leaned on the breakfast bar, watching Nicole pour two mugs of coffee. She followed her friend to the kitchen table and took a sip of the freshly brewed coffee, added sugar and half and half then stirred. She took another small sip and set down the mug.

"So, what happened?" Nicole asked, her hands wrapped around her own mug of coffee.

"Justin and I had a bad fight. I'm so mad, but I'm also scared."

"I can't imagine it could be the case, but he didn't try to hurt you, did he?" Nicole asked.

"Of course not. It wasn't like that. And I'm a little worried that I was wrong. But I was so angry. And then he left, and I don't know when I'll hear from him."

"What did you fight about?" Nicole asked as she took a sip.

London looked down and didn't answer right away. When she looked up, tears were threatening in her eyes.

"He said he wanted to go back to Afghanistan."

Nicole reached across the table and put her hand over London's.

"Billy and I . . . we've had that talk."

"Billy wants to go back in?"

"Yeah. I think if the right circumstances came up, he'd go back, too. It's upsetting, I know."

"I'm so mad that he wanted to leave me. I blew up at him. And it pissed him off."

"Why did it come up? I know Justin can't re-up because of health reasons."

"He ... he was down this morning. Like something bothered him. He said it was the anniversary of the ambush. I told him I was so glad he wasn't there anymore, and he said he wasn't glad. That he'd go back there if he could. I freaked out. We're supposed to be getting married, and he's thinking about how much he wants to be somewhere else? And he said I wouldn't understand."

"Yeah. It's hard. But they're warriors at heart. Think about what it must be like for them to leave someplace where what they do really matters. It's all life and death stuff. And we can't understand that, can we? We can try to picture what it was like for them over there. We can empathize. But we'll never *really* get it." She leaned on her elbows as she sipped her coffee.

"I'm so glad he's here and he's safe. I just can't imagine he'd want to be in danger again."

"I've felt all that. I've had to come to terms with it. With Billy, he doesn't have a medical condition to stop him. It's possible he could decide.... These guys are heroes. I'm proud of them."

"I don't think I can come to terms with it. And I don't even know what to say to him."

"I'm your friend. You know that, right? But I want to put this out there. You were surprised by what he said, but today was important to him. He not only lost friends in that ambush, but he lost his purpose. I think he needs to feel what he needs to feel. Maybe you should have the talk with him another day when he's not feeling so emotionally vulnerable."

"I wasn't a very good fiancée, was I?" London wiped at her eyes. "He said today wasn't about me, and I made it about me. I should have been there for him, and all I could think about was how upset I was. Do you think he'll forgive me? What do I do now?"

"He'll forgive you. I'm sure he already has. I think you should call him and go comfort your man."

She got up and put her arms around London. "He loves you. You love him. You can fix this."

Chapter 51

★ ★ ★

London's heart raced as she parked in front of Justin's apartment. Her hand shook as she knocked on the door.

When he answered, his face showed resignation. He stood aside as she entered, not speaking.

It would have made this so much easier if he'd smiled, or said something, but instead he stood silently looking at her.

"It's chilly in here," she said with a slight smile.

"I guess it is," he responded. "Can I get you anything?"

At least he's not throwing me out, she thought, daring to feel a small amount of encouragement. "No. I'm good."

She followed him into the kitchen, watching as he took two bottles of water out of the refrigerator.

"Thanks." She took the bottle and headed for the sofa in the living room.

"So," he said as he sat beside her.

"So." She couldn't look at him. "So, I was a complete jerk. I'm really, really sorry I responded the way I did. It's just that what you said came out of the blue."

He opened his mouth to speak, but she stopped him. "Let me finish."

She took his hand. "I know it's no excuse for my bad behavior. I shouldn't have made you feel bad about your . . . your words. It must be so hard for you to relive the experience. It changed your life forever, and all I could think about were my silly insecurities. It wasn't just what happened today. In the back of my mind, always, is the creeping fear that I could lose you to that damn bullet. That fear is enough to carry around. I overreacted. I'm sorry. Can you ever, ever forgive me?"

Her eyes welled up as she looked pleadingly into his face, hoping to see the forgiveness she so desperately wanted.

Justin looked down at his hands for a long moment, then he squeezed hers.

"It's a hard day. Maybe I overreacted, too."

The words were sparse, but the tension was eased. "I don't suppose . . ." She squirmed. "I don't suppose you'd tell me about that day."

He looked up at her, seeming to consider how he wanted to respond.

"It's okay if you don't want to," London said, not wanting to push.

He shrugged. "I'll tell you if you want to know. It's no secret." He sipped his water, settling back.

"Please," she said. "I really want to know."

He ran a hand through his hair, and leaned forward, resting his arms on his knees, his hands clasped, his head down. It took a moment before he started to talk. "One of our tanks hit an IED while on patrol. We were close behind and rushed up to give cover. As the tankers exited the vehicle, we started taking fire from a rooftop off to the side. Julio took one in the neck, and tumbled off the tank. Eric managed to make it to the ground but he was shot before he could get to cover. He didn't move after that. One of our guys, Danny Martino, raked his rifle across the roof as we scrambled to get out of the way. That's when another shooter popped out of a doorway and shot me. I didn't feel it right away and tried to keep running, but my legs gave out and I landed on my face. Billy grabbed hold of my jacket and pulled me out of the street. We managed to get inside a bombed-out shop. Billy tried to go back for Eric, but he took one in the leg, then dragged himself back inside. We held off the attackers until help arrived. It was hairy there for a time, but the shooters were hit and run guys, and scattered before our guys got there."

He took another sip. "Billy and I were airlifted to Germany and eventually back home."

"Billy saved you?"

"Yep. He's the reason I'm still among the living."

"You didn't mention Billy before our party. Didn't you keep in touch when you came back?"

"We talked a few times, and texted some. We both had our own things to deal with, our own ways to deal with our experiences. We didn't need to wallow in our memories."

"Oh." London laid her head on his shoulder.

Justin's smile was grim. "Anyway, that's it."

"But—"

"Look. Trust me when I tell you that you don't want that stuff in your head. It's not a pretty picture."

"I know, but—"

"No. You don't know. You can't comprehend it if you didn't live through it. I appreciate your concern. Honestly, I do. But let's just drop it. Okay?"

Reluctantly, London nodded. She leaned back and sipped her water silently. After a moment, she snuggled up under his arm.

"Is this okay? Or am I overstepping?" she asked softly.

"It's more than okay," he responded, his voice gruff. He pulled her into his arms and kissed her, then buried his face in her hair.

"Come here," she said. She lay back on the sofa and pulled him down with her. She nestled against him, cradling his head. She wanted nothing more than to comfort him, to shelter him. To keep him safe. Her heart swelled with emotion when she felt his breathing grow deeper as he fell asleep in her arms.

"I love you," she whispered, then closed her eyes.

Chapter 52

★ ★ ★

London shoved her feet into her running shoes and pulled her hair up into a ponytail. This morning she would run until she was mentally exhausted. Some serious soul searching was in order. She was ashamed of the way she had reacted when Justin had simply said he wanted to honor his memories of the day that had changed his life. He'd forgiven her for her selfishness, but was it enough? She was surprised at her own inability to hear the words he'd said. Instead, she'd heard the way the words he said affected her. Was she such a sniveling, self-absorbed little twit that she was incapable of compassion? Of deeper understanding? Even though he forgave her, could she forgive herself? She had to be honest. She knew herself well enough to realize that she'd never be completely selfless. The idea he'd inserted into her mind that he would even think about going back into the Army would most likely eat away at her. It would take a superhuman effort on her part to never let him know how much her heart ached.

Later at Nicole's, London shared the surprising information she'd learned from Justin.

"Did Billy tell you about the ambush?" she asked.

"Not with details. He doesn't like to talk about it."

"Justin doesn't either. But he told me that Billy saved his life."

"Billy saved Justin?"

"Yes. I always liked Billy. Now I love him."

"We're so lucky. Both of us have heroes to love."

"We do. You know what, though? I'm unsettled by what Justin said about wishing he could go back in. The thought of him risking his life, of maybe not making it out of there alive. It almost gives me nightmares."

Nicole looked pensive. "Can you blame them? Think how civilian life must measure up for them after the life and death stuff they dealt with every day over there. Dinner parties, shopping, watching TV. Doesn't exactly get their hearts racing."

"Oh, I know. How exciting can construction work be to someone who's saved lives? And I understand that as much as I can. But it doesn't mean the thought of it isn't horrifying to me. Aren't you scared, too?"

"Losing Billy would kill me. I love him. But I wouldn't stand in his way if he decided to go back in. I just wouldn't."

Chapter 53

★ ★ ★

When London finally allowed herself to examine the day at Venice Beach, and her conversation with Justin later, she saw that he wasn't planning his escape but had been venting his frustration at circumstances that had forced him to change the direction he had expected his life to take.

She vowed to follow the stern advice she'd given Justin so long ago. *If we're going to do this, then we have to do it with hope, and faith. And joy.* How could she have forgotten?

"Honey, I'm home," she called out as she opened the front door to her apartment and dropped the collection of *Bride* magazines she'd picked up at Barnes and Noble on the dining room table. She still needed to find that perfect dress.

"I'm in here," he called from the bedroom.

She unzipped her hoodie and tossed it on one of the chairs ringing the table, then headed for the bedroom. She flashed a smile as she put her arms around his neck and kissed him gently. "Sorry I'm late. I got caught up looking at wedding stuff and—"

"I have something for you," he said quietly. He opened his hand.

"Your dog tags?" She looked at them, puzzled, and lifted the chain out of his hand. "But—"

"I know you're worried. I don't want you to be afraid that I'm going to leave. Would you like to have them?"

"I'd be honored." She started to cry, touched by his gesture. She slipped the chain over her neck.

"I didn't mean to make you sad," he said, worry in his eyes.

"I'm not sad. I'm just so . . . my heart is so full. Your dog tags. You never take them off. And now you're giving them to me." She squeezed them. "I'll treasure them always."

Chapter 54

✯ ✯ ✯

Her cell phone rang. It was Justin's partner, Dave. "What's up?"

She listened, the color draining from her face. "I'll be right there," she said.

In a daze, she slipped the phone back into her handbag. It wasn't as if she hadn't known this was a possibility. In the back of her mind, that nagging fear was always waiting, hiding in some unexamined recess.

She tried to calm the panic that threatened to overwhelm her.

She wasn't completely successful, and the panic ate around the edges of her brain as she gathered her keys and rushed out the door.

Her insides were jittery and her voice shook as she called Nicole.

"Justin's in the hospital. Can you meet me there?"

In the twenty-minute drive to the hospital, London refused to believe what she feared would be true. That Justin was gone.

Like a dying person watching her life flash before her eyes, her life with Justin streamed through London's mind as silent tears fell.

"Don't go, Justin. Don't go," she pleaded again and again, squeezing her eyes to make the tears stop, and swiping her arm across her face to clear away the ones that blurred her vision.

She pulled haphazardly into the first parking space she saw, slamming the door and hurrying toward the entrance to the ER.

Nicole was already there, waiting outside, and they briefly embraced before heading through the Emergency Room doors.

"Justin Beckett. Is he here?" London asked at the desk. "I'm his fiancée. They told me he was being brought here."

"Have a seat, and I'll check for you."

"It was his heart. His friend said the EMTs thought it was his heart," she said, trying not to lose it in front of the nurse.

"Have a seat, please. When I know something, I'll tell you."

"How long can it take to look up a name?" London shrieked, coming undone.

The woman was implacable. Unruffled. She shook her head and looked at her screen. "He's in surgery, dear. The doctor will come find you when he has something to tell you. Now please have a seat."

"Come on. Let's go sit down," Nicole said, hoping to ease the tension. She led London to two seats by the wall. "Who called you? What did they say happened?"

"Justin just collapsed. He was on a worksite. Luckily, one of his crew saw it happen and called 911. Dave knew to call me. He said Justin was unresponsive when they put him in the ambulance." Fresh sobs choked her. When she finally had control of herself, she said, "I didn't want to believe it could happen, but it did." She waved away Nicole's attempts to calm her. "It was the shrapnel. He always feared it would get him."

Nicole sighed. "I hoped you'd never have to face this."

"The doctors told him that it could shift someday. That it could kill him." She looked away. "And now it has."

"You don't know that."

"No, but—"

"No buts. You wait until you hear it from the doctor. Don't give up on him."

It took over an hour before an ER doctor approached them. London jumped to her feet, her pale face reflecting her fear.

"Mr. Beckett is in surgery—"

"He's still alive?" London asked, almost afraid to let the hope in.

"Yes. It was necessary to operate immediately. He'll be moved to ICU after surgery, so you may want to wait in the ICU waiting room. It's more private there."

"I have to call his parents," London said to Nicole. "They'll be so upset."

"You're right. They should be here."

London pulled out her cell and dialed. No one answered, so she left a message that Justin was in the hospital and gave details of where she would be. Not a message anyone would want to receive.

The wait was endless. Billy arrived shortly after they moved to the ICU waiting room, and sat with his arm across Nicole's shoulders. He brought with him soothing words and affirmations that Justin was young and healthy and strong. London wanted to believe him so badly, but fear had her heart in its iron grip and she couldn't be comforted.

She needed to move, so she took a walk to find coffee. The machine coffee was bad, really bad, but that wasn't the point. It was distraction she craved at the moment.

"London?"

She looked over her shoulder to see a familiar face that took a minute for her to place. "Jack Slater? Hello."

"What are you doing here?"

"My—" She faltered, and tears started in her eyes. She quickly wiped them away.

He looked concerned and touched her shoulder sympathetically. "I'm sorry. I didn't mean—"

"No. It's okay. It's my fiancé. He . . . he was brought in a couple of hours ago after collapsing."

"I'm sorry to hear it."

"I don't know anything yet. I haven't talked to a doctor. He's still in surgery." Tears came again. This time, she let them fall.

"I think I'm the doctor who saw him when he came into the ER," Jack said. "He was in pretty bad shape, but I got him stabilized for the surgeon."

"You saw him?"

"Yes."

"Will he be okay?"

He indicated an empty waiting room. "Let's sit down a minute."

She sat, never taking her eyes off his face, and waited.

Jack cleared his throat. "I think he has a good chance. There was something, a foreign object of some kind, in his chest that may have been the reason for his collapse."

"It's shrapnel. From when he was in Afghanistan. He didn't want to make plans for the future because he thought he would die. He was afraid to get married. But I told him he had to have faith in us. And so he did. And then I went and jinxed it." She buried her face in her hands. "This is all my fault."

"Why would you say that? Whatever happened, you didn't cause it."

"Because I said everything was perfect. That we were blissfully happy. It was like drawing a bull's eye on us. On him."

"You know that's impossible, right? You can't jinx yourself. That's superstition."

"You can't know that. Even if it is just superstition that doesn't mean it can't be true."

"If that were true, no one would ever say they were happy. Would he want you to blame yourself? I'm pretty sure he wouldn't want that."

London turned to face him as an idea occurred to her. "Can you . . . do you think you could check on him to see what's happening? It hurts so much not knowing what's going on."

"Let me see what I can do. Why don't you go back to the ICU waiting area and I'll find you there."

London looked up as Jack entered the waiting room.

"They're wrapping up now. He should be moved to ICU within half an hour."

"Did the surgeon say if he's going to be okay?"

"The surgical team is doing all they can. But he's still alive, so there's reason to hope he'll be okay."

"Thanks. That helps. A little."

"I'll check back with you later to see how you're doing, okay?"

"Sure. That's fine." London stood and hugged him. "Thanks. I really appreciate your help."

Noticing Nicole, he said, "Nice to see you again."

"You, too," she responded.

He grinned somberly, and was gone.

"Who was that?" Billy asked.

"Someone Nicole sold a house to last year," London said.

"It was nice of him to check for you," Nicole said softly.

"At least I know he's still alive," London said, sitting down to resume her wait.

All three stood quickly when the surgeon appeared in the door of the waiting room. His friendly face looked grim, and London's chest clutched up in fear. She stepped forward and introduced herself.

"It was a tough go-round," the doctor said. "But he came through it."

"What . . . what happens next?" London asked.

"Now, we wait. He was in pretty bad shape, and there's a lot of healing he needs to do."

"What about the shrapnel?" London asked. "Is it still in there?"

"No. I removed the fragments. One came very close to his heart. Extremely close. But now we just have to see how he does."

"But is he going to be okay?" London's eyes were brimming with tears, and she wiped them away before they could fall.

"There's reason to hope. We'll know more when he wakes up. He was in good shape, so I feel good about his recovery."

London impulsively hugged him, and quickly stepped back in embarrassment. "I'm sorry. I'm just so relieved."

"No problem. I'm glad the news I had to deliver wasn't all bad."

"Can we see him now?"

"I'll have the nurse come get you when he can have visitors."

He looked so frail. Nothing like the buff, healthy man she knew. He was pale and still. She sat at his bedside and held his hand. When she squeezed, there was no response.

"Please, Justin," London whispered. She'd thought seeing him would make her feel better, but he looked so weak. She sat beside him, concentrating on breathing. Trying not to panic.

She asked the ICU nurse if her friends could come back, but hospital rules limited visitors to two. London joined Nicole and Billy in the waiting area.

"He can only have two visitors at a time, so I thought I'd come see if you'd like to see him."

Billy stood and waited for Nicole, but she said "You go ahead. I can see him when he gets moved to a room. I think it's more important for you and London to be there."

London gave her a grateful hug and then led the way back into the ICU.

Billy went right to the bedside.

"Hey, buddy," he said in a thick voice. "The worst is behind you now. We'll all be here waiting for you when you wake up. You're gonna be fine." He waited a moment, hoping for some reaction, but was met with silence.

London smiled sadly at him. "He'll be fine. He just needs to rest for a while."

"I know." He gave her a half smile. "Thanks." He turned and hugged her.

After a few minutes, Billy said he'd better get back to Nicole.

"You guys should go," London said. "I'll be okay here. I'll go say bye to Nic."

Nicole stood and searched their faces when they returned to the waiting room. "How is he?"

"He's hanging in there, but no change so far," London said. "Listen, I appreciate your being here, but it's going to be a long night. I'm going to stay here, but you guys should get some sleep. I'll call you if he wakes up."

"Did you hear anything from his family?"

"Not yet. I'll call again in a little while. I talked to my mom, and they're all concerned."

"What did she say?"

"She wants to help. She asked if she should come out, but I said I was okay. I'd let her know what was going on." She yawned, covering her mouth self-consciously. "You guys go on. The ICU nurses won't let all of us stay in there, and if you're going to be in the waiting room anyway you might as well be home. I'll see you tomorrow."

Nicole and Billy exchanged looks and Nicole nodded. "We'll see you in the morning then," she said. "My fingers are crossed that he'll be out of the woods by then."

Chapter 55

★ ★ ★

Alone with Justin, London pulled her chair closer and laid her head on his shoulder. The ICU had quieted down for the night.

"I got some news this morning. I could hardly wait to tell you. But now—"

She wiped at the tears in her eyes.

"I know you're going to be okay. I know you're going to wake up soon. Because you have to."

She put her hand over his. "It was fate for us to be together. How else can you explain how I picked your duffle bag to trip over at the airport? I never would have met you if the two of us hadn't been brought together at just that moment in time. We're meant to be. And fate wouldn't tear us apart so soon. You can see that, can't you? We're getting married. We have it all planned, so you have to be there."

She let the silent tears fall. "I love you," she whispered over and over.

London must have dozed off because she was startled by movement in the room. She wiped her eyes as she turned toward the visitor.

"Jack?" she asked.

"Just checking in," he said. "I didn't know you'd still be here. I wanted to see how the patient was doing."

"He hasn't woken up yet," London offered. "Is that normal? It's been a long time since the surgery."

"It hasn't, actually. Relatively speaking. But yes, it's normal. His body's gone through significant trauma, and needs time to heal."

"But when should I start to worry?" London asked.

"Let's wait and see what happens. Can I get you some more of that God-awful coffee while we wait?"

"Yeah, maybe." She looked at him for a moment. "We?"

"I thought I'd keep you company for a little while if that's okay."

"Sure, I guess."

"Great. I'll be back in a couple."

London went into the bathroom and splashed water on her face. Red, puffy eyes looked back at her from the mirror. She was pale and tired, and what little makeup she wore had been washed away by tears. She pulled a tube of lip balm out of her pocket, hoping it would help. She ran her fingers through her hair and stepped back into the room.

Jack was already there and handed her one of the cups. He sat in a chair on the opposite side of the bed from London. "So."

"So," she replied.

"Are you still mad that I bought your dream house? Nicole told me how jealous you were."

She laughed. "Well, I would be if I could have afforded it. Struggling writers usually rent."

"Actually, I'm going to be moving to New York in a couple of months. If your writing career picks up and you want me to save it for you, just say the word."

"That's very thoughtful of you. I'll keep it in mind."

She sipped her coffee silently, a look of sadness in her eyes.

He cleared his throat. "When are you getting married?" Jason asked.

"Christmas Eve. Like my parents did."

"That sounds nice."

"We're going to have a small, intimate ceremony. Justin's parents live in Pasadena and they've offered to host. They have a lovely large backyard that would be perfect."

"Well, congratulations."

"Thank you."

"Have his parents been to see him?"

"Not yet. I couldn't reach them when he was first brought in, so I left a message and they finally called. They were on vacation with some friends in Florida. They're flying home and should be here in the morning. I haven't heard back from his sister. I wish I could call and reassure them that everything's okay now, but it's not, is it?"

"There's every reason to think Justin is going to recover. Hopefully, by the time they arrive tomorrow, he'll be stronger."

"I know, but—"

"You have to wait. Time will tell how he's going to come out of this. Try to be patient."

"Patience isn't my middle name."

He laughed. "I have faith you can do it. Buck up."

When he stood to go, London said, "Thanks for the really bad coffee." He nodded with a smile and left.

She stared at the empty doorway for a moment before sighing deeply and taking Justin's hand.

"Please wake up, Justin. Please." But his eyes didn't open.

When the night nurse came in around three, London gazed at her with undisguised hope.

With gentle kindness, the nurse offered words of encouragement. "Honey, he'll wake up when his body's ready. It's healing, which is what it needs to do. His vitals are getting strong. Don't give up on him."

"I won't," London said gratefully. "Thank you."

"Did you hear that, love? The nurse said you're getting stronger." She watched his face. "Come on, honey, please come back to me."

She arched her back and stretched. Smoothing his bedcovers, she impulsively kissed him. No reaction.

"Your parents will be here in a few hours. It would be great if you could wake up and say hi to them. I'm sure they're very worried. Just like I am. It would be so great...."

She cried softly, and took a deep breath.

"I wanted to tell you something last night, but you were here, and you weren't listening. At least, it feels like you aren't listening. I hope you are, but it's not easy to carry on a conversation with someone who doesn't hold up their end."

She waited, not really expecting a response, but ever hopeful. "I had a doctor's appointment yesterday morning, and we're going to have a baby. So you have to be here. You have to see your little bundle of joy. And I don't want to be a single mother. I want our baby to have the most wonderful life. So you have to be here." She couldn't help the sobs that shook her then, and she buried her head on his shoulder, letting the tears flow. She felt so lonely, so disappointed.

London raised her head. "I was so excited to tell you my news. I was sure you would be so happy. I thought we'd be celebrating. In a million years, I didn't expect that, instead, I'd tell you about our baby and not even know if you could hear me."

She stood and walked to the window. In the dark hours of early morning, all she could see was the reflection of the hospital room and her tear-stained face. She wiped at her tears, and turned back to him.

"I didn't even tell Nicole. I wanted you to know before anyone else, so I didn't tell my best friend. I thought you and I would talk till dawn, about our future and what being parents would be like. We'd be too excited to sleep. And, now, it's just me, and I'm not sleeping but it's not because I'm excited. It's because I'm scared. Really. I'm scared to death that you aren't going to come back to me."

She squeezed the dog tags around her neck as she walked back to her chair. "There. I've said it. I'm scared you're going to leave me, Justin. That's why you have to fight. You have to fight to come back to me. You're the one true love of my life. So you can't leave me." She dug in her pocket for a tissue and wiped her eyes. "This is depressing. We need to change the subject. I have to keep my spirits up. My doctor said so. When you wake up, we have plans to make for our new baby. I think we need a new home. We need room for our growing family. I just heard about one we could look at. We can talk about that when you're you again. I mean, when you're back on your feet. I'm sorry. I can't help babbling." She laid her head down on the bed. "Wake me up if you want to talk."

All the tears made her eyes heavy. A good thing as it meant she was able to doze for a couple of hours. Around seven, the nurse shooed her out so she could check Justin's vital signs. London took the opportunity to freshen up. She wandered downstairs to the cafeteria for a quick breakfast of scrambled eggs and greasy cardboard bacon. She refilled her coffee cup and headed back up to the ICU.

As London approached, she saw his parents standing by his bed. She saw the anguish in their eyes, and wished she could ease their fears, but she could barely ease her own.

"London," Kathy said, wrapping her arms around her future daughter-in-law, "You must be so tired. We just got here. Do we know anything yet?"

"Not really. One of the nurses said some reassuring things about his body needing to heal, but that she expects he'll be okay. I was here all night, and he never woke up. Maybe today he'll open his eyes."

She hung back a little and watched as his parents bent over the bed and murmured to Justin. Giving them space, she walked to the nurse's station and asked if the doctor could update Justin's parents about his condition. She returned to his bedside just as Lindsay showed up.

"Sorry I wasn't here sooner. My phone battery died and I didn't notice it because I was so focused on the project I was working on. I came as soon as I found out. How is he?"

"I asked if the doctor could come talk to us. Hopefully, he'll be here soon. It's good to see you," London said. "I wish it was for a happy reason."

"It was so awful not being able to be here immediately. Of all the bad timing for us to be on vacation," Kathy said, a haunted look of guilt in her eyes. "Thank God for you, London. It would have been horrible if there were no one here for him."

London hugged her tightly, taking and giving the comfort they both needed.

Justin Senior put a supportive arm around Lindsay's waist. She smiled at him gratefully, then bent down and squeezed Justin's hand. "Hey, big brother. We're all here for you. Can you wake up so we can tell you how much we need you?" A tear slid down her cheek.

"You think he's going to be okay, don't you?" Kathy asked London.

"With all my heart, I believe it." She hoped her words concealed the fear that she might be wrong.

There was nothing to do but wait for the doctor. Luckily, it wasn't long before he appeared. He introduced himself, and cleared his throat.

"Mr. Beckett's vitals look good. The surgery was invasive, and it will take time for him to recover fully, but I'm hopeful. We got all the shrapnel out. That won't be a problem in the future. Things look good."

"But why hasn't he woken up?" London asked the question on everyone's minds.

"Maybe he's not ready. He's healing, after all."

"But isn't it bad the longer he doesn't wake up?" Lindsay asked.

"It's good if he wakes up soon. But each case is different. As I said, I think things look good." He paused, and said, "I'll stop in again this afternoon to check on him. Good day."

And he was gone, leaving everyone unsatisfied.

"He said things look good," Lindsay said.

"Yeah. I'm sure he would have told us if there was something really wrong," London replied.

"But still—" Lindsay started before her father put his hand on her shoulder. She looked up at him miserably.

"He'll be okay, Lindsay. We just have to wait."

Somehow, Senior's words and composure were comforting.

When the nurse reminded them that there were too many visitors in the room, London and Lindsay made a run to the coffee machine.

London wanted badly to spill her guts about the dread she was feeling. She wanted to cry out her fear and have someone say everything was fine, but she knew Lindsay was also trying to keep it together. London had to put on a brave front. They couldn't all be basket cases.

London and Lindsay sat in the waiting area with their coffee, giving Kathy and Senior time with Justin. The arrival of Nicole and Billy was immensely comforting. They breezed in with cheery hellos and words of encouragement, plopping into chairs next to London. She introduced them to Lindsay and gave them a synopsis of the doctor's words.

"Do you think we can go back?" Billy asked.

"Let's try. You can at least see him before the nurse brigade marches in to throw us out."

"We should be sneaky, though," Lindsay said with a smile.

Kathy looked up questioningly when the new visitors approached. In hushed tones, London introduced Billy and Nicole. Kathy smiled and moved away from the bedside to let Billy come close. He was solemn as he looked down at his friend before sitting down and picking up Justin's hand.

"Hey, buddy. Listen, you need to wake up. Take a look around this room at all the people who are going through hell waiting on you to open your eyes. I know you've got some healing to do but don't think it's okay to give up." Billy wiped at one of his eyes and hung his head for a moment. "Justin, dude. You can't let those bastards take you down, too. They got too many good men, and you beat 'em. You made it home. Now you need to wake up and come back to your loved ones."

He looked up, embarrassed by his display of emotion, and Nicole put her arms around him.

No one moved for a full minute.

"I'm surprised they haven't come in to kick some of us out," Lindsay said.

"I know," London said. "Until they do, let's send Justin all the healing thoughts we can."

Conversation was muted at first, but as they all became more comfortable in each other's presence, the mood lightened.

Kathy remained seated, holding her son's hand. At first, she didn't notice the cough, or the faint movement, but when a weak "What's going on?" came from the bed beside her, she gasped. The sound drew the attention of everyone else.

There was bewilderment in Justin's hooded eyes as he looked around, seeming not to focus on anything.

"*Justin,*" London almost shouted, rushing to the bedside. "Oh, Justin. You're awake."

He blinked once, and then again. "Where am I?" And then his eyes closed and his breathing smoothed out.

"Justin?" London said, getting no response. "Justin?" she asked again, this time with a sob.

Senior stood behind Kathy, his hand on her shoulder. Lindsay, Nicole and Billy stood like a halo around the bed searching for a sign that he was coming back to them. Nicole put her arms around London. "Please, God. Please," came from London's lips as tears streamed down her face.

London and Kathy exchanged looks, each hoping to see confidence in the other's eyes. But neither had confidence to give.

Billy slipped out the door, and was back within moments with a nurse in his wake. He explained that Justin had awakened but then fell back asleep. The nurse took Justin's vitals and opened his eyelids to check his pupils.

"His breathing and pulse are good. He doesn't have a temperature. This is a process he's going through until he's strong enough to wake up completely." She looked around at the fearful faces. "He'll come around when he's ready. Have faith." She smiled in a practiced, comforting way. "I'll check in on him again a little later." As she left, she turned and said, "I know you all want to be here, but there are other patients in the ICU and I can only give you another ten minutes before most of you must go back to the waiting area. We really need to keep the number of visitors down until he gets moved to a room of his own."

London stood by the window, looking out at a world going about its business, a world unaware of the anguish this room held. She traced a pattern on the glass with her index finger. She saw Justin's family and friends reflected back at her. It was both comforting and intrusive to have them all there. She wanted to be the one sitting by his bed, pouring out her heart to him. She knew it was a selfish thought. They all loved him. They all shared the same fear.

She thought about the new life growing within her. It would be so easy to turn around and tell everyone about the baby, but she couldn't bring herself to let anyone in. She wanted Justin to be the first one to know, and it was impossible to know if he'd heard her. She protectively hugged her belly and leaned her forehead against the glass.

"Are you all right?" Nicole appeared at her side and put an arm around her shoulders.

"I'm okay. At least as okay as I can be. I'm just scared."

"I know."

"How's Billy doing?"

"He's down. He's trying to hide it from me, but I know him well enough to see the pain."

"There's a lot of pain in this room. I feel so bad for his parents."

"I feel so bad for you," Nicole said softly.

Chapter 56

★ ★ ★

When the nurse came back to shoo them out of the room hours later, Lindsay asked if anyone was interested in going down to the cafeteria. Other than bad coffee, no one had eaten all day.

London was reluctant, but they could all use a break so she seconded Lindsay's suggestion. And she was starving. The baby needed food.

Fatigue spread through London's body as she sat in one of the uncomfortable plastic chairs, picking at the unappetizing meatloaf dinner in front of her. She yawned, setting off a chain reaction of yawns.

"Stop that." Kathy smiled. "Look what you started." In spite of themselves, everyone laughed.

It felt lighter, relaxing over the serviceable cafeteria food. The heavy cloud that had hung over them all day in the ICU wasn't quite as dark here. Or at least they were able to hold it at bay for a short while, knowing it was waiting for them to return.

Kathy glanced at her watch. "Do you think they'll let us stay tonight?"

"Probably not all of us," London said. She'd wondered if she was noble enough to let his parents spend the night in her place, but she knew it was the right thing to do. It was a struggle to think about not being with Justin, but it would be cruel to ask Kathy to leave.

Deciding on the high road, she said, "Lindsay, you can stay with me if you like. I imagine your parents will want to stay with Justin."

"Thank you, dear." Kathy patted London's hand. "I think that's a good idea. Why don't you go to London's? It doesn't take more than a couple of us to stay here." She smiled at Senior. "Don't you think so, dear?"

Lindsay's face hardened. Before Senior could respond, she said, "I'm not going anywhere. Sleeping in the visitor's lounge is fine for me."

London shrugged. "If it's good enough for Lindsay, it's good enough for me." She was privately glad to be staying. She wouldn't have been able to sleep at home, so far away from Justin if anything should happen.

But it was a long, uncomfortable night. The chairs weren't made for getting a good night's sleep.

London texted back and forth with Nicole before it got too late. Kind words from her sympathetic best friend were just what the doctor ordered.

Lindsay was as antsy as London. Dozing fitfully wasn't entirely satisfying, and sometime in the wee hours London told Lindsay she wanted to find a vending machine.

"I'm starving. Want to come with me?"

Lindsay pushed herself up from her chair and followed London out the door.

"Sorry about the zero dark thirty," London said. "I couldn't wait for daylight to find food."

They shuffled down the empty hallways, talking under their breath to avoid bothering any of the presumably sleeping patients in the rooms they passed.

Two vending machines with food-like items sat next to the soda machine. The *food-like* concept gave London pause, but she was hungry and her tiny pea baby needed food, too, so she spent a fairly decent amount of time checking out each possible choice.

"What's the holdup?" Lindsay asked. "Just get Cheetos."

London looked up at her from her bent-over scrutiny position and said, "I love Cheetos, but they aren't very healthy for my . . . uh . . . for my waistline. I have a wedding dress I have to fit into in a couple of months." She looked back at the vending machine and made a *that was close* face, quickly wiping it off before Lindsay could see her reflection in the glass front of the machine. Finally, she settled on cheese and crackers, two of them, acknowledging to Lindsay that she realized it was just a cut above Cheetos.

As London waited for Lindsay to make her selection, she was surprised when Jack Slater rounded the corner and almost collided with her.

"Whoa, I wasn't expecting to run into anyone here this time of night. Literally run into someone." He smiled. "How are you doing? How's Justin?"

Lindsay, Cheetos in hand, joined them and London introduced her to Jack, who immediately brightened his smile.

Noticing his scrubs, Lindsay was full of questions. She wanted to know if it was a bad sign that her brother had slipped back into sleep after waking up for a few moments.

His response was similar to what the nurse had told them. No surprise. London supposed they had the party-line they were supposed to adhere to. She started to say something but decided to listen instead. Something seemed to be happening between Lindsay and Jack. They were very focused on each other as they discussed Lindsay's brother's condition. Jack appeared perfectly content to stick around and chat with her, and Lindsay smiled coyly up at him. The thought crossed London's mind that they probably wouldn't even notice if she walked away, but just then Lindsay asked her something. Not really paying attention, London said "I'm sorry, what?"

"Should we get back?"

"Whenever you're ready."

Lindsay looked at Jack and said, "I suppose we should let you get back on your rounds, or whatever you're doing in the middle of the night."

"Sure. Maybe I'll drop in to check up on your brother tomorrow sometime," he said.

"I'll be here. I mean, we'll all be here. Thank you, Dr. Slater."

"London," he said with a head nod, and turned to the vending machines.

"We'll see you later," she said as she and Lindsay headed back to the waiting room.

London glanced once or twice at Lindsay, who was lost in thought as they walked. Under normal conditions, London would be teasing her about having a crush on Jack, but the hospital wasn't really a teasing atmosphere. Instead, when they were back in the waiting room, each ate her cheesy snack in silence. London stretched and yawned. "It's freezing in here," she said.

"It really is," Lindsay said with a shiver. She waited a beat and then said, "He seems nice."

"Who, Jack? He is. I think he likes you."

"Oh, no. I'm sure he was being polite."

"Maybe. Or maybe he likes you."

Next morning, there was no change in Justin's condition, although the nurse said his color was better. Settling in for another long day, London noticed Lindsay periodically looking at the doorway. Once, when Lindsay noticed London's gaze, her cheeks pinked up and she turned quickly away.

"I, uh, was thinking of getting something to eat," she said sheepishly. "Want to go?"

London smiled. "Sure."

"More Cheetos?" Lindsay asked. "Or cafeteria?"

"Let's just hit the machines."

London scanned the selections, silently chiding herself about eating more junk. *It's only for today. I'll get you real food later, pea baby.* It helped her guilt as she hit the button for a cake donut. *You believe me, right, pea baby?*

Lindsay chose something equally unhealthy. "So, how well did you know Dr. Slater?" She smiled. "I mean, did you . . . you know . . . ."

"No, I didn't 'you know.' I met him when Nicole sold him a house. I thought he was cute, but we never dated. He was Nicole's client so that wouldn't have been good."

"Well, do you still—"

"No, I do not *still* anything. In fact, I went on to date another guy after that and never looked back."

"What happened with the other guy?"

"Are you sure you want to hear all of this? I mean, I'm engaged to your brother. It's kind of weird, don't you think?"

"I'm sorry. Really. I don't mean to pry. It's just, here we are stuck in this hospital for hours, days even. I figured we might as well get to know each other. And I really only cared about your relationship with Dr. Slater anyway."

"And since I didn't have a relationship with Dr. Slater, it's fine. I've told Justin all of this. I'm not hiding anything. The other guy, Alex, ended up cheating on me. But it was the best thing that could have happened because right around then I met your brother. It was fate that my relationship with Alex ended when it did." She sighed. "So, listen. If you're interested in Jack, go for it. You have my blessing."

Lindsay smiled. "Thanks. And I'm sorry for prying. I'm a girl. We get curious, right?"

London smiled then, too. "Go, Sisterhood."

"Is there a wine machine around here? We should toast."

London laughed out loud. "Come on. Let's get back."

They noticed activity in the hallway outside the ICU. Kathy popped her head out the door when she saw them coming. "Hurry, hurry. He's awake. Justin's awake."

London sprinted the last few yards. She gave Kathy a quick hug as she moved past her into the room. "What—"

The doctor and a nurse were at his bedside, and Senior stood at the foot. A dazed-looking Justin was propped up in bed. When he saw London, he smiled weakly.

Tears sprang to her eyes as she knelt beside him and took his hand. "Oh, Justin. Are you okay?"

He started to speak, his voice hoarse and scratchy. He cleared his throat and the nurse stuck the straw from a glass of water into his mouth. He took a couple of sips, and pushed it away. He cleared his throat again, and said, "I'm okay."

He didn't say more, but his eyes spoke volumes as he looked at her. London lifted his hand to her lips and kissed it. "Thank God, thank God. Oh, Justin, thank God you're awake. We were so afraid."

She couldn't help the tears coursing down her cheeks. "I was so afraid."

Justin squeezed her hand. "I'd never leave you, London. Don't be afraid." He suddenly looked pale and exhausted.

London shot a panicked look at the doctor. "Not to worry," he said. "I think we're out of the woods now. He won't have a lot of energy for a while. We need to take this slow, but I think everything looks good."

Justin looked tiredly at Lindsay. "Hey, little sis."

Lindsay's voice caught, but she managed a smile. "Welcome back, bro. You had us worried." She leaned down and hugged him.

The doctor excused himself. London followed him out of the room. "Is he really going to be okay?"

"I believe he's turned the corner."

"Will he be able to come home soon?"

"If things keep looking good, maybe in another day or two."

"Are you sure the shrapnel, is . . . did you get it all out?"

"Yes. The scans showed that it was all clear."

"What happens now?"

"He needs to rest. He needs to get his strength up. His body has been fighting hard to recover. My recommendation is that you all take the night off and come back in the morning. It will do all of you good."

London stood in the doorway watching the happy scene. Justin's smile was weak but heartfelt. It was hard for her not to give in to tears again. Watching the man she loved, knowing she could finally breathe.

No one wanted to leave him alone that night, but London conveyed the doctor's statement that it was for Justin's own good. She gave him a hug and a kiss goodnight, promising to see him in the morning. As everyone filed from the room, she gave a final wistful look over her shoulder. Justin's eyes were already closed. She whispered *I love you* under her breath and followed the retreating family. *Tomorrow*, she thought. *Tomorrow will be the best day ever.*

London sent a quick text to Nicole asking if she and Billy wanted to grab a bite, and got an enthusiastic "yes" back.

The glass of wine was almost to her lips when London suddenly realized she couldn't drink the alcohol. Nicole didn't miss the expression on London's face as she quickly set the glass down.

"What's wrong? You look like you just smelled something particularly foul. Is your wine all right?"

"Yes. It's fine. I think my tummy's a little queasy from eating so much junk food the last few days. I'm gonna pass on the drinking." London gave an embarrassed smile and hoped her excuse sounded better out loud than it did in her head.

"You must be so relieved that Justin's awake," Nicole said. "I know we are. We'd have stayed at the hospital with you if you wanted us to."

"You were there when I needed you, and I appreciate it. I had plenty of company with his family there." Her hand absently reached for the wine, then changed course and picked up her water glass. "I really needed this," she said, then, realizing how it must have sounded, she continued, "I mean, I needed to relax with my friends, not a glass of water." She laughed, covering her mouth with her hand, ducking her head to conceal the tears that started in her eyes.

"Can I see him tomorrow?" Billy asked. "I gotta check on my bro."

"You can check on your bro. Of course you can. He's going to be in the hospital for another couple of days. I'm glad that when you see him this time you won't have to worry about him."

"Tell me about it."

"He's been pretty depressed worrying about Justin," Nicole said, squeezing Billy's hand. "We can all breathe again."

"Do you know what's going to happen when they cut him loose?" Billy asked. "I suppose he's going to your house?"

"I hope so. His mom probably would like to take him home with her. But I need to be with him. We'll see when the time comes."

When London arrived at the hospital the next morning, she learned that Justin had been moved into a private room. He sat propped up in bed surveying the covered dishes arrayed on the tray in front of him. He looked up and smiled.

London felt her heart catch in her throat. He looked so good. The pale, weak patient she had expected to see was nowhere in sight. She returned his smile and bent to kiss him, surprised when he met her lips with his own, in a kiss that lingered. "Welcome back, stranger," she said, her voice trembling.

She pulled a chair to his bedside. He looked so adorable, with the hair on one side of his head flat and on the other side sticking up in all directions. "You have quite the bedhead going on."

He laughed and ran his hand through his hair. "Yeah. About that."

"You look wonderful. You've never been more handsome."

"I find that hard to believe," he said with a skeptical smile.

London wanted to gush over him. She wanted to shower him with kisses and tell him she loved him over and over. Before she could leap onto the bed, however, his parents were at the door, followed closely by Lindsay.

"Doesn't your son look wonderful?" she asked.

The energy level in the room rose and everyone talked at once. London let his mother have the chair. Kathy thanked her, brushing quickly at a stray tear that had dared show itself.

Senior moved to the far side of the bed. "Son, glad to see you looking so well."

"Thanks, Dad."

"What's for breakfast?" Lindsay lifted the covers off the scrambled eggs and watery oatmeal, dry toast on the side. "I thought there would be Jell-O or something."

"Maybe that's what I get for dinner. I need something to look forward to."

"How soon can we sneak you in a Big Mac?" Lindsay asked.

"Soon, I hope," he said. "MREs would be more appetizing than this."

"Oh, stop complaining. If I knew you wanted MREs, I'd have brought some." Billy stepped forward hand outstretched.

Justin's smile was grateful and big as he clasped Billy's hand. "Hey, buddy."

"Hey, dude. It's about time you stopped lying around. Let's go grab a beer or something."

Justin laughed. "Maybe tomorrow."

Chapter 57

London was a jumble of emotions. Justin was being released in the morning and she was over the moon that he was going to be okay. She was apprehensive about telling him about the baby.

And she was devastated. Now that the shrapnel was gone, nothing stood in the way of his reenlisting. Her heart hurt at the thought of her love rejoining his unit. She'd heard everything he said about wanting to go back if he had the chance, and she knew he had meant what he said. She wanted to kick herself for feeling sorry for herself in the midst of his recovery. It was a fear she'd keep to herself. She would be supportive of whatever he decided to do.

She hugged her belly. "Pea Baby, your daddy's going to come home soon. He's going to be so happy to know about you. And he won't leave us ever." Then, feeling guilty for brainwashing her fetus, she added, "But if he does leave us, we'll keep the light on and welcome him home with open arms."

This isn't all about me, she thought. *I'll support him whatever he decides.*

London stood in the kitchen doorway watching Justin. He was lying on his side, covered with a blanket, his head on one of the sofa cushions, dozing in front of the television. He looked so peaceful. She put her hand on her heart, feeling joy at his closeness. He'd been out of the hospital for two days. He would stay with London until he felt up to going back to his own place. He slept a lot, which the doctor had told her to expect.

She loved taking care of him. Her heart overflowed with gratitude that he'd made it through the crisis. No more heavy clouds hung over their heads now that the surgeon had fixed him up. They could love freely without the fear that maybe their days together were numbered.

She hadn't told him about pea baby yet. He was still so weak. But Pea wouldn't be content to stay in the background for long. That was certain.

She heard him stir, and then he called out for her. The sound of his voice pierced her heart. She shivered at the memory of those silent days when she hadn't been sure she'd ever hear him speak again. "Hey," she responded. "You hungry yet?"

He threw back the blanket and sat up. London helped him to his feet and he padded down the hallway to the bathroom.

The table was set by the time he returned, and he took a seat as she served the chowder. She brought out a pitcher of ice water and filled the glasses.

Justin put a hand on her arm before she turned away. "Don't you want wine?" he asked. "Just because I'm on medication doesn't mean you have to abstain."

She smiled tentatively. "I sort of do."

Justin looked at her questioningly and she blushed. "Wait a minute." She disappeared into the kitchen and returned a moment later with two champagne flutes. She poured ice water into each flute and handed him one.

"I'm sorry this isn't real champagne," she said. "But I have to tell you something."

"If we should be using champagne, it must be great news."

"It is. I hope you think so, too. I actually told you the first night you were in the hospital, but I'm pretty sure you didn't hear me."

"I'm sorry I missed it. Everything was hazy for a while there."

"I know." She took his hand. "Justin, I'm pregnant."

He blinked and his mouth opened but no words came out. His eyes, however, reflected nothing but joy. He pushed back from the table and pulled London to her feet, kissing her with an intensity that left her weak.

He picked up his champagne flute and clinked it against hers. "I'll drink to that."

Chapter 58

There was a knock on her door. Justin looked up questioningly as London padded down the hallway to the front door. A grinning stranger stood on her porch.

"May I help you?"

"London Calloway?" he asked. "London Calloway, author of *The Hero*?"

"What's this about?" Apprehension filled her when she noticed the microphone in his hand, and the cameraman over his shoulder.

"I'm Bob Downey. From *You Gotta Know*. Perhaps you—"

"You're the tabloid. The trashy tabloid."

"I wouldn't say—"

"Well, I would." She started to slam the door in his face.

Bob blocked it with his foot. "Ow. That hurt." He pushed on the door and pulled back his foot. Before she could close it again, he quickly said, "I'm doing a follow up to our piece," shoving the microphone toward her face.

Angrily, London batted it away. "Your *hit* piece, you mean? I have nothing to say to you."

"You might want to know that Twitter is still blowing up. Everyone wants to know about you and the soldier. If you could—"

"How did you know where I live?"

"I can't reveal our source. It wouldn't be ethical."

"You think your story was ethical? The lies you printed, the invasion of our privacy? You don't have to tell me where you got your information. That opportunist was a thorn in my side from the day I met him."

"Look, I'm sorry you feel that way. Given the interest the first story generated, we'll be doing at least one follow-up, and I thought you might want to comment."

Justin appeared behind her. "What's going on here?"

A grin appeared on Bob's face. "Wow. In the flesh." Frantic cameras clicked in the background.

"Who is this?" Justin asked London, concerned at the anger on her face.

London pushed the door shut as Bob tucked his card into the doorjamb. "Call me if you want to tell your side," he said.

"With all that's been going on, I forgot about that damn story." She pushed off and headed back to the living room.

Justin sat beside her on the sofa. "What's going on? Who was that guy?"

"That guy is the reporter who wrote that crappy tabloid story."

"What did he want?"

"He's going to run a follow-up story. He said their social media went nuts over the first one. This is what I was always afraid would happen. Kyle thought if my *Hero* book got to be a bestseller then he could drag you out and parade you around."

"And that would benefit him how?"

"I'm not sure if it was his idea or David's. Revenge, maybe? I think he thought everyone would want to know about you if they thought the book was your story. Of course, the book wasn't about you, *per se*, but still . . . I don't know how much he got paid for the story. Maybe they have a big budget. And I'm sure David egged him on to create chaos in my life."

"I'll talk to Kyle and get him to shut up."

"No way. Knowing Kyle, he'd expand that into more press and keep the story going. It would be playing right into his hands."

"There has to be something we can do. He shouldn't get away with it." Justin slipped an arm around her shoulders.

"I think I should talk to an attorney and see if I can get an injunction or something."

"I don't know for sure, but I think if that was all there was to it there wouldn't be so many 'gotcha' celebrity stories out there. The tabloids would be afraid of all the lawsuits."

Justin ran his fingers through his hair. "I'm sorry. It was a mean-spirited story. The guy really is a piece of work." He kissed the top of her head. "Don't worry. We'll figure this out. You aren't fighting him alone this time."

London's cell vibrated. A glance told her it was Nicole.

Before Nicole could speak, London said, "I had a visit from the guy who wrote that story. I thought this would have died down by now."

"Bad pennies always keep turning up. Anyway, that's what they say. I forgot about the tabloid with what Justin was going through. I should find an assassin to take Kyle out."

"Too late. I've got one on order."

There was silence.

"I'm sorry. I don't know what to say."

"No one can control snake man."

"Snake man? How appropriate."

"You get brownie points for dumping him, and he's no longer your concern. I don't blame you, Nic. I love you. I have to figure out what to do now. The tabloid guy came to my *house*. I'm sure Kyle was happy to supply my address. They're going to run a follow-up story. What do they actually have to write about? He was giving me a chance to comment. I threw him out."

"London, I swear I didn't give him those pictures of you guys."

"I never thought you did. Kyle must be stalking me. Or David is. They're a couple of words I shouldn't say."

Another silence.

"Why don't you go on the offensive and beat him at his own game?"

"What do you mean?"

"Tell your story yourself. It's one for the ages. Can you imagine all the women out there who would die to have your life?"

"Tell it to whom?"

"Not the tabloid. But what about one of the women's magazines. Or *People*. Something everybody reads."

London was thoughtful. "I don't know."

"It couldn't hurt to look into it," Nicole said.

"There's something else I need to tell you."

"Good or bad?"

"Wonderful. It's wonderful. Justin and I are going to have a baby."

"Oh my God! That's incredible news. How are you feeling? Can I get you anything?"

"I feel fine, and I don't need you to wait on me. Although I appreciate the offer." She laughed. "I'm not an invalid, just pregnant."

"I know. I want to be there for you."

"You always are. It's kind of scary, but having you there will make having a baby a piece of cake."

Chapter 59

★ ★ ★

True to his word, Bob Downey's follow-up piece was in markets everywhere. London stood in line staring at a close-up grainy picture of her glowering face, with a caption that read "What's she hiding? What doesn't she want her soldier to know?"

There was a tap on her shoulder and a high-pitched excited voice asked, "Is that you?"

"I—" London started before leaving her groceries on the conveyor belt and squeezing out past the customers in front of her in line as she rushed to escape.

This time, she didn't allow herself to cry. She was ashamed for running away. She had nothing to hide. But it was too late to go back inside and stand up for herself, so she headed home.

Her cell dinged with texts from people she knew telling her there was another story. Nicole's text just said she was coming over.

"Okay, this has gone far enough," Justin said after London told him about the new story. "What did this article say?"

"I didn't read it. I fled the scene. Just like a criminal suspect would do. Damn it."

Nicole's knock on the door perked up London's spirits. Being surrounded by loved ones was the best medicine she could imagine in a situation like this.

"I brought it, just in case," Nicole offered, tossing the tabloid on the coffee table.

Justin picked it up and flipped to the page where the story continued. "London Calloway deflected our questions and refused to comment. Is that what an innocent person would do? It appears that things aren't on the up and up with *The Hero*. We ask again, does the soldier know how the author of the bestseller used him to promote herself?"

London turned to the page he'd read from, wanting to read it for herself. Bob Downey had thoughtfully included pictures of London shoving the microphone away and of her forcing the door closed. The angry expressions on her face were hardly attractive. Luckily, the pictures of Justin in the background were grainy and indistinct.

She handed the paper to Nicole, then leaned back and threw her hands up in exasperation. "How do I fight this? It's so unfair."

Justin squeezed her leg gently. "Take this for what it's worth. Let it go. In a few weeks, other stories will crowd this one out. A response from you is what the dirt bags want."

"That's what I thought after the last one. That it would all go away. But it didn't."

"I agree with Justin," Nicole said. "Ignore them. Hold your head high. You have nothing to be embarrassed about."

"Easier said than done."

"Yeah, but what isn't?" Nicole said.

"Then, he wins?" London couldn't help asking.

"Wins what? He's a slimy, evil creep. So he basks in his idea of glory for a couple of weeks. Then he goes back to being a slimy, evil creep," Nicole said.

"If they don't get a reaction from you, there's nothing to keep the story going. They had a few pictures and some made-up facts. If they make any slanderous statements, then we can sue them all." Justin ruffled her hair affectionately. "We're sticking together. Nothing he says can hurt you. Let it roll off your back. But he'd better hope our paths don't cross.

He might need dental work and a nose job."

London smiled. "My hero."

"And if I run into him," Nicole said, "I'll kick his ass."

"You're my hero, too," London said with a laugh.

Chapter 60

✯ ✯ ✯

The next time someone knocked on the door, London wasn't home, but Justin was. He opened the door to a stranger on the stoop. The woman held a mike and was backed up by a cameraman.

Justin rolled his eyes and sighed in exasperation. He started to close the door but instead glared at her until she squirmed uncomfortably.

"Mr. Beckett?" He didn't answer so she continued. "Mr. Beckett, I'm Patricia Connor. I'm with—"

"Which trashy tabloid is it this time?" Justin frowned. "Because I don't have anything to add to the hatchet job on my fiancée."

"Please, Mr. Beckett," she pleaded. There was something about her that caused him to hesitate. "My magazine isn't a tabloid, and I assure you I don't want to trash London Calloway. In fact, it's been the cruel attacks on her that prompted us to see if we could help in any way. We have quite a large reader base. We can counter-attack. If you're interested?"

"What magazine do you represent, then?"

"*People*. I'm sure you're familiar with us. You do realize, I hope, that our readership dwarfs *You Gotta Know*. We can drown them out. If you're interested, of course." She waited.

Justin ran a hand through his hair, contemplating. "I hope I don't come to regret this," he said, stepping aside to allow her in.

As Patricia and her sidekick scoped out the living room, Justin said, "London's not here."

Patricia paused, and smiled broadly. "Maybe that's even better. Would you be willing to let us interview you? I'm thinking how powerful a story might be on the hero telling his side and protecting his lady. I think our readers would eat it up."

"What, just me talking?"

"Well, we could talk to London if we needed to. How about you tell your story and we'll see how it goes."

"It seems odd that *People* would be interested in a tabloid story like this."

Patricia seemed caught off guard for a moment, and cleared her throat. "To be honest, here's the deal. I read *The Hero* when it first came out. I loved it. It was so romantic. When I saw the tabloid stories, that's the first I realized that there was a real soldier, you, behind the book. I was intrigued with the whole concept. Full disclosure, I wasn't assigned this story. I'm doing it on my own and hope to be able to sell my editors on it."

Justin was silent. Her honesty was refreshing, and some of his skepticism was eased. He shrugged. "Okay. Let's go for it. What do you want me to do?"

Patricia smiled. "Just tell your story."

Justin looked around. "Cool."

"Give Matt a few minutes to take a light reading and set up the frame. Do you want your coffee or a water bottle or anything?"

"Or a beer," Matt interjected.

"I'm good. Thanks."

He settled back on the sofa, waiting.

"I'm ready if you are," Patricia said. She flipped open a notebook, pulled up a dining room chair and faced him. "So, how did you two meet? Or did you know her before she wrote the book?"

"No. I didn't meet her until afterwards. London's nemesis, the perpetrator behind the tabloid stories, showed up at my parent's house when I was home on leave and told me a story about a woman who wrote a book about me and how he could make me a lot of money if I let him represent me. At first, I thought he was kidding. Then I was incensed at the intrusion. I paid a visit to London and pretty much ripped her a new one. Much later, she tripped over my bag at LAX and recognized me. She apologized and gave me her number and her book and told me to Google her."

"And you did."

"Yes."

He spent the next couple of hours talking. Patricia asked questions to fill in holes, then flipped her notebook closed.

"I appreciate your time, Justin. I'm so jealous of your fairytale romance."

"I wouldn't call it fairytale. We've definitely had our challenges. But I love her. And she loves me. And *because* she wrote a story about me, I get to spend the rest of my life with the woman who shows me every day how lucky I am. She calls it fate."

"Fate works for me. People are going to love this story."

Chapter 61

★ ★ ★

"What's this?" London asked when Justin handed her an envelope.

"I was interviewed by *People* a little while ago. The reporter was a big fan of your book and wanted to come to your rescue. This is the story she wrote. See what you think."

"You didn't tell me."

"I know. I wasn't sure anything would come of it. I didn't want you to get your hopes up."

"How did you get in touch with *People*?"

"I didn't. They showed up at our door. You weren't here. She convinced me that this would be good for us. So, what do you think?"

"Tell you in a minute." She sat on the sofa and began reading. Then she smiled. "You said some really nice things about me. And so did she."

The author London Calloway has been mostly unknown to the general public. Her latest novel, *The Hero*, may change that. The story of a Special Forces soldier in Afghanistan who saves the life of an American journalist and falls in love with her, *The Hero* has ignited a firestorm of interest on social media. Jason Westfall, the aforesaid hero of the book, is an iconic romantic figure. He's good-looking, brave, rugged, vulnerable, tender . . . I could go on and on. I'm one of a legion of readers who lost their hearts to this handsome soldier. Who wouldn't want to be rescued by such a man? Who wouldn't fall in love with such a man?

While undoubtedly this writer has a bright future, there are those who have tried to undermine her successful novel by insinuating that she exploited a real soldier. Self-serving warnings about Ms. Calloway's motives painted her as a greedy, manipulative opportunist.

I had the pleasure of meeting this soldier. He was understandably reluctant to talk on the record, but he fervently hoped to put a stop to the untruths and innuendos spread through a popular gossip magazine. Because he loves her.

Yes, there was a peaceful glow around this man as he talked about his fiancée. He seemed in awe that she was in his life. He said it was almost like fate brought them together, despite the odds against such an outcome.

"The first time I saw her, I yelled at her and told her to stay away from me or I'd sue her. She just stood there dumbfounded. Afterwards, I felt like a jerk. I had attacked her and didn't give her a chance to defend herself. You see, the person behind the tabloid attacks tracked me down and told me about London and her book. He said I would be famous and he could help me get rich. I didn't want fame, though. I wanted to be left alone.

"Luckily for me, she and I had a chance meeting months later and we both apologized. She asked me to read the book. I did, and finally gave her a chance to explain that she'd been inspired by a picture of me. We kind of hit it off, so we started seeing each other. I've come to know London, and I've come to love her. She rescued me from a dark place, and shined a light on my life. She had no intention of parading me around. But Kyle Nolan did, with prodding from his accomplice, David Rankin. That's why he leaked those tabloid stories."

"I'm the light of your life?" London asked with a smile.

"More than you know. You don't have to read all of it. It's more of the same. I go all mushy about how much I love you, and the reporter paints a picture of what a stud I am."

"I hope you weren't showing the reporter what a stud you are."

He laughed and pulled her into a bear hug.

"Okay. I believe you."

She frowned. "I don't know, though. Should we tell her to run the story or should we drop it?"

"It's a tradeoff. Even if we allow this article to be published, in another couple of weeks people will move on and we'll be right back where we were. But there's something to be said for fighting back. I think I'd get a kick out of rubbing Kyle's face in it, if you know what I mean."

"I do, and I agree. You don't know how much I've savored the idea of getting back at him."

"I named your nemesis in the story, and his pal, David. I also may have mentioned that your ex was a vindictive man."

"Woo hoo! But can we get in trouble for that?"

"Patricia said it wouldn't be a problem. If it were, they'd leave them unnamed. We should hear shortly whether *People* wants to run the story."

"You didn't say anything about the baby, did you? I mean, it's okay if you did, but—"

"No. That's private. So far, no one knows—"

"Well, Nicole knows. But she won't talk."

"Although we do need to tell our families."

"I know. But I wanted to wait, just in case. Not that I expect anything to happen, but I don't want to get everyone's hopes up. Let's wait a week or two."

Justin leaned forward and kissed her. "Why don't you put your feet up and let me spoil you a little bit."

"Who would turn down *that* offer?"

She edged into a corner of the sofa, lifted her legs and put her feet in his lap. He rubbed her legs gently and then massaged her feet. London's head lolled back on the cushion and she sighed in contentment. "I'm really gonna need this when I'm as big as a cow."

"I'm at your service. Nothing is too much for my girl."

London smiled, and sat up. "I just thought of something. My agent is going to be *very* excited that we're in *People*. It might be good for sales."

"I think it will be great for sales."

"It'll be *great* for sales," Sara said. "Your book has been selling well so far. Any press coverage we can get is a plus."

Within a week, Justin heard from Patricia. *People* was going to run her story, and wanted to interview London for a side-box. "It's a win-win for all of us," she gushed.

Sitting next to him on the sofa, London overheard Justin's side of the conversation and bounced excitedly as she waited for him to get off the phone.

"So, this is really happening?" she asked. She was nervous but also hopeful that the article would shut Kyle up for good. That was as far ahead as she wanted to look.

When Patricia interviewed her on the following Monday, London was happy to shine a light on Kyle and David's roles in the story. She didn't think her nemeses would be looking quite so bright and shiny in the public eye after the *People* feature appeared.

Justin hadn't mentioned his hospital stay. London did. She spoke of the fear she'd lived with those days while he was in a coma. Of being grateful when he came back to her. Of thanking the surgeon for saving his life by removing the shrapnel from his chest, and thanking God for every day she had with him.

Her pregnancy wasn't obvious yet, and neither she nor Justin mentioned it. The public could wait on that.

The story that ran was better than they could have hoped for. Patricia's emotional attachment to *The Hero* and to London and Justin gave it something extra that tugged at the heart strings. It was hard not to be caught up in her enthusiasm.

Pictures of the happy couple that accompanied the article put to rest any lagging residue of the tabloid hit pieces. Justin didn't look like a man who'd had the wool pulled over his eyes. And London didn't look like a devious, manipulative woman.

"I bought six copies." Nicole said. "It's so exciting to see my best friends staring out at me from my favorite magazine. Do people recognize you when you go out now?"

"It's happened," London said. "And people are so nice about it. Some of them have even asked me to sign the article. Who knew?"

"I haven't seen anything on the front page of *You Gotta Know*."

"Me neither. Bob Downey turned up at our front door again telling me how valuable it would be for me if I let him do a follow-up story. He offered me a nice chunk of money. I didn't waste any time slamming the door in his face. Stabbed me in the back twice. Why would he think I'd give him a chance to do it three times?"

"Have you heard anything from Kyle?"

"He wouldn't dare. But I think people will recognize him on the street now, too, and I doubt they will be as nice to him as they are to us."

"London, you really did it this time," Sara said. "Sales of your book are through the roof since the *People* story came out. This is just what you needed."

"Thanks. I know you were hoping this book would be a big seller."

"Not only do you have a blockbuster, you've been launched into a whole different league. I couldn't be more proud of you."

"I guess I need to thank you for nagging me."

"As your agent, there's something else I should tell you. Are you sitting down?"

"Why? What's going on? Is it good or bad."

"All good. London, two different studios contacted me. They want to buy the movie rights."

"Really?" Now London did sink into a chair. "Do you think—"

"Yes, I think. I think it will make a great movie. A blockbuster. Congratulations to my favorite novelist."

London stared dreamily out the kitchen window. When Justin came up behind her and squeezed her shoulders, she was excited to tell him the news.

"Wow. That's amazing."

"What's even more amazing is that we can lay this right at the feet of my favorite nemesis. What he tried to do to hurt me actually has put me on the verge of huge success. Silver lining, baby."

"I'll have to thank him next time I see him," Justin said with a big smile.

"Let's send flowers," she added. "You know, to thank him for his great work."

"You never know how things are going to turn out, do you?"

"No. It must have been fate."

Is it okay to be so happy? she wondered.

After an early dinner, Justin headed out to meet Billy at the gym. He'd been going several times a week since recovering from his ordeal. He looked buff and gorgeous.

He's healthy now. London sat on her bed staring at nothing. A tear slid from her eye. Suddenly, all the stress and fear and worry caught up with her and she curled into a ball. Sobs wracked her body and she cried until she was exhausted and gasping for breath. Stress and fear and worry and hormones. Her emotions were out of whack. She wondered if this was what PTSD was like.

He could go now if he wants. The thought caused a fresh torrent of tears. Until she heard the front door open and a cheery "Honey, I'm home." She jumped off the bed and locked herself in the bathroom, frantically washing her face, hoping to minimize the red leaky eyes.

"I'm in here," she called. "I'll be out in a minute."

As she futilely tried to apply mascara to wet lashes, there was a knock at the bathroom door.

"You okay in there? You sounded funny."

She sighed and put down the mascara wand. It wasn't working anyway. Slowly, she opened the door and could tell by his expression that she hadn't disguised her anguish.

"What—"

She brushed by him, but he caught her and turned her to face him. He put a hand under her chin and lifted it so he could look into her eyes. She glanced down quickly, her hand clasping the dog tags hanging around her neck.

"You're scaring me," he said.

She lifted the dog tags over her head and cradled them to her chest before pressing them into his hands. He looked down in confusion.

She took a deep breath. "I think you'll be needing these. Now that you've recovered, I know you've yearned to go back in. You're healthy. I want you to go do what your heart tells you to do."

He looked at her silently for a moment. He looked at the tags in his hand and then back at her.

"Come here," he said. He picked up her hand and gently handed them back to her. "How long have you been worried about this?"

"I've been so scared. I was happy, but I wasn't sure. Maybe you weren't. I know you want to go back. You and Billy. And now you can. I won't stop you."

He shook his head. "Don't you know by now how much I love you? My heart wants to be here, with you, and with our baby. I don't know what brought this on, but never doubt that I'll be here for you. For as long as you want me. What kind of man would I be if I walked out on my future wife and child?"

"But you were ready to go before."

"No. I wasn't. You caught me on a melancholy day. I was remembering my men and their sacrifices and their bravery. I felt a tug. I don't deny it. But trade you in for that life? That's never going to happen." He wiped away the tears brimming in her eyes. "Don't cry, baby. You're my life, my future, my everything." He patted her growing bump. "I'm going to have to work overtime to counteract all those hormones."

He took her hands in his. "How worried do I have to be about you?"

She felt foolish. "Can you go out and come in again? I want a do-over. Before you came home, I was in complete despair, but I won't ever go there again. I know you love me, and I know you're excited about our baby. Let's blame it on the hormones, okay?"

He laughed and headed out the door.

London wiped at her eyes and smoothed her hair as the door opened and she heard, "Honey, I'm home."

This time, she rushed into his arms and kissed him passionately. When he pulled back, he saw a face without any darkness. The face of the woman he loved.

He looked at her seriously. "Let's get married," he said.

"We are getting married, silly boy."

"I mean now. Let's get married now."

She tilted her head and looked at him in confusion. "But our families, our friends. Shouldn't we—"

"We can do it again for them. This time it will be for us."

Chapter 62

★ ★ ★

The morning was a blur for London. She spent a couple of hours shopping. Even if it wasn't their *formal* wedding, it was a real one, and she wanted to look amazing for her true love. And she wanted white.

At a local bridal boutique, with the help of a cheery consultant, she found a knee-length white silk sheath with an over-layer of white cotton lace. It was more garden party than wedding day, which was perfect. The dress didn't draw attention to the slight baby bump and was flattering to her still-slim figure. And London loved it. A little more shopping added strappy white sandals to the mix. She debated whether to add a hat or a veil, but chose not to, instead buying a pair of gold drop earrings and calling it good.

She texted Justin to see if he was ready, and he said he'd meet her back at home.

"I don't think so," she said.

"Why not?"

"It's bad luck to see the bride before the wedding. I want you to meet me on the steps of City Hall."

"Oookay," he said slowly.

"I know it's superstitious, but I want you to be surprised when you see me. And I don't want any bad juju."

He laughed. "No bad juju in our future. Check. See you at City Hall in an hour?"

"Thank you for understanding. I'll meet you there with bells on."

She watched his face light up as he climbed the steps of the courthouse to meet her. He took her hand and twirled her around before kissing her, and she felt the enveloping warmth of his love.

As they sat on a bench outside the office of the justice of the peace waiting to be called in, London looked at Justin's handsome profile. *I wonder if it's irony or fate*, she mused, *that the first sentence of the novel setting off the chain of events that brought us together is so meaningful now.*

"Most people never meet a real live hero, but I was in love with one." *And I'm marrying mine.*

THE END

Acknowledgments

I have to thank my usual suspects. They know who they are. ☺

But, for those who don't know, my usual suspects include my sisters, Sheila and Michelle, who are always ready to read and comment on multiple drafts of my stories, and my niece, Elise Crocker, all of whom are quick to offer suggestions and ideas. And many other supportive friends and family who keep my spirits up, so to speak.

My thanks also to Acorn Publishing, and the Acorn team, Jessica Therrien and Holly Kammier, Evelyn Lawhorn and Debbie Kennedy, plus others behind the scenes, who paved my path to publication.

As always, thanks to everyone who leaves me a review. Those just might tempt someone to read my books! And, who knows? With enough reviews, maybe I could make a few bestseller lists!

Made in the USA
Monee, IL
30 March 2025